We hope you enjoy th **D0314706**
Please return or rene
You can renew it at **www.** **es**
or by using our free library app. Otherwise you can
phone **0344 800 8020** - please have your library
card and pin ready.
You can sign up for email reminders too.

MURDER TAKES A HOLIDAY

TEN CLASSIC CRIME STORIES FOR SUMMER

Selected by Cecily Gayford

Arthur Conan Doyle · Dorothy L. Sayers
Anthony Berkeley · John Dickson Carr
Ngaio Marsh · R. Austin Freeman
Edmund Crispin · Ruth Rendell
Simon Brett · Michael Innes

P

PROFILE BOOKS

First published in Great Britain in 2020 by
PROFILE BOOKS LTD
29 Cloth Fair
London ECIA 7JQ
www.profilebooks.com

1 3 5 7 9 10 8 6 4 2

Typeset in Fournier by MacGuru Ltd
Printed and bound in Great Britain by CPI Group (UK) Ltd, Croydon CRO 4YY

The moral right of the authors has been asserted.

A CIP catalogue record for this book is available from the British Library.

ISBN 978 1 78816 575 4
eISBN 978 1 78283 730 5

Contents

The Adventure of the Devil's Foot

Arthur Conan Doyle

In recording from time to time some of the curious experiences and interesting recollections which I associate with my long and intimate friendship with Mr Sherlock Holmes, I have continually been faced by difficulties caused by his own aversion to publicity. To his sombre and cynical spirit all popular applause was always abhorrent, and nothing amused him more at the end of a successful case than to hand over the actual exposure to some orthodox official, and to listen with a mocking smile to the general chorus of misplaced congratulation. It was indeed this attitude upon the part of my friend and certainly not any lack of interesting material which has caused me of late years to lay very few of my records before the public. My participation in some of his adventures was always a privilege which entailed discretion and reticence upon me.

It was, then, with considerable surprise that I received a telegram from Holmes last Tuesday – he has never been known to write where a telegram would serve – in the following terms:

> Why not tell them of the Cornish horror– strangest case I have handled.

I have no idea what backward sweep of memory had brought the matter fresh to his mind, or what freak had caused him to desire that I should recount it; but I hasten, before another cancelling telegram may arrive, to hunt out the notes which give me the exact details of the case and to lay the narrative before my readers.

It was, then, in the spring of the year 1897 that Holmes's iron constitution showed some symptoms of giving way in the face of constant hard work of a most exacting kind, aggravated, perhaps, by occasional indiscretions of his own. In March of that year Dr Moore Agar, of Harley Street, whose dramatic introduction to Holmes I may some day recount, gave positive injunctions that the famous private agent lay aside all his cases and surrender himself to complete rest if he wished to avert an absolute breakdown. The state of his health was not a matter in which he himself took the faintest interest, for his mental detachment was absolute, but he was induced at last, on the threat of being permanently disqualified from work, to give himself a complete change of scene and air. Thus it was that in the early spring of that year we found ourselves together in a small cottage near Poldhu Bay, at the further extremity of the Cornish peninsula.

It was a singular spot, and one peculiarly well suited to the grim humour of my patient. From the windows of our little whitewashed house, which stood high upon a grassy headland, we looked down upon the whole sinister semicircle of Mounts Bay, that old death trap of sailing vessels, with its fringe of black cliffs and surge-swept reefs on which innumerable seamen have met their end. With a northerly breeze it lies placid and sheltered, inviting the storm-tossed craft to tack into it for rest and protection.

Then come the sudden swirl round of the wind, the blistering gale from the south-west, the dragging anchor, the lee shore, and the last battle in the creaming breakers. The wise mariner stands far out from that evil place.

On the land side our surroundings were as sombre as on the sea. It was a country of rolling moors, lonely and duncoloured, with an occasional church tower to mark the site of some old-world village. In every direction upon these moors there were traces of some vanished race which had passed utterly away, and left as its sole record strange monuments of stone, irregular mounds which contained the burned ashes of the dead, and curious earthworks which hinted at prehistoric strife. The glamour and mystery of the place, with its sinister atmosphere of forgotten nations, appealed to the imagination of my friend, and he spent much of his time in long walks and solitary meditations upon the moor. The ancient Cornish language had also arrested his attention, and he had, I remember, conceived the idea that it was akin to the Chaldean, and had been largely derived from the Phoenician traders in tin. He had received a consignment of books upon philology and was settling down to develop this thesis when suddenly, to my sorrow and to his unfeigned delight, we found ourselves, even in that land of dreams, plunged into a problem at our very doors which was more intense, more engrossing, and infinitely more mysterious than any of those which had driven us from London. Our simple life and peaceful, healthy routine were violently interrupted, and we were precipitated into the midst of a series of events which caused the utmost excitement not only in Cornwall but throughout the whole west of England. Many of my readers may retain some recollection of what was called at the time 'The Cornish Horror', though a most imperfect account of the matter reached the London press. Now, after thirteen years, I will give the true details of this inconceivable affair to the public.

I have said that scattered towers marked the villages which dotted this part of Cornwall. The nearest of these was the hamlet of Tredannick Wollas, where the cottages of a couple of hundred inhabitants clustered round an ancient, moss-grown church. The vicar of the parish, Mr Roundhay, was something of an archaeologist, and as such Holmes had made his acquaintance. He was a middle-aged man, portly and affable, with a considerable fund of local lore. At his invitation we had taken tea at the vicarage and had come to know, also, Mr Mortimer Tregennis, an independent gentleman, who increased the clergyman's scanty resources by taking rooms in his large, straggling house. The vicar, being a bachelor, was glad to come to such an arrangement, though he had little in common with his lodger, who was a thin, dark, spectacled man, with a stoop which gave the impression of actual, physical deformity. I remember that during our short visit we found the vicar garrulous, but his lodger strangely reticent, a sad-faced, introspective man, sitting with averted eyes, brooding apparently upon his own affairs.

These were the two men who entered abruptly into our little sitting-room on Tuesday, 16 March, shortly after our breakfast hour, as we were smoking together, preparatory to our daily excursion upon the moors.

'Mr Holmes,' said the vicar in an agitated voice, 'the most extraordinary and tragic affair has occurred during the night. It is the most unheard-of business. We can only regard it as a special Providence that you should chance to be here at the time, for in all England you are the one man we need.'

I glared at the intrusive vicar with no very friendly eyes; but Holmes took his pipe from his lips and sat up in his chair like an old hound who hears the view-halloa. He waved his hand to the sofa, and our palpitating visitor with his agitated companion sat side by side upon it. Mr Mortimer Tregennis was more self-contained than the clergyman, but the twitching of his thin hands and the brightness of his dark eyes showed that they shared a common emotion.

'Shall I speak or you?' he asked of the vicar.

'Well, as you seem to have made the discovery, whatever it may be, and the vicar to have had it second-hand, perhaps you had better do the speaking,' said Holmes.

I glanced at the hastily clad clergyman, with the formally dressed lodger seated beside him, and was amused at the surprise which Holmes's simple deduction had brought to their faces.

'Perhaps I had best say a few words first,' said the vicar, 'and then you can judge if you will listen to the details from

Mr Tregennis, or whether we should not hasten at once to the scene of this mysterious affair. I may explain, then, that our friend here spent last evening in the company of his two brothers, Owen and George, and of his sister Brenda, at their house of Tredannick Wartha, which is near the old stone cross upon the moor. He left them shortly after ten o'clock, playing cards round the dining-room table, in excellent health and spirits. This morning, being an early riser, he walked in that direction before breakfast and was overtaken by the carriage of Dr Richards, who explained that he had just been sent for on a most urgent call to Tredannick Wartha. Mr Mortimer Tregennis naturally went with him. When he arrived at Tredannick Wartha he found an extraordinary state of things. His two brothers and his sister were seated round the table exactly as he had left them, the cards still spread in front of them and the candles burned down to their sockets. The sister lay back stone-dead in her chair, while the two brothers sat on each side of her laughing, shouting and singing, the senses stricken clean out of them. All three of them, the dead woman and the two demented men, retained upon their faces an expression of the utmost horror – a convulsion of terror which was dreadful to look upon. There was no sign of the presence of anyone in the house, except Mrs Porter, the old cook and housekeeper, who declared that she had slept deeply and heard no sound during the night. Nothing had been stolen or disarranged, and there is absolutely no explanation of what the horror can be which has frightened a woman to death and two strong men out of their senses. There is the situation, Mr Holmes, in a nutshell, and if you can help us to clear it up you will have done a great work.'

I had hoped that in some way I could coax my companion back into the quiet which had been the object of our journey; but one glance at his intense face and contracted eyebrows told me how vain was now the expectation. He sat for some little time in silence, absorbed in the strange drama which had broken in upon our peace.'I will look into this matter,' he said at last. 'On the face of it, it would appear to be a case of a very exceptional nature. Have you been there yourself, Mr Roundhay?'

'No, Mr Holmes. Mr Tregennis brought back the account to the vicarage, and I at once hurried over with him to consult you.'

'How far is it to the house where this singular tragedy occurred?'

'About a mile inland.'

'Then we shall walk over together. But before we start I must ask you a few questions, Mr Mortimer Tregennis.'

The other had been silent all this time, but I had observed that his more controlled excitement was even greater than the obtrusive emotion of the clergyman. He sat with a pale, drawn face, his anxious gaze fixed upon Holmes, and his thin hands clasped convulsively together. His pale lips quivered as he listened to the dreadful experience which had befallen his family, and his dark eyes seemed to reflect something of the horror of the scene.

'Ask what you like, Mr Holmes,' said he eagerly. 'It is a bad thing to speak of, but I will answer you the truth.'

'Tell me about last night.'

'Well, Mr Holmes, I supped there, as the vicar has said, and my elder brother George proposed a game of whist afterwards. We sat down about nine o'clock. It was a quarter past ten when I moved to go. I left them all round the table, as merry as could be.'

'Who let you out?'

'Mrs Porter had gone to bed, so I let myself out. I shut the hall door behind me. The window of the room in which they sat was closed, but the blind was not drawn down. There was no change in door or window this morning, or any reason to think that any stranger had been to the house. Yet there they sat, driven clean mad with terror, and Brenda lying dead of fright, with her head hanging over the arm of the chair. I'll never get the sight of that room out of my mind so long as I live.'

'The facts, as you state them, are certainly most remarkable,' said Holmes. 'I take it that you have no theory yourself which can in any way account for them?'

'It's devilish, Mr Holmes, devilish!' cried Mortimer Tregennis. 'It is not of this world. Something has come into that room which has dashed the light of reason from their minds. What human contrivance could do that?'

'I fear,' said Holmes, 'that if the matter is beyond humanity it is certainly beyond me. Yet we must exhaust all natural explanations before we fall back upon such a theory as this. As to yourself, Mr Tregennis, I take it you were divided in some way from your family, since they lived together and you had rooms apart?'

'That is so, Mr Holmes, though the matter is past and done with. We were a family of tin-miners at Redruth, but we sold our venture to a company, and so retired with enough to keep us. I won't deny that there was some feeling about the division of the money and it stood between us for a time, but it was all forgiven and forgotten, and we were the best of friends together.'

'Looking back at the evening which you spent together, does anything stand out in your memory as throwing any possible light upon the tragedy? Think carefully, Mr Tregennis, for any clue which can help me.'

'There is nothing at all, sir.'

'Your people were in their usual spirits?'

'Never better.'

'Were they nervous people? Did they ever show any apprehension of coming danger?'

'Nothing of the kind.'

'You have nothing to add then, which could assist me?'

Mortimer Tregennis considered earnestly for a moment.

'There is one thing occurs to me,' said he at last. 'As we sat at the table my back was to the window, and my brother George, he being my partner at cards, was facing it. I saw him once look hard over my shoulder, so I turned round and looked also. The blind was up and the window shut, but I could just make out the bushes on the lawn, and it seemed to me for a moment that I saw something moving among them. I couldn't even say if it was man or animal, but I just thought there was something there. When I asked him what he was looking at, he told me that he had the same feeling. That is all that I can say.'

'Did you not investigate?'

'No; the matter passed as unimportant.'

'You left them, then, without any premonition of evil?'

'None at all.'

'I am not clear how you came to hear the news so early this morning.'

'I am an early riser and generally take a walk before breakfast. This morning I had hardly started when the doctor in his carriage overtook me. He told me that old Mrs Porter had sent a boy down with an urgent message. I sprang in beside him and we drove on. When we got there we looked into that dreadful room. The candles and the fire must have burned out hours before, and they had been sitting there in the dark until dawn had broken. The doctor said Brenda must have been dead at least six hours. There were no signs of violence. She just lay across the arm of the chair with that look on her face. George and Owen were singing snatches of songs and gibbering like two great apes. Oh, it was awful to see! I couldn't stand it, and the doctor was as white as a sheet. Indeed, he fell into a chair in a sort of faint, and we nearly had him on our hands as well.'

'Remarkable – most remarkable!' said Holmes, rising and taking his hat. 'I think, perhaps, we had better go down to Tredannick Wartha without further delay. I confess that I have seldom known a case which at first sight presented a more singular problem.'

Our proceedings of that first morning did little to advance the investigation. It was marked, however, at the outset by an incident which left the most sinister impression upon my mind. The approach to the spot at which the tragedy occurred is down a narrow, winding, country lane. While we made our way along it we heard the rattle of a carriage coming towards us and stood aside to let it pass. As it drove by us I caught a glimpse through the closed window of a horribly contorted, grinning face glaring out at us. Those staring eyes and gnashing teeth flashed past us like a dreadful vision.

'My brothers!' cried Mortimer Tregennis, white to his lips. 'They are taking them to Helston.'

We looked with horror after the black carriage, lumbering upon its way. Then we turned our steps towards this ill-omened house in which they had met their strange fate.

It was a large and bright dwelling, rather a villa than a cottage, with a considerable garden which was already, in that Cornish air, well filled with spring flowers. Towards this garden the window of the sitting-room fronted, and from it, according to Mortimer Tregennis, must have come that thing of evil which had by sheer horror in a single instant blasted their minds. Holmes walked slowly and thoughtfully among the flower-plots and along the path before we entered the porch. So absorbed was he in his thoughts, I remember, that he stumbled over the watering-pot, upset its contents, and deluged both our feet and the garden path. Inside the house we were met by the elderly Cornish housekeeper, Mrs Porter, who, with the aid of a young girl, looked after the wants of the family. She readily answered all Holmes's questions. She had heard nothing in the night. Her employers had all been in excellent spirits lately, and she had never known them more cheerful and prosperous. She had fainted with horror upon entering the room in the morning and seeing that dreadful company round the table. She had, when she recovered, thrown open the window to let the morning air in, and had run down to the lane, whence she sent a farm-lad for the doctor. The lady was on her bed upstairs if we cared to see her. It took four strong men to get the brothers into the asylum carriage. She would not herself stay in the house another day and was starting that very afternoon to rejoin her family at St Ives.

We ascended the stairs and viewed the body. Miss Brenda Tregennis had been a very beautiful girl, though now verging upon middle age. Her dark, clear-cut face was handsome, even in death, but there still lingered upon it something of that convulsion of horror which had been her last human emotion. From her bedroom we descended to the sitting-room, where this strange tragedy had actually occurred. The charred ashes of the overnight fire lay in the grate. On the table were the four guttered and burned-out candles, with the cards scattered over its surface. The chairs had been moved back against the walls, but all else was as it had been the night before. Holmes paced with light, swift steps about the room; he sat in the various chairs, drawing them up and reconstructing their positions. He tested how much of the garden was visible; he examined the floor, the ceiling and the fireplace; but never once did I see that sudden brightening of his eyes and tightening of his lips which would have told me that he saw some gleam of light in this utter darkness.

'Why a fire?' he asked once. 'Had they always a fire in this small room on a spring evening?'

Mortimer Tregennis explained that the night was cold and damp. For that reason, after his arrival, the fire was lit. 'What are you going to do now, Mr Holmes?' he asked.

My friend smiled and laid his hand upon my arm. 'I think, Watson, that I shall resume that course of tobacco-poisoning which you have so often and so justly condemned,' said he.

'With your permission, gentlemen, we will now return to our cottage, for I am not aware that any new factor is likely to come to our notice here. I will turn the facts over in my mind, Mr Tregennis, and should anything occur to me I will certainly communicate with you and the vicar. In the meantime I wish you both good-morning.'

It was not until long after we were back in Poldhu Cottage that Holmes broke his complete and absorbed silence. He sat coiled in his armchair, his haggard and ascetic face hardly visible amid the blue swirl of his tobacco smoke, his black brows drawn down, his forehead contracted, his eyes vacant and far away. Finally he laid down his pipe and sprang to his feet.

'It won't do, Watson!' said he with a laugh. 'Let us walk along the cliffs together and search for flint arrows. We are more likely to find them than clues to this problem. To let the brain work without sufficient material is like racing an engine. It racks itself to pieces. The sea air, sunshine and patience, Watson – all else will come.

'Now, let us calmly define our position, Watson,' he continued as we skirted the cliffs together. 'Let us get a firm grip of the very little which we DO know, so that when fresh facts arise we may be ready to fit them into their places. I take it, in the first place, that neither of us is prepared to admit diabolical intrusions into the affairs of men. Let us begin by ruling that entirely out of our minds. Very good. There remain three persons who have been grievously stricken by some conscious or unconscious human agency. That is firm ground. Now, when did this occur? Evidently, assuming his narrative to be true, it was immediately after Mr Mortimer

Tregennis had left the room. That is a very important point. The presumption is that it was within a few minutes afterwards. The cards still lay upon the table. It was already past their usual hour for bed. Yet they had not changed their position or pushed back their chairs. I repeat, then, that the occurrence was immediately after his departure, and not later than eleven o'clock last night.

'Our next obvious step is to check, so far as we can, the movements of Mortimer Tregennis after he left the room. In this there is no difficulty, and they seem to be above suspicion. Knowing my methods as you do, you were, of course, conscious of the somewhat clumsy water-pot expedient by which I obtained a clearer impress of his foot than might otherwise have been possible. The wet, sandy path took it admirably. Last night was also wet, you will remember, and it was not difficult – having obtained a sample print – to pick out his track among others and to follow his movements. He appears to have walked away swiftly in the direction of the vicarage.

'If, then, Mortimer Tregennis disappeared from the scene, and yet some outside person affected the card-players, how can we reconstruct that person, and how was such an impression of horror conveyed? Mrs Porter may be eliminated. She is evidently harmless. Is there any evidence that someone crept up to the garden window and in some manner produced so terrific an effect that he drove those who saw it out of their senses? The only suggestion in this direction comes from Mortimer Tregennis himself, who says that his brother spoke about some movement in the garden. That is certainly remarkable, as the night was rainy, cloudy and dark. Anyone who had the design to alarm these people would be compelled to place his very face against the glass before he could be seen. There is a three-foot flower-border outside this window, but no indication of a footmark. It is difficult to imagine, then, how an outsider could have made so terrible an impression upon the company, nor have we found any possible motive for so strange and elaborate an attempt. You perceive our difficulties, Watson?'

'They are only too clear,' I answered with conviction.

'And yet, with a little more material, we may prove that they are not insurmountable,' said Holmes. 'I fancy that among your extensive archives, Watson, you may find some which were nearly as obscure. Meanwhile, we shall put the case aside until more accurate data are available, and devote the rest of our morning to the pursuit of neolithic man.'

I may have commented upon my friend's power of mental detachment, but never have I wondered at it more than upon that spring morning in Cornwall when for two hours he discoursed upon Celts, arrowheads and shards, as lightly as if no sinister mystery were waiting for his solution. It was not until we had returned in the afternoon to our cottage that we found a visitor awaiting us, who soon brought our minds back to the matter in hand. Neither of us needed to be told who that visitor was. The huge body, the craggy and deeply seamed face with the fierce eyes and hawk-like nose, the grizzled hair which nearly brushed our cottage ceiling, the beard – golden at the fringes and white near the lips, save for the nicotine stain from his perpetual cigar –all these were as well known in London as in Africa, and could only be associated with the tremendous personality of Dr Leon Sterndale, the great lion-hunter and explorer.

We had heard of his presence in the district and had once or twice caught sight of his tall figure upon the moorland paths. He made no advances to us, however, nor would we have dreamed of doing so to him, as it was well known that it was his love of seclusion which caused him to spend the greater part of the intervals between his journeys in a small bungalow buried in the lonely wood of Beauchamp Arriance. Here, amid his books and his maps, he lived an absolutely lonely life, attending to his own simple wants and paying little apparent heed to the affairs of his neighbours. It was a surprise to me, therefore, to hear him asking Holmes in an eager voice whether he had made any advance in his reconstruction of this mysterious episode. 'The county police are utterly at fault,' said he, 'but perhaps your wider experience has suggested some conceivable explanation. My only claim to being taken into your confidence is that during my many residences here I have come to know this family of Tregennis very well – indeed, upon my Cornish mother's side I could call them cousins – their strange fate has naturally been a great shock to me. I may tell you that I had got as far as Plymouth upon my way to Africa, but the news reached me this morning, and I came straight back again to help in the inquiry.'

Holmes raised his eyebrows.

'Did you lose your boat through it?'

'I will take the next.'

'Dear me! That is friendship indeed.'

'I tell you they were relatives.'

'Quite so – cousins of your mother. Was your baggage aboard the ship?'

'Some of it, but the main part at the hotel.'

'I see. But surely this event could not have found its way into the Plymouth morning papers.'

'No, sir; I had a telegram.'

'Might I ask from whom?'

A shadow passed over the gaunt face of the explorer.

'You are very inquisitive, Mr Holmes.'

'It is my business.'

With an effort Dr Sterndale recovered his ruffled composure.

'I have no objection to telling you,' he said. 'It was Mr Roundhay, the vicar, who sent me the telegram which recalled me.'

'Thank you,' said Holmes. 'I may say in answer to your original question that I have not cleared my mind entirely on the subject of this case, but that I have every hope of reaching some conclusion. It would be premature to say more.'

'Perhaps you would not mind telling me if your suspicions point in any particular direction?'

'No, I can hardly answer that.'

'Then I have wasted my time and need not prolong my visit.' The famous doctor strode out of our cottage in considerable ill-humour, and within five minutes Holmes had followed him. I saw him no more until the evening, when he returned with a slow step and haggard face which assured me that he had made no great progress with his investigation. He glanced at a telegram which awaited him and threw it into the grate.

'From the Plymouth hotel, Watson,' he said. 'I learned the name of it from the vicar, and I wired to make certain that Dr Leon Sterndale's account was true. It appears that he did indeed spend last night there, and that he has actually allowed some of his baggage to go on to Africa, while he returned to be present at this investigation. What do you make of that, Watson?'

'He is deeply interested.'

'Deeply interested – yes. There is a thread here which we had not yet grasped and which might lead us through the tangle. Cheer up, Watson, for I am very sure that our material has not yet all come to hand. When it does we may soon leave our difficulties behind us.'

Little did I think how soon the words of Holmes would be realised, or how strange and sinister would be that new development which opened up an entirely fresh line of investigation. I was shaving at my window in the morning when I heard the rattle of hoofs and, looking up, saw a dog-cart coming at a gallop down the road. It pulled up at our door, and our friend, the vicar, sprang from it and rushed up our garden path. Holmes was already dressed, and we hastened down to meet him.

Our visitor was so excited that he could hardly articulate, but at last in gasps and bursts his tragic story came out of him.

'We are devil-ridden, Mr Holmes! My poor parish is devil-ridden!' he cried. 'Satan himself is loose in it! We are given over into his hands!' He danced about in his agitation, a ludicrous object if it were not for his ashy face and startled eyes. Finally he shot out his terrible news.

'Mr Mortimer Tregennis died during the night, and with exactly the same symptoms as the rest of his family.'

Holmes sprang to his feet, all energy in an instant.

'Can you fit us both into your dog-cart?'

'Yes, I can.'

'Then, Watson, we will postpone our breakfast. Mr Roundhay, we are entirely at your disposal. Hurry – hurry, before things get disarranged.'

The lodger occupied two rooms at the vicarage, which were in an angle by themselves, the one above the other. Below was a large sitting-room; above, his bedroom. They looked out upon a croquet lawn which came up to the windows. We had arrived before the doctor or the police, so that everything was absolutely undisturbed. Let me describe exactly the scene as we saw it upon that misty March morning. It has left an impression which can never be effaced from my mind.

The atmosphere of the room was of a horrible and depressing stuffiness. The servant who had first entered had thrown up the window, or it would have been even more intolerable. This might partly be due to the fact that a lamp stood flaring and smoking on the centre table. Beside it sat the dead man, leaning back in his chair, his thin beard projecting, his spectacles pushed up on to his forehead, and his lean dark face turned towards the window and twisted into the same distortion of terror which had marked the features of his dead sister. His limbs were convulsed and his fingers contorted as though he had died in a very paroxysm of fear. He was fully clothed, though there were signs that his dressing had been done in a hurry. We had already learned that his bed had been slept in, and that the tragic end had come to him in the early morning.

One realised the red-hot energy which underlay Holmes's phlegmatic exterior when one saw the sudden change which came over him from the moment that he entered the fatal apartment. In an instant he was tense and alert, his eyes shining, his face set, his limbs quivering with eager activity. He was out on the lawn, in through the window, round the room, and up into the bedroom, for all the world like a dashing foxhound drawing a cover. In the bedroom he made a rapid cast around and ended by throwing open the window, which appeared to give him some fresh cause for excitement, for he leaned out of it with loud ejaculations of interest and delight. Then he rushed down the stair, out through the open window, threw himself upon his face on the lawn, sprang up and into the room once more, all with the energy of the hunter who is at the very heels of his quarry. The lamp, which was an ordinary standard, he examined with minute care, making certain measurements upon its bowl. He carefully scrutinised with his lens the talc shield which covered the top of the chimney and scraped off some ashes which adhered to its upper surface, putting some of them into an envelope, which he placed in his pocketbook. Finally, just as the doctor and the official police put in an appearance, he beckoned to the vicar and we all three went out upon the lawn.

'I am glad to say that my investigation has not been entirely barren,' he remarked. 'I cannot remain to discuss the matter with the police, but I should be exceedingly obliged, Mr Roundhay, if you would give the inspector my compliments and direct his attention to the bedroom window and to the sitting-room lamp. Each is suggestive, and together they are almost conclusive. If the police would desire further information I shall be happy to see any of them at the cottage. And now, Watson, I think that, perhaps, we shall be better employed elsewhere.'

It may be that the police resented the intrusion of an amateur, or that they imagined themselves to be upon some hopeful line of investigation; but it is certain that we heard nothing from them for the next two days. During this time Holmes spent some of his time smoking and dreaming in the cottage; but a greater portion in country walks which he undertook alone, returning after many hours without remark as to where he had been. One experiment served to show me the line of his investigation. He had bought a lamp which was the duplicate of the one which had burned in the room of Mortimer Tregennis on the morning of the tragedy. This he filled with the same oil as that used at the vicarage, and he carefully timed the period which it would take to be exhausted. Another experiment which he made was of a more unpleasant nature, and one which I am not likely ever to forget.

'You will remember, Watson,' he remarked one afternoon, 'that there is a single common point of resemblance in the varying reports which have reached us. This concerns the effect of the atmosphere of the room in each case upon those who had first entered it. You will recollect that Mortimer Tregennis, in describing the episode of his last visit to his brother's house, remarked that the doctor on entering the room fell into a chair? You had forgotten? Well I can answer for it that it was so. Now, you will remember also that Mrs Porter, the housekeeper, told us that she herself fainted upon entering the room and had afterwards opened the window.

In the second case – that of Mortimer Tregennis himself – you cannot have forgotten the horrible stuffiness of the room when we arrived, though the servant had thrown open the window. That servant, I found upon inquiry, was so ill that she had gone to her bed. You will admit, Watson, that these facts are very suggestive. In each case there is evidence of a poisonous atmosphere. In each case, also, there is combustion going on in the room – in the one case a fire, in the other a lamp. The fire was needed, but the lamp was lit – as a comparison of the oil consumed will show – long after it was broad daylight. Why? Surely because there is some connection between three things – the burning, the stuffy atmosphere and, finally, the madness or death of those unfortunate people. That is clear, is it not?'

'It would appear so.'

'At least we may accept it as a working hypothesis. We will suppose, then, that something was burned in each case which produced an atmosphere causing strange toxic effects. Very good. In the first instance – that of the Tregennis family – this substance was placed in the fire. Now the window was shut, but the fire would naturally carry fumes to some extent up the chimney. Hence one would expect the effects of the poison to be less than in the second case, where there was less escape for the vapour. The result seems to indicate that it was so, since in the first case only the woman, who had presumably the more sensitive organism, was killed, the others exhibiting that temporary or permanent lunacy which is evidently the first effect of the drug. In the second case the result was complete. The facts, therefore, seem to bear out the theory of a poison which worked by combustion.

'With this train of reasoning in my head I naturally looked about in Mortimer Tregennis's room to find some remains of this substance. The obvious place to look was the talc shelf or smoke-guard of the lamp. There, sure enough, I perceived a number of flaky ashes, and round the edges a fringe of brownish powder, which had not yet been consumed. Half of this I took, as you saw, and I placed it in an envelope.'

'Why half, Holmes?'

'It is not for me, my dear Watson, to stand in the way of the official police force. I leave them all the evidence which I found. The poison still remained upon the talc had they the wit to find it. Now, Watson, we will light our lamp; we will, however, take the precaution to open our window to avoid the premature decease of two deserving members of society, and you will seat yourself near that open window in an armchair unless, like a sensible man, you determine to have nothing to do with the affair. Oh, you will see it out, will you? I thought I knew my Watson. This chair I will place opposite yours, so that we may be the same distance from the poison and face to face. The door we will leave ajar. Each is now in a position to watch the other and to bring the experiment to an end should the symptoms seem alarming. Is that all clear? Well, then, I take our powder – or what remains of it – from the envelope, and I lay it above the burning lamp. So! Now, Watson, let us sit down and await developments.'

They were not long in coming. I had hardly settled in my chair before I was conscious of a thick, musky odour, subtle and nauseous. At the very first whiff of it my brain and my imagination were beyond all control. A thick, black cloud swirled before my eyes, and my mind told me that in this cloud, unseen as yet, but about to spring out upon my appalled senses, lurked all that was vaguely horrible, all that was monstrous and inconceivably wicked in the universe. Vague shapes swirled and swam amid the dark cloud-bank, each a menace and a warning of something coming, the advent of some unspeakable dweller upon the threshold, whose very shadow would blast my soul. A freezing horror took possession of me. I felt that my hair was rising, that my eyes were protruding, that my mouth was opened, and my tongue like leather. The turmoil within my brain was such that something must surely snap. I tried to scream and was vaguely aware of some hoarse croak which was my own voice, but distant and detached from myself. At the same moment, in some effort of escape, I broke through that cloud of despair and had a glimpse of Holmes's face, white, rigid and drawn with horror – the very look which I had seen upon the features of the dead. It was that vision which gave me an instant of sanity and of strength. I dashed from my chair, threw my arms round Holmes, and together we lurched through the door, and an instant afterwards had thrown ourselves down upon the grass plot and were lying side by side, conscious only of the glorious sunshine which was bursting its way through the hellish cloud of terror which had girt us in. Slowly it rose from our souls like the mists from a landscape until peace and reason had returned, and we were sitting upon the grass, wiping our clammy foreheads, and looking with apprehension at each other to mark the last traces of that terrific experience which we had undergone.

'Upon my word, Watson!' said Holmes at last with an unsteady voice, 'I owe you both my thanks and an apology. It was an unjustifiable experiment even for one's self, and doubly so for a friend. I am really very sorry.'

'You know,' I answered with some emotion, for I have never seen so much of Holmes's heart before, 'that it is my greatest joy and privilege to help you.'

He relapsed at once into the half-humorous, half-cynical vein which was his habitual attitude to those about him. 'It would be superfluous to drive us mad, my dear Watson,' said he. 'A candid observer would certainly declare that we were so already before we embarked upon so wild an experiment. I confess that I never imagined that the effect could be so sudden and so severe.' He dashed into the cottage, and, reappearing with the burning lamp held at full arm's length, he threw it among a bank of brambles. 'We must give the room a little time to clear. I take it, Watson, that you have no longer a shadow of a doubt as to how these tragedies were produced?'

'None whatever.'

'But the cause remains as obscure as before. Come into the arbour here and let us discuss it together. That villainous stuff seems still to linger round my throat. I think we must admit that all the evidence points to this man, Mortimer Tregennis, having been the criminal in the first tragedy, though he was the victim in the second one. We must remember, in the first place, that there is some story of a family quarrel, followed by a reconciliation. How bitter that quarrel may have been, or how hollow the reconciliation we cannot tell. When I think of Mortimer Tregennis, with the foxy face and the small shrewd, beady eyes behind the spectacles, he is not a man whom I should judge to be of a particularly forgiving disposition. Well, in the next place, you will remember that this idea of someone moving in the garden, which took our attention for a moment from the real cause of the tragedy, emanated from him. He had a motive in misleading us. Finally, if he did not throw the substance into the fire at the moment of leaving the room, who did do so? The affair happened immediately after his departure. Had anyone else come in, the family would certainly have risen from the table. Besides, in peaceful Cornwall, visitors did not arrive after ten o'clock at night. We may take it, then, that all the evidence points to Mortimer Tregennis as the culprit.'

'Then his own death was suicide!'

'Well, Watson, it is on the face of it a not impossible supposition. The man who had the guilt upon his soul of having brought such a fate upon his own family might well be driven by remorse to inflict it upon himself. There are, however, some cogent reasons against it. Fortunately, there is one man in England who knows all about it, and I have made arrangements by which we shall hear the facts this afternoon from his own lips. Ah! he is a little before his time. Perhaps you would kindly step this way, Dr Leon Sterndale. We have been conducting a chemical experiment indoors which has left our little room hardly fit for the reception of so distinguished a visitor.'

I had heard the click of the garden gate, and now the majestic figure of the great African explorer appeared upon the path. He turned in some surprise towards the rustic arbour in which we sat.

'You sent for me, Mr Holmes. I had your note about an hour ago, and I have come, though I really do not know why I should obey your summons.'

'Perhaps we can clear the point up before we separate,' said Holmes. 'Meanwhile, I am much obliged to you for your courteous acquiescence. You will excuse this informal reception in the open air, but my friend Watson and I have nearly furnished an additional chapter to what the papers call the Cornish Horror, and we prefer a clear atmosphere for the present. Perhaps, since the matters which we have to discuss will affect you personally in a very intimate fashion, it is as well that we should talk where there can be no eavesdropping.'

The explorer took his cigar from his lips and gazed sternly at my companion.

'I am at a loss to know, sir,' he said, 'what you can have to speak about which affects me personally in a very intimate fashion.'

'The killing of Mortimer Tregennis,' said Holmes.

For a moment I wished that I were armed. Sterndale's fierce face turned to a dusky red, his eyes glared, and the knotted, passionate veins started out in his forehead, while he sprang forward with clenched hands towards my companion. Then he stopped, and with a violent effort he resumed a cold, rigid calmness, which was, perhaps, more suggestive of danger than his hot-headed outburst.

'I have lived so long among savages and beyond the law,' said he, 'that I have got into the way of being a law to myself. You would do well, Mr Holmes, not to forget it, for I have no desire to do you an injury.'

'Nor have I any desire to do you an injury, Dr Sterndale. Surely the clearest proof of it is that, knowing what I know, I have sent for you and not for the police.'

Sterndale sat down with a gasp, overawed for, perhaps, the first time in his adventurous life. There was a calm assurance of power in Holmes's manner which could not be withstood. Our visitor stammered for a moment, his great hands opening and shutting in his agitation.

'What do you mean?' he asked at last. 'If this is bluff upon your part, Mr Holmes, you have chosen a bad man for your experiment. Let us have no more beating about the bush. What do you mean?'

'I will tell you,' said Holmes, 'and the reason why I tell you is that I hope frankness may beget frankness. What my next step may be will depend entirely upon the nature of your own defence.'

'My defence?'

'Yes, sir.'

'My defence against what?'

'Against the charge of killing Mortimer Tregennis.'

Sterndale mopped his forehead with his handkerchief. 'Upon my word, you are getting on,' said he. 'Do all your successes depend upon this prodigious power of bluff?'

'The bluff,' said Holmes sternly, 'is upon your side, Dr Leon Sterndale, and not upon mine. As a proof I will tell you some of the facts upon which my conclusions are based. Of your return from Plymouth, allowing much of your property to go on to Africa, I will say nothing save that it first informed me that you were one of the factors which had to be taken into account in reconstructing this drama –'

'I came back –'

'I have heard your reasons and regard them as unconvincing and inadequate. We will pass that. You came down here to ask me whom I suspected. I refused to answer you. You then went to the vicarage, waited outside it for some time, and finally returned to your cottage.'

'How do you know that?'

'I followed you.'

'I saw no one.'

'That is what you may expect to see when I follow you. You spent a restless night at your cottage, and you formed certain plans, which in the early morning you proceeded to put into execution. Leaving your door just as day was breaking, you filled your pocket with some reddish gravel that was lying heaped beside your gate.'

Sterndale gave a violent start and looked at Holmes in amazement.

'You then walked swiftly for the mile which separated you from the vicarage. You were wearing, I may remark, the same pair of ribbed tennis shoes which are at the present moment upon your feet. At the vicarage you passed through the orchard and the side hedge, coming out under the window of the lodger Tregennis. It was now daylight, but the household was not yet stirring. You drew some of the gravel from your pocket, and you threw it up at the window above you.'

Sterndale sprang to his feet.

'I believe that you are the devil himself!' he cried.

Holmes smiled at the compliment. 'It took two, or possibly three, handfuls before the lodger came to the window.

You beckoned him to come down. He dressed hurriedly and descended to his sitting-room. You entered by the window. There was an interview – a short one – during which you walked up and down the room. Then you passed out and closed the window, standing on the lawn outside smoking a cigar and watching what occurred. Finally, after the death of Tregennis, you withdrew as you had come. Now, Dr Sterndale, how do you justify such conduct, and what were the motives for your actions? If you prevaricate or trifle with me, I give you my assurance that the matter will pass out of my hands for ever.'

Our visitor's face had turned ashen grey as he listened to the words of his accuser. Now he sat for some time in thought with his face sunk in his hands. Then with a sudden impulsive gesture he plucked a photograph from his breast-pocket and threw it on the rustic table before us.

'That is why I have done it,' said he.

It showed the bust and face of a very beautiful woman. Holmes stooped over it.

'Brenda Tregennis,' said he.

'Yes, Brenda Tregennis,' repeated our visitor. 'For years I have loved her. For years she has loved me. There is the secret of that Cornish seclusion which people have marvelled at. It has brought me close to the one thing on earth that was dear to me. I could not marry her, for I have a wife who has left me for years and yet whom, by the deplorable laws of England, I could not divorce. For years Brenda waited. For years I waited. And this is what we have waited for.' A terrible sob shook his great frame, and he clutched his throat under his brindled beard. Then with an effort he mastered himself and spoke on:

'The vicar knew. He was in our confidence. He would tell you that she was an angel upon earth. That was why he telegraphed to me and I returned. What was my baggage or Africa to me when I learned that such a fate had come upon my darling? There you have the missing clue to my action, Mr Holmes.'

'Proceed,' said my friend.

Dr Sterndale drew from his pocket a paper packet and laid it upon the table. On the outside was written 'Radix pedis diaboli' with a red poison label beneath it. He pushed it towards me. 'I understand that you are a doctor, sir. Have you ever heard of this preparation?'

'Devil's-foot root! No, I have never heard of it.'

'It is no reflection upon your professional knowledge,' said he, 'for I believe that, save for one sample in a laboratory at Buda, there is no other specimen in Europe. It has not yet found its way either into the pharmacopoeia or into the literature of toxicology. The root is shaped like a foot, half human, half goatlike; hence the fanciful name given by a botanical missionary. It is used as an ordeal poison by the medicine-men in certain districts of West Africa and is kept as a secret among them. This particular specimen I obtained under very extraordinary circumstances in the Ubangi country.' He opened the paper as he spoke and disclosed a heap of reddish-brown, snuff-like powder.

'Well, sir?' asked Holmes sternly.

'I am about to tell you, Mr Holmes, all that actually occurred, for you already know so much that it is clearly to my interest that you should know all. I have already explained the relationship in which I stood to the Tregennis family.

For the sake of the sister I was friendly with the brothers. There was a family quarrel about money which estranged this man Mortimer, but it was supposed to be made up, and I afterwards met him as I did the others. He was a sly, subtle, scheming man, and several things arose which gave me a suspicion of him, but I had no cause for any positive quarrel.

'One day, only a couple of weeks ago, he came down to my cottage and I showed him some of my African curiosities. Among other things I exhibited this powder, and I told him of its strange properties, how it stimulates those brain centres which control the emotion of fear, and how either madness or death is the fate of the unhappy native who is subjected to the ordeal by the priest of his tribe. I told him also how powerless European science would be to detect it. How he took it I cannot say, for I never left the room, but there is no doubt that it was then, while I was opening cabinets and stooping to boxes, that he managed to abstract some of the devil's-foot root. I well remember how he plied me with questions as to the amount and the time that was needed for its effect, but I little dreamed that he could have a personal reason for asking.

'I thought no more of the matter until the vicar's telegram reached me at Plymouth. This villain had thought that I would be at sea before the news could reach me, and that I should be lost for years in Africa. But I returned at once. Of course, I could not listen to the details without feeling assured that my poison had been used. I came round to see you on the chance that some other explanation had suggested itself to you. But there could be none. I was convinced that Mortimer Tregennis was the murderer; that for the sake of money, and with the idea, perhaps, that if the other members of his family were all insane he would be the sole guardian of their joint property, he had used the devil's-foot powder upon them, driven two of them out of their senses, and killed his sister Brenda, the one human being whom I have ever loved or who has ever loved me. There was his crime; what was to be his punishment?

'Should I appeal to the law? Where were my proofs? I knew that the facts were true, but could I help to make a jury of countrymen believe so fantastic a story? I might or I might not. But I could not afford to fail. My soul cried out for revenge. I have said to you once before, Mr Holmes, that I have spent much of my life outside the law, and that I have come at last to be a law to myself. So it was even now. I determined that the fate which he had given to others should be shared by himself. Either that or I would do justice upon him with my own hand. In all England there can be no man who sets less value upon his own life than I do at the present moment.

'Now I have told you all. You have yourself supplied the rest. I did, as you say, after a restless night, set off early from my cottage. I foresaw the difficulty of arousing him, so I gathered some gravel from the pile which you have mentioned, and I used it to throw up to his window. He came down and admitted me through the window of the sitting-room. I laid his offence before him. I told him that I had come both as judge and executioner. The wretch sank into a chair, paralysed at the sight of my revolver. I lit the lamp, put the powder above it, and stood outside the window, ready to carry out my threat to shoot him should he try to leave the room. In five minutes he died. My God! how he died! But my heart was flint, for he endured nothing which my innocent darling had not felt before him. There is my story, Mr Holmes. Perhaps, if you loved a woman, you would have done as much yourself. At any rate, I am in your hands. You can take what steps you like. As I have already said, there is no man living who can fear death less than I do.'

Holmes sat for some little time in silence.

'What were your plans?' he asked at last.

'I had intended to bury myself in central Africa. My work there is but half finished.'

'Go and do the other half,' said Holmes. 'I, at least, am not prepared to prevent you.'

Dr Sterndale raised his giant figure, bowed gravely, and walked from the arbour. Holmes lit his pipe and handed me his pouch.

'Some fumes which are not poisonous would be a welcome change,' said he. 'I think you must agree, Watson, that it is not a case in which we are called upon to interfere. Our investigation has been independent, and our action shall be so also. You would not denounce the man?'

'Certainly not,' I answered.

'I have never loved, Watson, but if I did and if the woman I loved had met such an end, I might act even as our lawless lion-hunter has done. Who knows? Well, Watson, I will not offend your intelligence by explaining what is obvious. The gravel upon the window-sill was, of course, the starting-point of my research. It was unlike anything in the vicarage garden. Only when my attention had been drawn to Dr Sterndale and his cottage did I find its counterpart. The lamp shining in broad daylight and the remains of powder upon the shield were successive links in a fairly obvious chain. And now, my dear Watson, I think we may dismiss the matter from our mind and go back with a clear conscience to the study of those Chaldean roots which are surely to be traced in the Cornish branch of the great Celtic speech.'

The Entertaining Episode of the Article in Question

Dorothy L. Sayers

The unprofessional detective career of Lord Peter Wimsey
was regulated (though the word has no particular propriety
in this connection) by a persistent and undignified inquisi-
tiveness. The habit of asking silly questions – natural,
though irritating, in the immature male – remained with him
long after his immaculate man, Bunter, had become attached
to his service to shave the bristles from his chin and see to
the due purchase and housing of Napoleon brandies and
Villar y Villar cigars. At the age of thirty-two his sister Mary
christened him Elephant's Child. It was his idiotic inquiries
(before his brother, the Duke of Denver, who grew scarlet
with mortification) as to what the Woolsack was really stuffed
with that led the then Lord Chancellor idly to investigate the
article in question, and to discover, tucked deep within its

recesses, that famous diamond necklace of the Marchioness of Writtle which had disappeared on the day Parliament was opened and been safely secreted by one of the cleaners. It was by a continual and personal badgering of the Chief Engineer at 2LO on the question of 'What is Oscillation and How is it Done?' that his lordship incidentally unmasked the great Ploffsky gang of Anarchist conspirators, who were accustomed to converse in code by a methodical system of howls, superimposed (to the great annoyance of listeners in British and European stations) upon the London wavelength and duly relayed by 5XX over a radius of some five or six hundred miles. He annoyed persons of more leisure than decorum by suddenly taking into his head to descend to the Underground by way of the stairs, though the only exciting things he ever actually found there were the blood-stained boots of the Sloane Square murderer; on the other hand, when the drains were taken up at Glegg's Folly, it was by hanging about and hindering the plumbers at their job that he accidentally made the discovery which hanged that detestable poisoner, William Girdlestone Chitty.

Accordingly, it was with no surprise at all that the reliable Bunter, one April morning, received the announcement of an abrupt change of plan.

They had arrived at the Gare Saint-Lazare in good time to register the luggage. Their three months' trip to Italy had been purely for enjoyment, and had been followed by a pleasant fortnight in Paris. They were now intending to pay a short visit to the Duc de Sainte-Croix in Rouen on their way back to England. Lord Peter paced the Salle des Pas Perdus for some time, buying an illustrated paper or two and eyeing the crowd. He bent an appreciative eye on a slim, shingled creature with the face of a Paris *gamin,* but was forced to admit to himself that her ankles were a trifle on the thick side; he assisted an elderly lady who was explaining to the bookstall clerk that she wanted a map of Paris and not a *carte postale,* consumed a quick cognac at one of the little green tables at the far end, and then decided he had better go down and see how Bunter was getting on.

In half an hour Bunter and his porter had worked themselves up to the second place in the enormous queue – for, as usual, one of the weighing-machines was out of order. In front of them stood an agitated little group – the young woman Lord Peter had noticed in the Salle des Pas Perdus, a sallow-faced man of about thirty, their porter, and the registration official, who was peering eagerly through his little *guichet.*

'*Mais je te répète que je ne les ai pas,*' said the sallow man heatedly. '*Voyons, voyons. C'est bien toi qui les as pris, n'est-ce pas? Eh bien, alors, comment veux-tu que je les aie, moi?*'

'*Mais non, mais non, je te les ai bien donnés là-haut, avant d'aller chercher les journaux.*'

'*Je t'assure que non. Enfin, c'est évident! J'ai cherché partout, que diable! Tu ne m'as rien donné, du tout, du tout.*'

'*Mais puisque je t'ai dit d'aller faire enregistrer les bagages! Ne faut-il pas que je t'aie bien remis les billets? Me prends-tu pour un imbécile? Va! On n'est pas dépourvu de sens! Mais regarde l'heure! Le train part à 11 h. 20 m. Cherche un peu, au moins.*'

'*Mais puisque j'ai cherché partout – le gilet, rien! Le jacquet rien, rien! Le pardessus – rien! rien! rien! C'est toi—*'

Here the porter, urged by the frantic cries and stamping of the queue, and the repeated insults of Lord Peter's porter, flung himself into the discussion.

'*P't-être qu' m'sieur a bouté les billets dans son pantalon,*' he suggested.

'*Triple idiot!*' snapped the traveller, '*je vous le demande – est-ce qu'on a jamais entendu parler de mettre des billets dans son pantalon? Jamais—*'

The French porter is a Republican, and, moreover, extremely ill-paid. The large tolerance of his English colleague is not for him.

'*Ah!*' said he, dropping two heavy bags and looking round for moral support. '*Vous dîtes? En voilà du joli! Allons, mon p'tit, ce n'est pas parce qu'on porte un faux col qu'on a le droit d'insulter les gens.*'

The discussion might have become a full-blown row, had not the young man suddenly discovered the missing tickets – incidentally, they were in his trousers-pocket after all – and continued the registration of his luggage, to the undisguised satisfaction of the crowd.

'Bunter,' said his lordship, who had turned his back on the group and was lighting a cigarette, 'I am going to change the tickets. We shall go straight on to London. Have you got that snapshot affair of yours with you?'

'Yes, my lord.'

'The one you can work from your pocket without anyone noticing?'

'Yes, my lord.'

'Get me a picture of those two.'

'Yes, my lord.'

'I will see to the luggage. Wire to the Duc that I am unexpectedly called home.'

'Very good, my lord.'

Lord Peter did not allude to the matter again till Bunter was putting his trousers in the press in their cabin on board the *Normania*. Beyond ascertaining that the young man and woman who had aroused his curiosity were on the boat as second-class passengers, he had sedulously avoided contact with them.

'Did you get that photograph?'

'I hope so, my lord. As your lordship knows, the aim from the breast-pocket tends to be unreliable. I have made three attempts, and trust that one at least may prove to be not unsuccessful.'

'How soon can you develop them?'

'At once, if your lordship pleases. I have all the materials in my suitcase.'

'What fun!' said Lord Peter, eagerly tying himself into a pair of mauve silk pyjamas. 'May I hold the bottles and things?'

Mr Bunter poured three ounces of water into an eight-ounce measure, and handed his master a glass rod and a minute packet.

'If your lordship would be so good as to stir the contents of the white packet slowly into the water,' he said, bolting the door, 'and, when dissolved, add the contents of the blue packet.'

'Just like a Seidlitz powder,' said his lordship happily. 'Does it fizz?'

'Not much, my lord,' replied the expert, shaking a quantity of hypo crystals into the hand-basin.

'That's a pity,' said Lord Peter. 'I say, Bunter, it's no end of a bore to dissolve.'

'Yes, my lord,' returned Bunter sedately. 'I have always found that part of the process exceptionally tedious, my lord.'

Lord Peter jabbed viciously with the glass rod.

'Just you wait,' he said, in a vindictive tone, 'till we get to Waterloo.'

Three days later Lord Peter Wimsey sat in his book-lined sitting-room at 110A Piccadilly. The tall bunches of daffodils on the table smiled in the spring sunshine, and nodded to the breeze which danced in from the open window. The door opened, and his lordship glanced up from a handsome edition of the *Contes de la Fontaine,* whose handsome hand-coloured Fragonard plates he was examining with the aid of a lens.

'Morning, Bunter. Anything doing?'

'I have ascertained, my lord, that the young person in question has entered the service of the elder Duchess of Medway. Her name is Celestine Berger.'

'You are less accurate than usual, Bunter. Nobody off the stage is called Celestine. You should say "under the name of Celestine Berger". And the man?'

'He is domiciled at this address in Guilford Street, Bloomsbury, my lord.'

'Excellent, Mr Bunter. Now give me *Who's Who.* Was it a very tiresome job?'

'Not exceptionally so, my lord.'

'One of these days I suppose I shall give you something to do which you *will* jib at,' said his lordship, 'and you will leave me and I shall cut my throat. Thanks. Run away and play. I shall lunch at the club.'

The book which Bunter had handed his employer indeed bore the words *Who's Who* engrossed upon its cover, but it was to be found in no public library and in no bookseller's shop. It was a bulky manuscript, closely filled, in part with the small print-like handwriting of Mr Bunter, in part with Lord Peter's neat and altogether illegible hand. It contained biographies of the most unexpected people, and the most unexpected facts about the most obvious people. Lord Peter turned to a very long entry under the name of the Dowager Duchess of Medway. It appeared to make satisfactory reading, for after a time he smiled, closed the book, and went to the telephone. 'Yes – this is the Duchess of Medway. Who is it?' The deep, harsh old voice pleased Lord Peter. He could see the imperious face and upright figure of what had been the most famous beauty in the London of the sixties. 'It's Peter Wimsey, duchess.'

'Indeed, and how do you do, young man? Back from your Continental jaunting?'

'Just home – and longing to lay my devotion at the feet of the most fascinating lady in England.'

'God bless my soul, child, what do you want?' demanded the duchess. 'Boys like you don't flatter an old woman for nothing.'

'I want to tell you my sins, duchess.'

'You should have lived in the great days,' said the voice appreciatively. 'Your talents are wasted on the young fry.'

'That is why I want to talk to you, duchess.'

'Well, my dear, if you've committed any sins worth hearing I shall enjoy your visit.'

'You are as exquisite in kindness as in charm. I am coming this afternoon.'

'I will be at home to you and to no one else. There.'

'Dear lady, I kiss your hands,' said Lord Peter, and he heard a deep chuckle as the duchess rang off.

'You may say what you like, duchess,' said Lord Peter from his reverential position on the fender-stool, 'but you are the youngest grandmother in London, not excepting my own mother.'

'Dear Honoria is the merest child,' said the duchess. 'I have twenty years more experience of life, and have arrived at the age when we boast of them. I have every intention of being a great-grandmother before I die. Sylvia is being married in a fortnight's time, to that stupid son of Attenbury's.'

'Abcock?'

'Yes. He keeps the worst hunters I ever saw, and doesn't know still champagne from sauterne. But Sylvia is stupid, too, poor child, so I dare say they will get on charmingly. In my day one had to have either brains or beauty to get on – preferably both. Nowadays nothing seems to be required but a total lack of figure. But all the sense went out of society with the House of Lords' veto. I except you, Peter. You have talents. It is a pity you do not employ them in politics.'

'Dear lady, God forbid.'

'Perhaps you are right, as things are. There were giants in my day. Dear Dizzy. I remember so well, when his wife died, how hard we all tried to get him – Medway had died the year before – but he was wrapped up in that stupid Bradford woman, who had never even read a line of one of his books, and couldn't have understood 'em if she had. And now we have Abcock standing for Midhurst, and married to Sylvia!'

'You haven't invited me to the wedding, duchess dear. I'm so hurt,' sighed his lordship.

'Bless you, child, *I* didn't send out the invitations, but I suppose your brother and that tiresome wife of his will be there. You must come, of course, if you want to. I had no idea you had a passion for weddings.'

'Hadn't you?' said Peter. 'I have a passion for this one. I want to see Lady Sylvia wearing white satin and the family lace and diamonds, and to sentimentalise over the days when my fox-terrier bit the stuffing out of her doll.'

'Very well, my dear, you shall. Come early and give me your support. As for the diamonds, if it weren't a family tradition, Sylvia shouldn't wear them. She has the impudence to complain of them.'

'I thought they were some of the finest in existence.'

'So they are. But she says the settings are ugly and old-fashioned, and she doesn't like diamonds, and they won't go with her dress. Such nonsense. Whoever heard of a girl not liking diamonds? She wants to be something romantic and moonshiny in pearls. I have no patience with her.'

'I'll promise to admire them,' said Peter – 'use the privilege of early acquaintance and tell her she's an ass and so on. I'd love to have a view of them. When do they come out of cold storage?'

'Mr Whitehead will bring them up from the Bank the night before,' said the duchess, 'and they'll go into the safe in my room. Come round at twelve o'clock and you shall have a private view of them.'

'That would be delightful. Mind they don't disappear in the night, won't you?'

'Oh, my dear, the house is going to be over-run with policemen. Such a nuisance. I suppose it can't be helped.'

'Oh, I think it's a good thing,' said Peter. 'I have rather an unwholesome weakness for policemen.'

On the morning of the wedding-day, Lord Peter emerged from Bunter's hands a marvel of sleek brilliance. His primrose-coloured hair was so exquisite a work of art that to eclipse it with his glossy hat was like shutting up the sun in a shrine of polished jet; his spats, light trousers and exquisitely polished shoes formed a tone-symphony in monochrome. It was only by the most impassioned pleading that he persuaded his tyrant to allow him to place two small photographs and a thin, foreign letter in his breast-pocket. Mr Bunter, likewise immaculately attired, stepped into the taxi after him. At noon precisely they were deposited beneath the striped awning which adorned the door of the Duchess of Medway's house in Park Lane. Bunter promptly disappeared in the direction of the back entrance, while his lordship mounted the steps and asked to see the dowager.

The majority of the guests had not yet arrived, but the house was full of agitated people, flitting hither and thither, with flowers and prayer-books, while a clatter of dishes and cutlery from the dining-room proclaimed the laying of a sumptuous breakfast. Lord Peter was shown into the morning-room while the footman went to announce him, and here he found a very close friend and devoted colleague, Detective-Inspector Parker, mounting guard in plain clothes over a costly collection of white elephants. Lord Peter greeted him with an affectionate hand-grip.

'All serene so far?' he inquired.

'Perfectly OK.'

'You got my note?'

'Sure thing. I've got three of our men shadowing your friend in Guilford Street. The girl is very much in evidence here. Does the old lady's wig and that sort of thing. Bit of a coming-on disposition, isn't she?'

'You surprise me,' said Lord Peter. 'No' – as his friend grinned sardonically – 'you really do. Not seriously? That would throw all my calculations out.'

'Oh, no! Saucy with her eyes and her tongue, that's all.'

'Do her job well?'

'I've heard no complaints. What put you on to this?'

'Pure accident. Of course I may be quite mistaken.'

'Did you receive any information from Paris?'

'I wish you wouldn't use that phrase,' said Lord Peter peevishly. 'It's so of the Yard – yardy. One of these days it'll give you away.'

'Sorry,' said Parker. 'Second nature, I suppose.'

'Those are the things to beware of,' returned his lordship, with an earnestness that seemed a little out of place. 'One can keep guard on everything but just those second-nature tricks.' He moved across to the window, which overlooked the tradesmen's entrance. 'Hullo!' he said, 'here's our bird.'

Parker joined him, and saw the neat, shingled head of the French girl from the Gare Saint-Lazare, topped by a neat black bandeau and bow. A man with a basket full of white narcissi had rung the bell, and appeared to be trying to make

46

a sale. Parker gently opened the window, and they heard Celestine say with a marked French accent, 'No, nossing today, sank you.' The man insisted in the monotonous whine of his type, thrusting a big bunch of the white flowers upon her, but she pushed them back into the basket with an angry exclamation and flirted away, tossing her head and slapping the door smartly to. The man moved off muttering. As he did so a thin, unhealthy-looking lounger in a check cap detached himself from a lamp-post opposite and mouched along the street after him, at the same time casting a glance up at the window. Mr Parker looked at Lord Peter, nodded, and made a slight sign with his hand. At once the man in the check cap removed his cigarette from his mouth, extinguished it, and, tucking the stub behind his ear, moved off without a second glance.

'Very interesting,' said Lord Peter, when both were out of sight. 'Hark!'

There was a sound of running feet overhead – a cry –and a general commotion. The two men dashed to the door as the bride, rushing frantically downstairs with her bevy of bridesmaids after her, proclaimed in a hysterical shriek: 'The diamonds! They're stolen! They're gone!'

Instantly the house was in an uproar. The servants and the caterer's men crowded into the hall; the bride's father burst out from his room in a magnificent white waistcoat and no coat; the Duchess of Medway descended upon Mr Parker, demanding that something should be done; while the butler, who never to the day of his death got over the disgrace, ran out of the pantry with a corkscrew in one hand and a priceless bottle of crusted port in the other, which he shook with all the vehemence of a town-crier ringing a bell. The only dignified entry was made by the dowager duchess, who came down like a ship in sail, dragging Celestine with her, and admonishing her not to be so silly.

'Be quiet, girl,' said the dowager. 'Anyone would think you were going to be murdered.'

'Allow me, your grace,' said Mr Bunter, appearing suddenly from nowhere in his usual unperturbed manner, and taking the agitated Celestine firmly by the arm. 'Young woman, calm yourself.'

'But what is to be *done?*' cried the bride's mother. 'How did it happen?'

It was at this moment that Detective-Inspector Parker took the floor. It was the most impressive and dramatic moment in his whole career. His magnificent calm rebuked the clamorous nobility surrounding him.

'Your grace,' he said, 'there is no cause for alarm. Our measures have been taken. We have the criminals and the gems, thanks to Lord Peter Wimsey, from whom we received inf —'

'Charles!' said Lord Peter in an awful voice.

'Warning of the attempt. One of our men is just bringing in the male criminal at the front door, taken red-handed with your grace's diamonds in his possession.' (All gazed round, and perceived indeed the check-capped lounger and a uniformed constable entering with the flower-seller between them.) 'The female criminal, who picked the lock of your grace's safe, is — here! No, you don't,' he added, as Celestine, amid a torrent of apache language which nobody, fortunately, had French enough to understand, attempted to whip out a revolver from the bosom of her demure black dress.

'Celestine Berger,' he continued, pocketing the weapon, 'I arrest you in the name of the law, and I warn you that anything you say will be taken down and used as evidence against you.'

'Heaven help us,' said Lord Peter; 'the roof would fly off the court. And you've got the name wrong, Charles. Ladies and gentlemen, allow me to introduce you to Jacques Lerouge, known as Sans-culotte – the youngest and cleverest thief, safe-breaker and female impersonator that ever occupied a dossier in the Palais de Justice.'

There was a gasp. Jacques Sans-culotte gave vent to a low oath and cocked a *gamin* grimace at Peter.

'*C'est parfait,*' said he; '*toutes mes félicitations, milord,* what you call a fair cop, *bein?* And now I know him,' he added, grinning at Bunter, 'the so-patient Englishman who stand behind us in the queue at Saint-Lazare. But tell me, please, how you know me, that I may correct it *next time.*'

'I have mentioned to you before, Charles,' said Lord Peter, 'the unwisdom of falling into habits of speech. They give you away. Now, in France, every male child is brought up to use masculine adjectives about himself. He says: *Que je suis beau!* But a little girl has it rammed home to her that she is female; she must say: *Que je suis belle!* It must make it beastly hard to be a female impersonator. When I am at a station and I hear an excited young woman say to her companion, *"Me prends-tu pour* un *imbécile"* – the masculine article arouses curiosity. And that's that!' he concluded briskly. 'The rest was merely a matter of getting Bunter to take a photograph and communicating with our friends of the Sûreté and Scotland Yard.'

Jacques Sans-culotte bowed again.

'Once more I congratulate milord. He is the only Englishman I have ever met who is capable of appreciating our beautiful language. I will pay great attention in future to the article in question.'

With an awful look, the Dowager Duchess of Medway advanced upon Lord Peter.

'Peter,' she said, 'do you mean to say you *knew* about this, and that for the last three weeks you have allowed me to be dressed and undressed and put to bed by a *young man?*'

His lordship had the grace to blush.

'Duchess,' he said humbly, 'on my honour I didn't know absolutely for certain till this morning. And the police were so anxious to have these people caught red-handed. What can I do to show my penitence? Shall I cut the privileged beast in pieces?'

The grim old mouth relaxed a little.

'After all,' said the dowager duchess, with the delightful consciousness that she was going to shock her daughter-in-law, 'there are very few women of my age who could make the same boast. It seems that we die as we have lived, my dear.'

For indeed the Dowager Duchess of Medway had been notable in her day.

The Mystery of Horne's Copse

Anthony Berkeley

Chapter I

The whole thing began on the 29 May.

It is over two years ago now and I can begin to look at it in its proper perspective; but even still my mind retains some echo of the incredulity, the horror, the dreadful doubts as to my own sanity and the sheer, cold-sweating terror which followed that ill-omened 19 May.

Curiously enough the talk had turned for a few minutes that evening upon Frank himself. We were sitting in the drawing-room of Bucklands after dinner, Sir Henry and Lady Rigby, Sylvia and I, and I can remember the intensity with which I was trying to find a really convincing excuse to get Sylvia alone with me for half an hour before I went home. We had only been engaged a week then and the longing for solitary places with population confined to two was tending to increase rather than diminish.

I think it was Lady Rigby who, taking advantage of a pause in her husband's emphatic monologue on phosphates (phosphates were at the time Sir Henry's chief passion), asked me whether I had heard anything of Frank since he went abroad.

'Yes,' I said. 'I had a picture postcard from him this morning. An incredibly blue Lake Como in the foreground and an impossibly white mountain at the back, with Cadenabbia sandwiched microscopically in between. Actually, though, he's in Bellagio for a few days.'

'Oh,' said Sylvia with interest and then looked extremely innocent. Bellagio had been mentioned between us as a possible place for the beginning of our own honeymoon.

The talk passed on to the Italian lakes in general. 'And Frank really does seem quite settled down now, Hugh, does he?' Lady Rigby asked casually, a few minutes later.

'Quite, I think,' I replied guardedly; for Frank had seemed quite settled several times, but had somehow become unsettled again very soon afterwards.

Frank Chappell was my first cousin and incidentally, as I had been an only child and Ravendean was entailed, my heir. Unfortunately he had been, till lately, most unsatisfactory in both capacities. Not that there was anything bad in him, I considered he was merely weak; but weakness, in its results, can be as devastating as any deliberate villainy. It was not really his fault. He derived on his mother's side from a stock which was, to put it frankly, rotten and Frank took after his mother's family. He had not been expelled from Eton, but only by inches; he had been sent down from Oxford and his departure from the Guards had been a still more serious affair. The shock of this last killed my uncle and Frank had come into the property. It was nothing magnificent, falling far short of the resources attached to Ravendean, but plenty to allow a man to maintain his wife in very tolerable comfort. Frank had run through it in three years.

He had then, quite unexpectedly, married one of his own second cousins and, exchanging extravagance for downright parsimony, settled down with her to make the best of a bad job and put his heavily mortgaged property on its feet once more. In this, I more than suspected, he was directed by his wife. Though his cousin on the distaff side, Joanna showed none of the degeneracy of the Wickhams. Physically a splendid creature, tall and lithe and with a darkness of colouring that hinted at a Spanish ancestor somewhere in the not too remote past, she was no less vigorous mentally; under the charm of her manner one felt at once a well-balanced intelligence and a will of adamant. She was exactly the right wife for Frank and I had been delighted.

It was a disappointment to me that Sylvia did not altogether share my liking for Joanna. The Rigbys' property adjoined mine and Frank's was less than twenty miles away, so that the three families had always been on terms of intimacy. Sylvia did not actually dislike Joanna but it was clear that, if the thing were left to her, they would never become close friends and as Frank had always had a hearty dislike for me, it seemed that relations between Ravendean and Moorefield would be a little distant. I cannot say that the thought worried me. So long as I had Sylvia, nothing else could matter.

Frank had now been married something over two years and, to set the wreath of domestic virtue finally on his head, his wife six months ago had given birth to a son. The recuperation of Moorefield, moreover, had proceeded so satisfactorily that three weeks ago the pair had been able to set out on a long wandering holiday through Europe, leaving the child with his foster-mother. I have had to give Frank's history in this detail, because of its importance in the strange business which followed that homely scene in the drawing-room of Bucklands that evening.

Sylvia and I did get our half-hour together in the end and no doubt we spent it as such half-hours always have been spent. I know it seemed a very short time before I was sitting at the wheel of my car, one of the new six-cylinder Dovers, and pressing the self-starter. It failed to work. On such trivialities do our destinies hang.

'Nothing doing?' said Sylvia. 'The wiring's gone, I expect. And you won't be able to swing her; she'll be much too stiff.' Sylvia's grasp of the intricacies of a car's interior had always astonished me. 'You'd better take Emma.' Emma was her own two-seater.

'I think I'll walk,' I told her. 'Through Horne's Copse it's not much over a mile. It'll calm me down.'

She laughed, but it was quite true. I had proposed to Sylvia as a sort of forlorn hope and I had not nearly become accustomed yet to the idea of being actually engaged to her.

It was a lovely night and my thoughts, as I swung along, turned as always then upon the amazing question: what did Sylvia see in me? We had a few tastes in common, but her real interest was cars and mine the study of early civilisations, with particularly kindly feelings towards the Minoan and Mycenean. The only reason I had ever been able to get out of her for her fondness was: 'Oh well, you see, Hugh darling, you're rather a lamb, aren't you? And you *are* such a perfect old idiot.' It seemed curious, but I knew our post-war generation has the reputation of being unromantic.

My eyes had become accustomed to the moonlight, but inside Horne's Copse everything was pitch black. It was hardly necessary for me to slacken my pace, however, for I knew every turn and twist of the path. The copse was not more than a couple of hundred yards long and I had reached, as I judged, just about the middle when my foot struck against an obstacle right in the middle of the track which nearly sent me flying to the ground.

I recovered my balance with an effort, wondering what the thing could be. It was not hard, like a log of wood, but inertly soft. I struck a match and looked at it. I do not think I am a particularly nervous man, but I felt a creeping sensation in the back of my scalp as I stood staring down by the steady light of the match. The thing was a body – the body of a man; and it hardly took the ominous black hole in the centre of his forehead, its edges spangled with red dew, to tell me that he was very dead indeed.

But that was not all. My match went out and I nerved myself to light another and hold it close above the dead face to assure myself that I had been mistaken. But I had not been mistaken. Incredibly, impossibly, the body was that of my cousin, Frank.

Chapter II

I took a grip on myself. This was Frank and he was dead –
probably murdered. Frank was not in Bellagio. He was here,
in Horne's Copse, with a bullet-hole in his forehead. I must
not lose my head. I must remember the correct things to do
in such a case and then I must do them. 'Satisfy oneself that
life is extinct.' From some hidden reserve of consciousness
the phrase emerged and, almost mechanically, I proceeded
to act on it. But it was really only as a matter of form that
I touched the white face, which was quite cold and horribly
clammy.

One arm was doubled underneath him, the other lay flung
out at his side, the inside of the wrist uppermost. I grasped
the latter gingerly, raising the limp hand a little off the
ground as I felt the pulse, or rather, where the pulse should
have been; for needless to say, nothing stirred under the cold,
damp skin. Finally, with some half-buried recollection that
as long as a flicker of consciousness remains, the pupils of
the eyes will react to light, I moved one of my last matches
backwards and forwards and close to and away from the
staring eyes. The pupils did not contract the hundredth of a
millimetre as the match approached them.

I scrambled to my feet.

Then I remembered that I should make a note of the exact
time and this I did too. It was precisely eleven minutes and
twenty seconds past twelve.

Obviously the next thing to do was to summon the police.

Not a doctor first, for the poor fellow was only too plainly
beyond any doctor's aid.

I am a magistrate and certain details of routine are familiar to me. I knew, for instance, that it was essential that the body should not be touched until the police had seen it; but as I had no one with me to leave in charge of it, that must be left to chance; in any case it was not probable that anyone else would be using the right-of-way through Horne's Copse so late. I, therefore made my way, as fast as I dared in that pitch darkness, out of the copse and then ran at top speed the remaining half-mile to the house. As always I was in sound condition and I dare swear that nobody has ever covered a half-mile, fully clothed, in much quicker time.

I had told Parker, the butler, not to sit up for me and I, therefore, had to let myself in with my own latch-key. Still panting, I rang up the police station in Salverton, about three miles away and told them briefly what I had discovered. The constable who answered the telephone, of course, knew me well and Frank too, and was naturally shocked by my news. I cut short his ejaculations, however, and asked him to send someone out to Ravendean at once, to take official charge. He undertook to rouse his sergeant immediately and asked me to wait at the house in order to guide him to the spot. I agreed to do so – and it was a long time before I ceased to regret it. It is easy to blame oneself after the event and easy for others to blame one too; but how could I possibly have foreseen an event so extraordinary?

The interval of waiting I filled up by rousing Parker and ringing up my doctor. The latter had not yet gone to bed and promised to come round at once. He was just the kind of man I wanted, for myself rather than Frank; my nervous system has never been a strong one and it had just received a considerable shock. Gotley was his name and he was a great hulking young man who had been tried for England at rugger while he was still at Guy's and, though just failing to get his cap, had been accounted as a good a forward as any outside the team. For a man of that type he had imagination, too, intelligence and great charm of manner, he was moreover a very capable doctor. He had been living in the village for about four years now and I had struck up quite a friendship with him, contrary to my usual practice, for I do not make friends easily.

His arrival was a relief – and so was the whisky and soda with which Parker immediately followed his entrance into the library where I was waiting.

'This sounds a bad business, Chappell,' he greeted me. 'Hullo, man, you look as white as a sheet. You'd better have a drink and a stiff one at that.' He manipulated the decanter.

'I'm afraid it has rather upset me,' I admitted. Now that there was nothing to do but wait I did feel decidedly shaky.

With the plain object of taking my mind off the gruesome subject Gotley embarked on a cheerful discussion of England's chances in the forthcoming series of test matches that summer, which he kept going determinedly until the arrival of the police some ten minutes later.

These were Sergeant Afford whom, of course, I knew well and a young constable. The sergeant was by no means of the doltish, obstinate type which the writers of detective fiction invariably portray, as if our country police forces consisted of nothing else; he was a shrewd enough man and at this moment he was a tremendously excited man too. This fact he was striving nobly to conceal in deference to my feelings for, of course, he knew Frank as well as myself and by repute as well as in person; but it was obvious that the practical certainty of murder, and in such a circle, had roused every instinct of the blood-hound in him: he was literally quivering to get on the trail. No case of murder had ever come his way before and in such a one as this there was, besides the excitement of the hunt, the certainty that publicity galore, with every chance of promotion, would fall to the lot of Sergeant Afford – *if* only he could trace the murderer before his Superintendent had time to take the case out of his hands.

As we hurried along the sergeant put such questions as he wished, so that by the time we entered the copse he knew almost as much of the circumstances as I did myself. There was now no need to slacken our pace, for I had a powerful electric torch to guide our steps. As we half ran, half walked along I flashed it continuously from side to side, searching the path ahead for poor Frank's body. Somewhat surprised, I decided that it must lie further than I had thought; though, knowing the copse intimately as I did, I could have sworn that it had been lying on a stretch of straight path, the only one, right in the very middle; but we passed over the length of it and it was not there.

A few moments later we had reached the copse's further limit and came to an irresolute halt.

'Well, sir?' asked the sergeant, in a tone studiously expressionless.

But I had no time for nuances. I was too utterly bewildered. 'Sergeant,' I gasped, 'it – it's *gone.*'

Chapter III

There was no doubt that Frank's body had gone, because it was no longer there; but that did not explain its remarkable removal. 'I can't understand it, Sergeant. I know within a few yards where he was: on that straight bit in the middle. I wonder if he wasn't quite dead after all and managed to crawl off the path somewhere.'

'But I thought you were quite sure he was dead, sir?'

'I was. Utterly sure,' I said in perplexity, remembering how icy cold that clammy, clay-like face had been.

The constable, who had not yet uttered a word, continued to preserve his silence. So also did Gotley. After a somewhat awkward pause the sergeant suggested that we should have a look round.

'Well, I can show you where he was, at any rate,' I said. 'We can recognise the place from the dead matches I left there.'

We turned back again and the sergeant, taking my torch, examined the ground. The straight stretch was not more than a dozen yards long and he went slowly up it one side and back the other. 'Well, sir, that's funny; there isn't a match anywhere along here.'

'Are you sure?' I asked incredulously. 'Let me look.'

I took the torch, but it was a waste of time: not a match-stalk could I find.

'Rum go,' muttered Gotley.

I will pass briefly over the next hour, which was not one of triumph for myself. Let it be enough to say that search as we might on the path, in the undergrowth and even beyond the confines of the copse, not a trace could we discover of a body, a match-stalk, or anything to indicate that these things had ever been there.

As the power of my electric torch waned so did the sergeant's suspicions of my good faith obviously increase. More than once he dropped a hint that I must have been pulling his leg and wasn't it about time I brought a good joke to an end.

'But I did see it, Sergeant,' I said desperately, when at last we were compelled to give the job up as a bad one and turn homewards. 'The only way I can account for it is that some man came along after I'd gone, thought life might not be extinct and carried my cousin bodily off with him.'

'And your burnt matches as well, sir, I suppose,' observed the sergeant woodenly.

Gotley and I parted with him and his constable outside the house; he would not come in, even for a drink. It was clear that he was now convinced that I had been playing a joke on him and was not by any means pleased about it. I had to let him carry the delusion away with him.

When they had gone I looked inquiringly at Gotley, but he shook his head. 'My goodness, no, I'm not going. I want to go into this a little deeper. I'm coming in with you, whether you like it or not.'

As a matter of fact I did. It was nearly half-past one, but sleep was out of the question. I wanted to talk the thing out with Gotley and decide what ought to be done.

We went into the library and Gotley mixed us each another drink.

I certainly needed the one he handed to me.

'Nerves still a bit rocky?' Gotley remarked, looking at me with a professional eye.

'A bit,' I admitted. I may add in extenuation that I was supposed to have been badly shell-shocked during the war. Certainly my nervous system had never been the same since. 'I'm glad you don't want to go. I want your opinion on this extraordinary business. I noticed you didn't say much up there.'

'No, I thought better not.'

'Well, it'll be light in just over an hour. I want to get back and examine that copse by daylight, before anyone else gets there. I simply can't believe that there aren't some indications that I was telling the truth.'

'My dear chap, I never doubted for one moment that you were telling what you sincerely thought was the truth.'

'No?' This sounded to me rather oddly put, but I didn't question it for the moment. 'Well, the sergeant did. Look here, are you game to stay here and come up with me?'

'Like a shot. If any message comes for me, they know at home where I am. In the meantime, let's try to get some sort of a line on the thing. I thought your cousin was abroad?'

'So did I,' I replied helplessly. 'In fact, I had a card from him only this morning, from Bellagio.'

'Did he give the name of his hotel?'

'Yes, I think so. Yes, I'm sure he mentioned it.'

'Then I should wire there directly the post office opens and ask if he's still there.'

'But he isn't,' I argued stupidly. 'How can he be?'

Gotley contemplated his tumbler. 'Still, you know,' he said airily – rather too airily, 'still, I should wire.'

The hour passed more quickly than I could have expected. I knew now that Gotley did not consider that I had been deliberately romancing, he suspected me merely of seeing visions; but he did not give himself away again and discussed the thing with me as gravely as if he had been as sure as I was that what I had seen was fact and not figment. As soon as the dawn began to show we made our way to the copse; for no message had arrived from the police station to throw any light on the affair.

Our journey, let me say briefly, was a complete failure. Not a single thing did we find to bear out my story – not a burnt match, a drop of blood, nor even a suspicious footprint on the hard ground.

I could not with decency retain Gotley any longer, especially as he was having more and more difficulty in concealing from me his real opinion. I made no comment or protestation. His own suggestion of the telegram to Bellagio could be left to do that; for I had now determined to adopt it in sheer self-defence, to prove that there was at least the fact of Frank's absence to support me. If he had been in Horne's Copse he could not be in Bellagio and, conversely, if he had suddenly left Bellagio, he could have appeared in Horne's Copse.

I did not go to bed till past eight o'clock, at which hour I telephoned my telegram.

The rest of the day dragged. Sylvia telephoned after lunch to say that the chauffeur had now put my car right, but I put her off with a non-committal answer. The truth was that nothing would induce me to leave the house until the answer to my telegram had arrived.

Just after six o'clock it came.

I tore open the flimsy envelope with eager fingers. 'Why

the excitement?' it ran. 'Here till tomorrow, then Grand Hotel, Milan. Frank.'

So Gotley had been right. I *had been* seeing visions.

Chapter IV

I sank into a chair, the telegram between my fingers. But I had *not* been imagining the whole thing. It was out of the question. The details had been too vivid, too palpable. No, Gotley was wrong. I had seen someone – it might not have been Frank.

I hurried to the telephone and rang up Sergeant Afford. Had he heard anything more about last night's affair? I might possibly have been mistaken in thinking the dead man my cousin. Had any other disappearance been reported? The sergeant was short with me. Nothing further had developed. He had been himself to the scene of the alleged death that morning and found nothing. He advised me, not too kindly, to think no more about the affair.

I began to feel annoyed. Now that it was proved that the body could not possibly have been Frank's, my feeling towards it was almost resentment. Only by the chance of a defective wire on my car had I stumbled across it and the contact had resulted in suspicion on the part of the police of an uncommonly callous practical joke and the conviction on the part of my doctor that I was mentally unbalanced. The more I thought about it, the more determined I was that the mystery must be unveiled. I resolved to tell Sylvia the whole story that very evening.

Unlike Gotley, Sylvia asked plenty of questions; still more unlike him she accepted what I said as a statement of fact.

'Rot, Hugh,' she said bluntly, when I told her of that young man's suspicions. 'If you say you saw it, you did see it. And anyhow, how could you possibly imagine such a thing? Hugh, this is terribly exciting. What are we going to do about it?' She took her own part in any subsequent action for granted.

I looked at her pretty grey eyes sparkling with excitement and, in spite of the gravity of the affair, I could not help smiling. 'What do you suggest, dear?' I asked.

'Oh, we must get to the bottom of it, of course. We'll make inquiries in the neighbourhood and go round all the hospitals, oh and everything.' As I had often noticed before, Sylvia had been able to translate into realities ideas which to me had remained a trifle nebulous.

So for the next few days we played at being detectives inquiring into a mysterious murder and travelled all over the country in pursuit of our ridiculous but delightful theories. We enjoyed ourselves tremendously; but if real detectives got no further in their cases than we did, the number of undetected murders would see a remarkable increase; for we discovered exactly nothing at all. No man resembling Frank had been seen in the vicinity; there was not the vaguest report of a man with a bullet wound in his forehead.

All we really did determine was that the man must have been dead (for that he had been dead I was absolutely convinced) for about four to six hours because, though the body was cold, the wrist I had held was still limp, which meant that *rigor mortis* had not set in. This information came from Gotley who gave it with a perfectly grave face and then quite spoilt the effect by advising us to waste no more time on the business. Sylvia was most indignant with him.

Perhaps it is not true to say that we discovered nothing at all, for one rather curious fact did come to light. Although we knew now that the man must have been dead at least four hours, must have died, that is, not later than eight o'clock, we found no less than three persons who had passed over the path between that hour and midnight; and at none of those times had he been there.

'There's a gang in it,' Sylvia pronounced with enjoyment. 'He was shot miles away, brought to the copse and then carried off again, all by the gang.'

'But why?' I asked, wondering at these peripatetic activities.

'Heaven only knows,' Sylvia returned helplessly.

And there, in the end, we had to leave it.

At least a month passed and my mysterious adventure gradually became just a curious memory. Gotley ceased to look at me thoughtfully and when I met him at the local flower show even Sergeant Afford showed by his magnanimous bearing that he had forgiven me.

At first, I must confess, I had tended to avoid Horne's Copse at night, although it was much the shortest route between Bucklands and Ravendean. Then, as the memory faded, reason reasserted itself. By 3 July I had shed the last of my qualms.

That 3 July!

There is a saying that history repeats itself. It did that night with a vengeance. Once again I had been dining at Bucklands. Before leaving home my chauffeur had found a puncture in one of the back tyres of the Dover and had put the spare wheel on. I risked the short journey without a spare, only to find, when it was time to go home, that another puncture had developed.

Once again Sylvia offered me her own car: once again I refused, saying that I should enjoy the walk. Once again I set out with my mind busy with the dear girl I had just left and the happiness in store for me. That very evening we had fixed our wedding provisionally for the middle of September.

Indeed, so intent was I upon these delightful reflections, that I had got a third of the way through Horne's Copse before I even called to mind the sinister connection which the place now held for me. It was not quite such a dark night as that other one, but inside the copse the blackness was as dense as before as I turned the last twist before the stretch of straight path in the centre.

'It was just about six yards from here,' I reflected idly as I walked along, 'that my foot struck, with that unpleasant thud, against —' I stopped dead, retaining my balance this time with ease, as if I had subconsciously been actually anticipating the encounter. For my foot had struck, with just such another unpleasant thud, against an inert mass in the middle of the path.

With a horrible creeping sensation at the back of my scalp, I struck a match and forced myself to look at the thing in my way, though I knew well enough before I did so what I should see. And I was right. Lying across the path, with unnaturally disposed limbs and, this time, a small dagger protruding from his chest, was my cousin Frank.

Chapter V

The match flickered and went out and still I stood, rigid and gasping, striving desperately to conquer the panic which was threatening to swamp my reason.

Gradually, in the darkness, I forced my will to control my trembling limbs. Gradually I succeeded in restoring my brain to its natural functions. Here, I told myself deliberately, was the real thing. As for the other – vision, pre-knowledge, clairvoyance, or whatever it might have been, I had at the moment no time to find explanations; here I was in the presence of the real thing and I must act accordingly.

I suppose it can really have been scarcely more than a couple minutes before, restored to the normal, I felt myself not merely calm but positively eager to investigate. With fingers that no longer quivered I struck another match and bent over my unfortunate cousin. It did not even repel me this time to touch the cold, clammy face, glistening in the match-light with unnatural moisture, as I made sure that he really was dead.

It was with an odd sense of familiarity that I made my swift examination. Except for the dagger in his chest and the bloodstained clothes around it instead of the bullet wound in his forehead, everything was exactly the same as before and my own actions followed more or less their previous course. There was the same outflung arm, cold wrist uppermost, whose motionless pulse I could conveniently feel for; there were the staring eyes, unresponsive to the movements of my match; there was the damp, chilled skin of his face. It was only too plain that he was dead, without it being necessary for me to disarrange his clothing to feel his heart and I was again unwilling to do this, knowing how much the police dislike a body to be tampered with before they have examined it themselves.

But one thing further I did this time. I made sure that the

body was, beyond all possibility of dispute, that of Frank himself. Frank had a scar on his left temple, just at the edge of the hair. I looked for the scar and I found it. Then I hurried home at the best speed I could, to ring up Sergeant Afford and Gotley. I was conscious as I did so of a rather ignoble feeling of triumph. But after all, self-vindication *is* a pleasant feeling.

Sergeant Afford himself was not at the police station, but to Gotley I spoke directly. 'Right-ho,' he said with enthusiasm. 'Really has happened this time, has it?'

'Yes,' I replied. 'There's no doubt this time. I shall want to go into that other affair with you sometime. It must have been a vision of some kind, I suppose.'

'Yes, extraordinary business. And apparently not quite an accurate one. What about getting the Psychical Research Society on to it?'

'We might. In the meantime, I'm going back to the copse now. Meet me there. I'm taking no risks this time.'

Gotley promised to do so and we rang off.

As I passed out of the front door I looked at my watch. The time was three minutes to twelve. It had been twenty-one minutes to the hour within a few seconds, when I left the body. I walked back at a good pace and the journey took me about twelve minutes. In all, then, I was absent from the centre of Horne's Copse for about half an hour. The importance of these figures will be apparent later.

I am not sure what motive prompted my return alone to the spot where I had left the body. I think I wanted, in some vague way, to keep guard over it, almost as if it might run away if left to itself. Anyhow I certainly had the feeling, as

I had mentioned to Gotley, that this time I would take no chances.

I had my torch with me now and I turned it on as I reached the copse. It threw a powerful beam and as I turned the corner on to the straight path I directed the light along to the further end. The whole dozen yards of straight path was thus illuminated, the undergrowth at the sides and the dense green foliage beyond the twist at the end. But that was all. Of Frank's body there was no sign.

Incredulously I hurried forward, thinking that I must have been mistaken in my bearings; the body must have lain round the further corner. But neither round the corner was there any sign of it, nor anywhere along the path right to the further edge of the copse. Filled with horror, I retraced my steps, sweeping the surface of the ground with my beam. It was as I feared. Again there was not even a litter of spent matches to show where I had knelt by Frank's remains.

In the middle of the path I halted, dazed with nameless alarm. Was my reason going? The thing was fantastic, inexplicable. If I had had my suspicions about the reality of my former experience, I had none concerning this one. I *knew* there had been a body; I *knew* I had handled it, physically and materially; I *knew it* was Frank's – Frank who was supposed to be that moment in Rome. I knew all these things as well as I knew my own name, but ... But the alternative simply did not bear thinking about.

But for all that, hallucinations ...

And yet I felt as sane as ever I had been in my life. There *must* be some ordinary, simple, logical explanation ...

I was still trying to find it when the police and Gotley arrived together.

I turned to meet them. 'It's gone!' I shouted. 'Would you believe it, but the damned thing's gone again. I saw him as plainly as I see you, with the dagger in his chest and the blood all round the wound – I touched him! And now there isn't a sign that he was ever there at all. Damn it, the very matches have disappeared too.' I laughed, for really if you looked at it one way, the thing was just absurd.

Sergeant Afford eyed me austerely. 'Is that so, sir?' he said, in his most wooden voice.

He was going to say more, but Gotley brushed him aside and took me by the arm.

'That's all right, Chappell, old man,' he said, very soothingly. 'Don't you worry about it any more tonight. I'm going to take you home and fill you up with bromide and tomorrow we'll go into it properly.'

Gotley thought I was mad, of course. After all it was only to be expected.

Chapter VI

'Ought I to marry, then?' I asked drearily. I had been trying for some minutes to summon up the courage to put this question.

It was the next evening and Gotley and I had been talking for over an hour. He had succeeded in convincing me. I had seen nothing, felt nothing, imagined everything. To pacify me he had telegraphed that morning to Frank in Rome; the answer, facetiously couched, had left no room for doubt.

Gotley had been perfectly open with me during the last

hour. It was better, he said, to face this sort of thing frankly. The thing was not serious; I must have been overworking, or suffering from nervous strain of some kind. If I took things easily for a bit these hallucinations would disappear and probably never return. Above all, I must not brood over them.

'Ought I to marry, then, Gotley?' I repeated.

'Oh dear, yes. In time. No need to hurry about it.'

'You mean, not in September?'

'Well, perhaps not quite so soon. But later, oh, yes.'

'Is it fair? I mean, if there are children.'

'My dear chap,' Gotley said with great cheerfulness, 'it's nothing as bad as that. Nothing but a temporary phase.'

'I shall tell Sylvia.'

'Ye-es,' he agreed, though a little doubtfully. 'Yes, you could tell Miss Rigby; but let me have a word with her too. And look here, why not go away somewhere with her and her mother for a bit of a holiday? That's what you want. Drugs can't do anything for you, but a holiday, with the right companionship, might do everything.'

And so, the next day, it was arranged.

I told Sylvia everything. She, of course, was her own loyal self and at first refused to believe a word of Gotley's diagnosis. If I thought I had seen a body, then a body I had seen, and felt, and examined. Even Frank's facetious telegram did not shake her. But her private talk with Gotley did, a little. She was not convinced, but she went so far as to say that there might be something in it, conceivably. In any case there was no reason why I should not have a holiday with herself and her mother, if that was what everyone seemed to want; but neither Sir Henry nor Lady Rigby were to be told a word about anything else. To this, though somewhat reluctantly, I agreed.

Nevertheless, rumours of course arose. Not that Gotley said a word, but I cannot think that Sergeant Afford was so discreet. When we got back, in August, from Norway, I was not long in gathering, from the curious looks which everywhere greeted me, that some at any rate of the cat had escaped from its bag.

I saw Gotley at once and he expressed his satisfaction with my condition. 'You'll be all right now,' he predicted confidently. 'I shouldn't go to that place at night for a bit yet, but you'd be all right now really, in any case.'

A couple of days later I had a letter from Frank. It was in answer to one I had written him from Norway, asking him, just as a matter of curiosity, exactly what he had been doing just before midnight on the 3 July, as I had had rather a strange dream about him just at that time. He apologised for not having answered earlier, but the hotel in Rome had been slow in forwarding my letter, which had only just now caught him up in Vienna, from which town his own letter was written. So far as he could remember, he was just coming out of a theatre in Rome at the time I mentioned: was that what I wanted? My recovery had been so far complete that I could smile at a couple of very typical spelling mistakes and then dismiss the matter from my mind.

That was on 9 August. The next morning was a blazing day, the sort of shimmering, cloudless day that one always associates with the month of August and, about once in three years, really gets. I made a leisurely breakfast, read the newspaper for a little and then set off to keep an appointment with a farmer, a tenant of mine, concerning the re-roofing of his barn. The farm adjoined the Bucklands estate and lay about three miles away by road, but little over a mile if one cut through Horne's Copse. It was a little hot for walking and I had intended to take the Dover, but a message reached me from the garage that something had gone mysteriously wrong with the carburettor and a new float would have to be obtained before I could take her out. Rather welcoming the necessity for exercise, I set off on foot.

As I approached Horne's Copse I reflected how complete my recovery must be, for instead of feeling the slightest reluctance to pass through it I positively welcomed its prospect of cool green shade. Strolling along, my thoughts on the coming interview and as far as they well could be from the unhappy memories that the place held for me, I turned the last corner which hid from me the little length of straight path which had played so sinister a part in those memories – even, I think, whistling a little tune.

Then the tune froze abruptly on my lips and the warmth of the day was lost in the icy sweat of sheer terror which broke out all over me. For there at my feet, incredibly, impossibly, lay the body of Frank, the blood slowly oozing round the dagger that projected from his heart.

This time I stayed to make no examination. In utter panic I took to my heels and ran. Whither, or with what idea, I had no notion. My one feeling was to get away from the place and as soon and as quickly as possible.

Actually I came to my senses in a train, bound for London, with a first-class ticket clutched in my hand. How I had got there I had no conception but the vaguest. It had been a blind flight.

Fortunately the compartment was an empty one and I was able to take measures to control the trembling of my limbs before trying to take stock of the situation. I was not cured, then. Far from it. What was I to do?

One thing I determined. I would stay a few days in London now that I was already on the way there and, when I felt sufficiently recovered to tell my story coherently, consult some experienced alienist. Obviously I was no longer a case for Gotley.

It was no doubt (as I reflected in a strangely detached way), a part of my mania that I did not go to my usual hotel, where I was known, but sought out the most obscure one I could find. In an effort to shake off my obsession and complete the process of calming myself I turned after the meal into a dingy little cinema and tried to concentrate for three hours on the inanities displayed on the screen.

'Shocking murder in a wood!' screamed a newsboy almost in my ear, as I stood blinking in the sunlight outside again. Mechanically I felt for a copper and gave it to him. It was in a wood that I had seen ...

And it was an account of the finding of Frank's body that I read there and then, on the steps of that dingy cinema – Frank who had been found that morning in Horne's Copse with a dagger in his heart.

'The police,' concluded the brief account, 'state that they would be grateful if the dead man's cousin, Mr Hugh Chappell, who was last seen boarding the 11.19 train to London, would put himself in touch with them as soon as possible.'

Chapter VII

I turned and began to walk quickly, but quite aimlessly, along the pavement. The one idea in my mind at the moment was that nobody should guess, from any anxiety I might display, that *I* was the notorious Hugh Chappell with whom the police wished to get in touch as soon as possible. It never occurred to me to doubt that I was notorious, that my name was already on everyone's lips and that not merely every policeman but even every private citizen was eagerly looking for me. Such is the effect of seeing one's name, for the first time, in a public news sheet.

By and by my mind recovered from this temporary obsession and I began to think once more. So this time my hallucination had not been a hallucination at all. Frank *had* been killed – murdered, almost certainly: it *was* his body I had seen that morning. But what, then, of the two previous times I had seen that same body and even handled it? Or so I had fancied at the time. Obviously they were not the meaningless delusions that Gotley and, finally, I myself, had believed them to be; they really were definite pre-visions of the real event. It was most extraordinary.

In any case, be that as it might, my own immediate action was clear. I must return at once to Ravendean and offer Sergeant Afford any help in my power.

It did not take me much over half an hour to ring up my hotel, cancel my room and make my way to Paddington. There I found that a train was luckily due to start in ten minutes and, having taken my ticket, I strolled to the bookstall to see if any later edition with fuller details was yet on sale. As I approached the stall I noticed a figure standing in front of it which looked familiar to me. The man turned his head and I recognised him at once as a fellow who had been on my staircase at Oxford, though I had never known him well: his name was Sheringham and I had heard of him during the last few years as a successful novelist with an increasing reputation, Roger Sheringham.

I had not the least wish, at the present juncture, to waste time renewing old acquaintances, but as the man was now staring straight at me I could hardly do less than nod, with what pleasantness I could muster and greet him by name.

His response surprised me enormously. 'Hullo, Hugh!' he said warmly, indeed with a familiarity I resented considering that we had never been on terms of anything but surnames before. 'Come and have a drink.' And he actually took me by the arm.

'I'm sorry,' I said, a little stiffly, 'I have a train to catch.' And I endeavoured to release myself.

'Nonsense!' he said loudly. 'Plenty of time for a quick one.' I was going to reply somewhat peremptorily when, to my astonishment, he added in a hissing sort of whisper without moving his lips: 'Come *on*, you damned fool.'

I allowed him to lead me away from the bookstall, completely bewildered.

'Phew!' he muttered, when we had gone about thirty yards. 'That was a close shave. Don't look round. That man in the grey suit who was just coming up on the left is a Scotland Yard man.'

'Indeed?' I said, interested but perplexed. 'Looking for someone, you mean?'

'Yes,' Sheringham said shortly. 'You. One of a dozen in

this very station at this very minute. Let's get out – if we can!'

I was surprised to hear that so many detectives were actually looking for me. Evidently the police considered my evidence of the first importance. I wondered how Sheringham knew and asked him.

'Oh, I'm in touch with those people,' he said carelessly. 'Lord,' he added, more to himself than to me, 'I wish I knew what to do with you now I've got you.'

'Well,' I smiled, 'I'm afraid you can't do anything at the moment. If you're in touch with Scotland Yard, you'll have heard about my poor cousin?' He nodded and I explained my intentions.

'I thought so,' he nodded, 'seeing you here. Well, that confirms my own opinion.'

'What opinion?'

'Oh, nothing. Now look here, Chappell, I don't want you to take this train. There's another a couple of hours later which will do you just as well; there's no particular urgency so far as you're concerned. In the interval, I want you to come back with me to my rooms at the Albany.'

'But why?'

'Because I want to talk to you – or rather, hear you talk. And I may say I was about to travel down to your place by that same train for just that purpose.'

This was the most surprising news I had yet received. I demurred, however, at missing the train, but Sheringham was so insistent that at last I agreed to accompany him.

'We'd better get a taxi, then,' I remarked with, I fear, no very good grace.

'No,' Sheringham retorted. 'We'll go by tube.'

And by tube we went.

Sheringham took me into a very comfortable panelled sitting-room and we sat down in two huge leather armchairs.

'Now,' he said, 'don't think me impertinent, Chappell, or mysterious, and remember that I'm not only in touch with Scotland Yard but I have on occasions even worked with them. I want you to tell me, from beginning to end, in as much detail as you can, your story of this extraordinary business of your cousin's death. And believe me, it's entirely in your own interests that I ask you to do so, though for the present you must take that on trust.'

The request seemed to me highly irregular, but Sheringham appeared to attach such importance to it that I did, in fact, comply. I told him the whole thing.

'I see,' he said. 'Thank you. And you proposed to go down and give the police what help you could. Very proper. Now I'll tell you something, Chappell. What do you think they want you for? Your help? Not a bit of it. They want you in order to arrest you, for killing your cousin.'

'What!' I could only gasp.

'I have it from their own lips. Shall I tell you what the police theory is? That your two false alarms were the results of hallucinations, which left you with the delusion that you had a divine mission to kill your cousin and that, meeting him accidentally in the flesh in that same place you, under the influence of this mania, actually did kill him.'

Chapter VIII

For a minute or two Sheringham's revelation of this hideous

79

suggestion left me quite speechless with horror. I was beginning to stammer out a repudiation when he waved me into silence.

'My dear chap, it's all right: *I* don't believe anything of the sort. I never did and now I've seen and talked to you I do still less. You're not mad. No, I'm convinced the business isn't so simple as all that. In fact, I think there's something pretty devilish behind it. That's why I was on my way down to try to find you before the police did and ask you if I could look into things for you.'

'Good heavens,' I could only mutter, 'I'd be only too grateful if you would. I've no wish to end my days in a madhouse. This is really terrible. Have you any ideas at all?'

'Only that those first two occasions were no more delusions than the last. You did see something that you were meant to see – either your cousin or somebody made up to resemble him. And the plot which I'm quite certain exists is evidently aimed against you as well as against your cousin. For some reason a certain person or persons do want you locked up in an asylum. At least, that seems the only possible explanation, with the result that the police are thinking exactly what they have been meant to think. Now, can you tell me of anyone who would benefit if you were locked up in a madhouse?'

'No one,' I said in bewilderment. 'But Sheringham, how can it possibly be a deliberate plot? It was only by the merest chance on all those three occasions that I went through Horne's Copse at all. Nobody could possibly have foreseen it.'

'Are you sure? On each occasion, you remember, you had

to pass from one point to another, with Horne's Copse as the nearest route, provided you were on foot. And on each occasion, you also remember, your car just happened to be out of action. You think that's coincidence? I don't.'

'You mean – you think my car had been tampered with?'

'I intend to have a word or two with your chauffeur; but I'm ready to bet a thousand pounds here and now what the implications of his answers will be – though doubtless he won't realize it himself. What sort of a man is he, by the way? Sound?'

'Very. A first-rate mechanic and an excellent fellow. In fact, he has rather a sad story. Not that he's ever told me a word himself; actually I had it from Frank who sent him along to me, not being able to find a job for him himself. He's a public school and University man whose people lost all their money while he was up at Cambridge, where Frank knew him slightly. So, having a bent for engineering, he buckled down to it, worked his way through the shops and turned himself into a most efficient chauffeur.'

'Stout fellow,' Sheringham commented. 'We may find him very useful. Now look here, Chappell, you're absolutely convinced that the man you saw each time in Horne's Copse was your cousin? You're sure it wasn't somebody disguised as him?'

'I'm practically certain,' I replied.

'Yes; well, we must check up on that; which means that someone must go abroad and cover the ground.'

'But you forget the telegrams I had from Frank.'

'Indeed I don't,' Sheringham retorted. 'A telegram's no evidence at all.'

'But who is to go?'

'There you have me,' he admitted. 'I simply can't spare the time myself if I'm to go into things properly at this end, and we've got none of it to lose. I want to get the case cleared up before the police find you and we don't know when that may be.'

'Oh! I'm to go into hiding, then?'

'Well, of course. Once arrested it's the dickens of a job to get free again. We must put it off as long as we possibly can.'

'But where am I to hide?'

'Why, I thought here. Meadows, my man, is perfectly safe. Any objection?'

'None, indeed. This is extraordinarily good of you, Sheringham. I needn't say how very grateful I am.'

'That's all right, that's all right. Now then, if I'm to do any good down in your neighbourhood I must put a few questions before I leave you. I'm going to catch that train.'

Sheringham hurriedly put his queries, some concerning my own affairs and Frank's and some upon local conditions and personages and rushed off to catch his train. Before he went I obtained his promise to see Sylvia and secretly inform her of my plans and whereabouts, together with his own hopes of getting me out of this trouble, which I urged him to put as high as possible to save the poor girl anxiety. This he undertook to do and I was left alone.

It need not be said that my reflections were not pleasant ones; but rack my brains as I might, I could see no possible solution of the mystery of my cousin's death, nor even discover the least bit of evidence to support Sheringham's theory that some person or persons unknown, having murdered Frank, were now trying to get me confined as a homicidal lunatic. Who was there who could possibly benefit by this double crime?

To all practical purposes I was a prisoner in the Albany for an indefinite period. Outside the shelter of Sheringham's rooms I did not dare to put my nose. And for all the company that the silent-footed, respectfully taciturn Meadows proved himself, I might just as well have been completely alone. The time hung heavily on my hands, in spite of the numbers of newspapers I examined, Meadows silently bringing me each fresh edition as it appeared. There was, however, little fresh to be found in the reports so far as real information went, though columns of balderdash were printed concerning myself, Frank and everything relevant and irrelevant to the case. The only piece of complete news was that the dagger with which Frank had been stabbed had been identified as my own dagger, from the wall in my library, a fact which lent superficial support to the police theory but, to me, more to Sheringham's.

The latter had not been able to say how long he would be absent. Actually it was nearly forty-eight hours before he returned, looking considerably graver than when he departed.

I had jumped up eagerly to question him as to his success and his reply was anything but reassuring.

'I've found out a little, but not much. And the police have found out a good deal more. They've got evidence now which has made them change their theory completely. You'd better prepare for a shock, Chappell. They think now that you feigned the first two hallucinations in order to create the impression that you were mad and then, having established that, killed your cousin in extremely sane cold blood in accordance with a careful plan of murder, knowing that as a homicidal maniac you couldn't be executed but would get off with a year or so in Broadmoor before proving that you'd recovered your sanity. That's what we're up against now.'

Chapter IX

I had still found no words to answer Sheringham's appalling news when the door behind him opened and Sylvia herself appeared. 'Oh, Hugh!' she said, with a little cry and ran to me.

'She would come,' Sheringham said gloomily. 'I couldn't stop her. Well, I'll go and unpack.' He left us alone together.

'Hugh dear,' Sylvia said, when our first disjointed greetings were over, 'what does this terrible business all mean? Frank dead and you suspected of killing him! I knew all the time there was something dreadful behind those "hallucinations" of yours, as that idiot of a Dr Gotley would call them.'

'I can tell you one thing it must mean, darling,' I said sadly, 'and that is that our engagement must be broken off. It wouldn't be fair to you. Though when I'm cleared I shall—'

'Hugh!' she interrupted me indignantly. 'How dare you say such a thing to me! What kind of a girl do you imagine I am? Engagement broken off indeed. Do you know *why* I've come up with Mr Sheringham?'

'Well, no,' I had to admit.

But I was not destined to learn just then exactly why Sylvia had come up to London, for Sheringham himself followed his own discreet tap on the door into the room.

We settled down into a council of war.

'There's no disguising the fact,' Sheringham said gravely, 'that the position's uncommonly serious, Chappell. The hunt for you is up, with a vengeance.'

'Look here,' I returned, 'in that case I must leave your rooms. You could get into serious trouble for harbouring a wanted man, you know.'

'Oh, that,' Sheringham said scornfully. 'Yes, you can go all right, but you'll have to knock me out first. I'll hold you here if necessary by main force.'

Sylvia's face, which had become highly apprehensive at my remark, lightened again and she shot a grateful smile at our host.

'Then you really don't think I should surrender to the police and let them hold me while you're working?' I asked anxiously, for, magistrate as I was, the way in which I was evading arrest seemed to me just then almost more reprehensible than the ridiculous charge which was out against me.

'I do not,' Sheringham replied bluntly. 'That is, not unless you want to turn a short story into a long one. Give me just a few days and I'll clear the mystery up – granted one thing only.'

'And what's that?'

'Why, that the agent we send abroad is able to establish the fact that your cousin was *not* at his hotel abroad on those first two occasions; because unless you're completely mistaken in your identification, there can't be any doubt about that, as a fact.'

'But wait a minute!' Sylvia cried. 'Mr Sheringham, that would mean that that – that his wife is in it too.'

'Oh, yes,' Sheringham agreed carelessly. 'Naturally.'

'Joanna!' I exclaimed. 'Oh, that's impossible.'

'I wouldn't put it past her,' said Sylvia. 'But why "naturally", Mr Sheringham? Have you got a theory that brings her in?'

'Yes. My idea is that so far as your cousin and his wife were concerned, Chappell, the thing was a joke, just to give you a fright. Rather a gruesome joke, perhaps, but nothing more. He was home on business for a day or two and, with the help of somebody else, rigged himself up as a sham corpse. *Then* that unknown third person turned the joke against him most effectively by really killing him the third time. All we've got to do, therefore, is to find this mysterious person (which, with your cousin's wife's help, shouldn't be difficult), and we've got the murderer.'

'Joanna's on her way home now, of course,' Sylvia told me. 'They expect her to arrive tonight or tomorrow. Mr Sheringham's going down again to see her.'

'I understand,' I said slowly, though I was not altogether sure that I did. 'And supposing that she says that Frank was with her all the time and our agent confirms that?'

'Well, in that case there's only one possible explanation: your identification was mistaken.'

'I'm sure it wasn't,' I said. 'And what's more I'm equally sure that Frank was dead the first time of all – quite dead. I tell you, his face was icy cold and his heart wasn't beating; I felt his pulse most carefully. It's impossible that I could have been mistaken.'

'That does make things a little more difficult,' Sheringham murmured.

There was a gloomy little pause, which I broke to ask Sheringham what this fresh evidence was which the police imagined they had discovered against me. Apparently it amounted to the facts that, according to Jefferson, my chauffeur, the car had on each occasion shown every sign of having been deliberately tampered with (which Sheringham had expected), and by myself (which he had not); that the police had obtained my finger-prints from articles in the house and the finger-prints on the dagger corresponded with them; and that I had been heard to use threatening language as regards Frank – which so far as his escapades before marriage were concerned, was possibly in some degree true, though I could not in any way account for the finger-prints. 'Whom are you going to send abroad for us, Mr Sheringham?' Sylvia asked suddenly, when our discussion on these points was over.

'Well, I've been thinking about that. It must be someone who knew the dead man and all the circumstances. In my opinion the very best thing would be for Hugh to go and act as his own detective. We can easily lay a trail to make the police think he's still in London, so the foreign forces won't be warned.'

'Hugh!' Sylvia echoed in surprise. 'Well, really, that mightn't be at all a bad idea. Though as to detecting … Still, I can do that part of it.'

'You?' we exclaimed in unison.

'Oh, yes,' said Sylvia serenely. 'I shall go with him, of course.'

'But, darling,' I was beginning to expostulate.

'Which brings me back to my real reason for coming up to

London, Hugh,' Sylvia went on with the utmost calmness. 'It was so that we can get married at once, of course. Or at any rate, within the usual three days. It will have to be in false names, I'm afraid, owing to this fuss, but it's just as legal and we can go through a ceremony again in our own names if you like after it's all over. I've applied for the special licence already, in the name of—' She began to giggle and dived into her handbag, from which she extracted a crumpled piece of paper. 'Yes, Miss Arabella Whiffen. And you, darling, are Mr Penstowe Stibb.'

Chapter X

And so, in spite of my misgivings, Sylvia and I actually were married three days later. In my own defence I may say that when Sylvia has really made her mind up to a thing …

How we got safely out of the country, while the police were feverishly chasing clues ingeniously laid by Sheringham to show that I was still in London, I do not propose to say. In the public interest such things are better kept quiet.

It was a strange honeymoon upon which we embarked, with its object of finding out whether or not Frank really had been abroad at the time when I had seen him (as I was now more convinced than ever that I had), lying dead in Horne's Copse. Nor was there any time to lose. With only one night to break the journey in Bâle on the way, we went straight through to the Italian lakes. We did not, however, stay in Bellagio, where Frank had been (or said he had been), but at Cadenabbia opposite. For all we knew, we might encounter an English detective in Bellagio and we did not intend to remain in the danger zone longer than necessary.

We arrived at Cadenabbia late at night. The next morning, before crossing the lake to Bellagio, I received a letter from Sheringham, addressed to me in the assumed name in which we were travelling. Its contents were most disturbing:

DEAR STIBB,

I am keeping in close touch with S.Y. and they still have no doubt that London is the place. Meanwhile here is news.

Both the police and I have seen J. and she tells the same story to both of us: that her husband never came back to England at all, until the day before his death, when he had to return for a few hours to see in person to some business connected with the estate and left saying that he was going straight to you to ask you to put him up. That is bad enough, but this is worse. The police now think they have found a definite motive for you. They say you were in love with J. (Your late marriage, of course, would be put down to an act of panic.)

Now this information can have come from one person only, J. herself, so I tackled her about it. She was very reluctant to tell me anything but finally, while admitting the possibility that she might have been totally mistaken, did hint that in her opinion your attentions to her since her marriage have been a good deal more marked than one might have expected in the case of a man engaged to another girl. I need not tell you my own opinion that J. is a vain hussy and all this is pure moonshine due to her inordinate conceit; but I must admit that it would not sound at all a pretty story in court.

I am more than ever certain that everything now hinges on your being able to establish that F. was not where he pretended to be. So do your level best.

Yours, R.S.

P.S. J. is very bitter against you. She seems to have no doubt in her empty head that you did the deed.

'Well, I am blessed!' I exclaimed and showed the letter to Sylvia. 'Really, I can't imagine how Joanna can have got such an extraordinary idea into her head. I'm quite certain I never gave her the least grounds for it.'

Sylvia read the letter through carefully. 'I never did like Joanna,' was all she said.

It can be imagined that, after this news, we were more anxious than ever to succeed in the object of our journey. It was, therefore, with a full realisation of the fateful issues involved that we approached the Grand Hotel in Bellagio, which Frank had given as his address there.

While Sylvia engaged the reception clerk in a discussion regarding terms for a mythical stay next year I, as if idly, examined the register. My heart sank. There was the entry for the date in question. 'Mr and Mrs Francis Chappell', unmistakably in Joanna's handwriting. Apparently they had only stayed for two nights.

Concealing my disappointment, I turned to the clerk. 'I believe some friends of ours were staying here last May. English, of course. I don't suppose you remember them. The lady was very dark, with quite black hair and her husband was just about my build and not at all unlike me in face, except that he had a scar just here.' I touched my right temple.

'Was he a gentleman of fast temper – no, quick temper,

your friend?' asked the clerk, who spoke excellent English, with a slight smile.

'Yes,' I agreed. 'Occasionally perhaps he is. Why?'

'Oh, nothing. It was nothing at all,' said the clerk hastily. Too hastily, for it was evidently something. 'Just something that displeased the gentleman. Quite natural. Yes, Signor, I remember your friends very well. Their name is Chappell, is it not? And they went on from here to Milan. I remember he told me he got the scar playing cricket when a boy. Is it not so?'

'It is,' I said gloomily.

'You have a very good memory,' remarked Sylvia.

'It is my business,' beamed the clerk, evidently pleased with the compliment.

Disconsolately we made our way back across the lake to our hotel, where Sylvia vanished indoors to write a letter.

Rather to my surprise, considering how urgent our business was, Sylvia refused to go on to Rome the next day, nor even the day after that. She had always wanted to see the Italian lakes, she said and now she was here she was going to see them all. And see them all we did, Lugano, Maggiore and the rest at the cost of a day apiece. It was almost a week later before at last we found ourselves in Rome.

And there it seemed that our inquiries were to meet with just the same fate. The conversation with the hotel clerk was repeated almost word for word. Did he remember my friend? Certainly he did and again by name as well as behaviour (Frank seemed from the hints we had had to have travelled across Europe blazing a trail of fiery temper). There was no doubt at all about his having been there. Even the scar was once more in evidence.

Sylvia drew something out of her bag and pushed it across the counter. I saw what it was as she did so. It was a small but excellent photograph of Frank himself.

'Is that anything like Mr Chappell?' she asked, almost carelessly.

The clerk took the photograph up and looked at it carefully. 'It is like him, just a little. But it is not Mr Chappell himself, as the Signora well knows. Oh, no.'

Sylvia glanced at me. 'I knew you'd need someone with you to do the real detecting,' she said calmly, though her eyes were dancing.

Chapter XI

But that was not the end of my surprises. Sylvia was contemplating the clerk thoughtfully. 'Are you ever able to get away from here for the weekend?' she asked. 'A long weekend?'

The man shook his head regretfully. 'No, never. We do not have the English weekend in Italy.'

'Oh!' said Sylvia.

'Only a week's holiday in a year we have. My holiday begins in three days' time. I shall not be sorry.'

Sylvia brightened. 'Look here, how would you like to go to England for your week's holiday, all expenses paid?'

The man's voluble answer left no doubt of his liking for the idea. Sylvia arranged the details with him there and then.

'My darling,' I said, when at last we were seated in a café a few streets away and could talk properly, 'what on earth is it you're doing and how did you know the man with Joanna wasn't Frank at all?'

She gave me a superior smile. 'It didn't strike you as curious, Hugh, that both those men remembered Frank so well, what with his temper and his scar, about which he was so confidential, and the rest? It didn't occur to you to wonder whether they remembered all the visitors at their hotels quite so thoroughly? It didn't strike you as though Frank had almost gone out of his way to be remembered at those two places so clearly?'

'Go on. Rub it in. No, it didn't.'

'Poor lamb! Well, why should it have? You haven't got such a suspicious mind as I have. But all those things struck me. Also the fact that it was Joanna who signed the register. Very fishy, I thought. So I wrote off to Mr Sheringham to get hold somehow of a photograph of Frank and send it to me *poste restante* at Rome. That's why I insisted on staying so long on the lakes, to give it time to arrive.'

'Well, well,' I said. 'I'm quite glad I married you. So what is our programme now?'

'I must write to Mr Sheringham at once and tell him what we've discovered and that we're bringing the witness back with us in two or three days' time.'

'But why are we doing that?'

'I'm not going to let him go off on his holiday where we can't get hold of him,' Sylvia retorted. 'Besides, aren't there things called affidavits that he'll have to swear? Something like that. Anyhow, Mr Sheringham will know, so to Mr Sheringham he's going.'

And to Mr Sheringham, three days later, the man went. I think I have already hinted in this chronicle that when Sylvia makes up her mind to a thing ...

Sheringham seemed scarcely less pleased to see him than us. He handed him over to Meadows with as much care as if he had been made of glass and might fall into pieces at any moment.

As soon as he had gone and Sylvia had received Sheringham's congratulations on her perspicacity, I asked eagerly whether anything further had come to light at this end of the affair.

Sheringham smiled, as if not ill-pleased with himself. 'I think I've made some progress, but I'd rather not say anything just at the moment. I've arrived at one decision, though, Chappell, and that is that you must now come out in the open.'

'Stop skulking?' I said. 'I shall be only too pleased. I've nothing to hide and I dislike this hole and corner atmosphere I've been living in.'

'But is it safe?' Sylvia asked anxiously.

'On that we've got to take a chance,' Sheringham told her. 'Personally, I think it will be. In any case, since getting your letter I've arranged a conference here this evening. I'm going to do my best to bring everyone into the open and with any luck developments may result.'

'Who's coming?' I asked, a little uneasily. I was not sure that I cared for the sound of the word 'conference'.

'Well, Mrs Chappell, for one.'

'Joanna? Really, Sheringham, do you think it advisable—'

'And her brother, for another,' he interrupted me. 'You know him, I expect?'

'Well, very slightly. I met him at the wedding. That's all. I've heard of him, of course. Rather a – a—'

'Bad egg?'

'Exactly.'

'Well, bad egg or not he's coming to support his sister in my omelette.'

'Yes, but what have you found out, Mr Sheringham?' Sylvia insisted. 'What have you been doing these last ten days?'

'What have I found out?' Sheringham repeated whimsically. 'Well, where to buy ice in your neighbourhood, for one thing. Very useful, in this hot weather.'

Sylvia's eyes dilated. 'Mr Sheringham, you don't mean that Frank was killed right back in May and – and—'

'And kept on ice till August?' Sheringham laughed. 'No, I certainly don't. The doctor was quite definite that he hadn't been dead for more than a couple of hours at the outside when he was found.

'And now don't ask me any more questions, because I'm determined not to spoil my conference for you.'

It was by then nearly dinner time and Sheringham, refusing to satisfy our curiosity any further, insisted on our going off to dress. We had to take what heart we could from the fact that he certainly seemed remarkably confident.

Joanna and her brother, Cedric Wickham, were to arrive at nine o'clock. Actually they were a minute or two early.

The meeting, I need hardly say, was constrained in the extreme. From the expression of acute surprise on their faces it was clear that the other two had had no idea that we were to be present, a fact which Sheringham must have purposely concealed from us. Recovering themselves, Joanna greeted us with the faintest nod, her brother, a tall, good-looking fellow, with a scowl. As if noticing nothing in the least amiss, Sheringham produced drinks.

Not more than three minutes later there was a ring at the front door bell. The next moment the door of the room was opened, a large, burly man was framed in the doorway and Meadows announced: 'Detective Chief Inspector Moresby.'

Expecting as I did to be arrested on the spot, I put as good a face on the encounter as I could, though I had a task to appear altogether normal as the CID man, after a positively benevolent nod to the others, advanced straight towards me. But all he did was to put out a huge hand and say: 'Good evening, Mr Chappell. And how are you, sir? I've been wanting to meet you for some time.' His blue eyes twinkled genially.

I returned his smile as we shook hands – a proceeding which Joanna and her brother watched decidedly askance. They too, I think, had been expecting to see me led off, so to speak, in chains.

'Now,' said Sheringham briskly, 'I'm glad to say I've got news for you. A new witness. No credit to me, I'm afraid. Mrs Hugh Chappell is responsible. We'll have him in straight away, shall we, and hear what he's got to say.' He pressed the bell.

The Chief Inspector, as it were casually, strolled over to a position nearer the door.

I think our little Italian thoroughly enjoyed his great moment, though his English suffered a little under the strain. He stood for a moment in the doorway, beaming at us and then marched straight up to Cedric Wickham.

'Ah, it is a pleasure to meet antique faces again, *non è vero?* Good evening, Mr Frank Chappell!'

Chapter XII

Joanna, her brother and Chief Inspector Moresby had gone. Almost immediately, as it seemed, after the little Italian clerk's identification of Cedric Wickham as the impersonator of Frank at Bellagio and Rome the room had appeared to fill with burly men, before whom the Chief Inspector had arrested Joanna and Cedric, the latter as the actual perpetrator of the murder and the former as accessory to it both before and after the fact. My own chauffeur, whose real name I now learned was Harvey, not that under which I had engaged him on poor Frank's recommendation, was already under arrest as a further accessory.

It was a terrible story that Sheringham told Sylvia and myself later that evening.

'There were two plots in existence,' he said when we were settled in our chairs and the excitement of the treble arrest had begun to calm down. 'The first was invented by your cousin himself, who called in his wife, his brother-in-law and Harvey to help him carry it out. The second was an adaptation by these three aimed against the originator of the first. Both, of course, were aimed against you too.

'This was the first plot. I'm not quite clear myself yet on some of its details, but – '

At this point the telephone bell in the hall rang and Sheringham went out to answer it.

He was away a considerable time and when he returned it was with a graver face even than before.

'Mrs Chappell has confessed,' he said briefly. 'She puts all the blame on the other two. I have every doubt of that and so have the police, but I can give you her whole story now. It fills up the gaps in my knowledge of the case.' He sat down again in his chair.

'The first plot, then,' he resumed, 'was aimed against you, Chappell, by your cousin. It did not involve murder, although it was designed to put your possessions in his hands. To put it shortly, Frank had worked hard for two years and he didn't like it: what is more, he did not intend to work any longer. He determined to anticipate his inheritance from you. But, rotter though he was, he drew the line at murder. To get you shut up in a lunatic asylum for the rest of your life, with the result that he as your heir and next-of-kin would have the administering of your estate, was quite enough for his purpose.

'To achieve this result he hit on the idea of causing you several times to come across his apparently dead body, knowing that you would give the alarm and then, when the searchers and the police came, have no body to show for it. When this had happened three or four times, the suspicion that you were mad would become a certainty and the rest would follow. I think it only too likely that if the plan had been left at that it would almost certainly have succeeded.'

'The devil!' Sylvia burst out indignantly.

'I'm quite sure it would,' I agreed soberly. 'The police were taken in and Gotley too and, upon my word, I was ready to wonder myself whether I wasn't mad. But what I can't understand is how he copied death so well. I hadn't the slightest suspicion that he wasn't dead. He not only looked dead, he *felt* dead.'

'Yes – in the parts you did feel, which were the ones you were meant to feel. If you'd slipped your hand inside his shirt and felt his actual heart, instead of only the pulse in his wrist, you'd have felt it beating at once.

'Anyhow, the way he and Harvey went about it was this. About an hour before you were expected, Frank gave himself a stiff injection of morphia. They couldn't use chloroform, because of the smell. Harvey meantime was watching for you to start, having, of course, already put the car out of action so as to ensure your walking and through Horne's copse at that. As soon as you set out or looked like doing so, Harvey ran on ahead at top speed for the copse, which he would reach about ten minutes before you.

'Ready waiting for him there was a tourniquet, a bottle of atropine drops and a block of ice fashioned roughly to the shape of a mask and wrapped in a blanket. He clapped the ice over your cousin's face and another bit over his right hand and wrist and fastened it there, put the tourniquet on his right arm above the elbow and slipped off the ice mask for a moment, when his hand was steadier, to put a few of the atropine drops into Frank's eyes to render the pupils insensible to light. Then he arranged the limbs with the dead pulse invitingly upwards and so on, waited till he could actually hear you coming, and then whipped off the ice blocks and retreated down the path. After you'd gone to give the alarm, of course, he cleared the ground of your traces, match-stalks and so on and carried Frank out of the way, coming back to smooth out any footprints he might have made in so doing.

'In the meantime, Joanna's brother was impersonating Frank abroad, just in the unlikely event of your making any inquiries over there, though, as your wife very shrewdly spotted, he overdid his attempts to impress the memory of himself on the hotel staff. And, of course, she answered your telegrams. By the way, as an example of their thoroughness I've just heard that your cousin engaged two single rooms instead of one double one through the whole tour, so that the fact of it being done at Bellagio and Rome, where it was necessary, wouldn't appear odd afterwards. Well, that's the first plot and, as I say, it very nearly came off.

'The second was, in my own opinion, most probably instigated by Joanna herself, or Joanna and Harvey. Frank didn't know, when he brought into his own scheme a man who would help because he was in love with Frank's wife, that Frank's wife was in love with him. You told me yourself that the Wickhams are rotten stock, though you didn't think that Joanna was tainted. She was, worse than any of them (except perhaps her own brother), but morally, not physically. To take advantage of Frank's plot by having him actually killed in the hope that you (if the evidence was rigged a little on the spot, which Harvey was in a position to do) would be hanged for his murder, was nothing to her.'

'Is that what was really intended?' Sylvia asked, rather white.

Sheringham nodded. 'That was the hope, in which event, of course, her infant son would inherit and she would more or less administer things for him till he came of age, marrying Harvey at her leisure and with a nice fat slice of the proceeds earmarked for brother Cedric. If things didn't go so well as that, there was always Frank's original scheme to fall back on, which would give almost as good a result, though with that there was always the danger of your being declared sane again.'

'And the police,' I exclaimed, 'were for a time actually bamboozled!'

'No,' Sheringham laughed. 'We must give Scotland Yard its due. I learned today that, though puzzled, they never seriously suspected you, and what's more, they knew where you were the whole time and actually helped you to get abroad, hoping you'd help them to clear up their case for them, and in fact you did.'

'How silly of them,' Sylvia pronounced. 'When we were out of the country they lost track of us.'

'Yes?' said Sheringham. 'By the way, did you make any friends on the trip?'

'No. At least, only one. There was quite a nice man staying at Cadenabbia who was actually going on to Rome the same day as we did. He was very helpful about trains and so on. We took quite a fancy to him, didn't we, Hugh?'

'He is a nice fellow, isn't he?' Sheringham smiled.

'Oh, do you know him? No, of course you can't; you don't even know who I mean.'

'Indeed I do,' Sheringham retorted. 'You mean Detective Inspector Peters of the CID, though I don't think you knew that yourself, Mrs Chappell.'

Invisible Hands

John Dickson Carr

He could never understand afterwards why he felt uneasiness, even to the point of fear, before he saw the beach at all.

Night and fancies? But how far can fancies go?

It was a steep track down to the beach. The road, however, was good, and he could rely on his car. And yet, half-way down, before he could even taste the sea-wind or hear the rustle of the sea, Dan Fraser felt sweat on his forehead. A nerve jerked in the calf of his leg over the foot brake.

'Look, this is damn silly!' he thought to himself. He thought it with a kind of surprise, as when he had first known fear in wartime long ago. But the fear had been real enough, no matter how well he concealed it, and they believed he never felt it.

A dazzle of lightning lifted ahead of him. The night was too hot. This enclosed road, bumping the springs of his car, seemed pressed down in an airless hollow.

After all, Dan Fraser decided, he had everything to be thankful for. He was going to see Brenda; he was the luckiest man in London. If she chose to spend weekends as far away as North Cornwall, he was glad to drag himself there – even a day late.

Brenda's image rose before him, as clearly as the flash of lightning. He always seemed to see her half-laughing, half-pouting, with light on her yellow hair. She was beautiful; she was desirable. It would only be disloyalty to think any trickiness underlay her intense, naive ways.

Brenda Lestrange always got what she wanted. And she had wanted him, though God alone knew why: he was no prize package at all. Again, in imagination, he saw her against the beat and shuffle of music in a night club. Brenda's shoulders rose from a low-cut silver gown, her eyes as blue and wide-spaced as the eternal Eve's.

You'd have thought she would have preferred a dasher, a roaring bloke like Toby Curtis, who had all the women after him. But that, as Joyce had intimated, might be the trouble. Toby Curtis couldn't see Brenda for all the rest of the crowd. And so Brenda preferred –

Well, then, what was the matter with him?

He would see Brenda in a few minutes. There ought to have been joy bells in the tower, not bats in the – *Easy!*

He was out in the open now, at sea-level. Dan Fraser drove bumpingly along scrub grass, at the head of a few shallow terraces leading down to the private beach. Ahead of him, facing seaward, stood the overlarge, overdecorated bungalow which Brenda had rather grandly named 'The King's House'.

And there wasn't a light in it – not a light showing at only a quarter past ten.

Dan cut the engine, switched off the lights, and got out of the car. In the darkness he could hear the sea charge the beach as an army might have charged it.

Twisting open the handle of the car's boot, he dragged out his suitcase. He closed the compartment with a slam which echoed out above the swirl of water. This part of the Cornish coast was too lonely, too desolate, but it was the first time such a thought had ever occurred to him.

He went to the house, round the side and towards the front. His footsteps clacked loudly on the crazy-paved path on the side. And even in a kind of luminous darkness from the white of the breakers ahead, he saw why the bungalow showed no lights.

All the curtains were drawn on the windows – on this side, at least.

When Dan hurried round to the front door, he was almost running. He banged the iron knocker on the door, then hammered it again. As he glanced over his shoulder, another flash of lightning paled the sky to the west.

It showed him the sweep of grey sand. It showed black water snakily edged with foam. In the middle of the beach, unearthly, stood the small natural rock formation – shaped like a low-backed armchair, eternally facing out to sea – which for centuries had been known as King Arthur's Chair.

The white eye of the lightning closed. Distantly there was a shock of thunder.

This whole bungalow couldn't be deserted! Even if Edmund Ireton and Toby Curtis were at the former's house some distance along the coast, Brenda herself must be here. And Joyce Ray. And the two maids.

Dan stopped hammering the knocker. He groped for and found the knob of the door.

The door was unlocked.

He opened it on brightness. In the hall, rather overdecorated like so many of Brenda's possessions, several lamps shone on gaudy furniture and a polished floor. But the hall was empty too.

With the wind whisking and whistling at his back Dan went in and kicked the door shut behind him. He had no time to give a hail. At the back of the hall a door opened. Joyce Ray, Brenda's cousin, walked towards him, her arms hanging limply at her sides and her enormous eyes like a sleepwalker's.

'Then you did get here,' said Joyce, moistening dry lips. 'You did get here, after all.'

'I—'

Dan stopped. The sight of her brought a new realisation.

It didn't explain his uneasiness or his fear – but it did explain much.

Joyce was the quiet one, the dark one, the unobtrusive one, with her glossy black hair and her subdued elegance. But she was the poor relation, and Brenda never let her forget it. Dan merely stood and stared at her. Suddenly Joyce's eyes lost their sleepwalker's look. They were grey eyes, with very black lashes; they grew alive and vivid, as if she could read his mind.

'Joyce,' he blurted, 'I've just understood something. And I never understood it before. But I've got to tell—'

'Stop!' Joyce cried.

Her mouth twisted. She put up a hand as if to shade her eyes.

'I know what you want to say,' she went on. 'But you're not to say it! Do you hear me?'

'Joyce, I don't know why we're standing here yelling at each other. Anyway, I – I didn't mean to tell you. Not yet, anyway. I mean, I must tell Brenda—'

'You can't tell Brenda!' Joyce cried.

'What's that?'

'You can't tell her anything, ever again,' said Joyce. 'Brenda's dead.'

There are some words which at first do not even shock or stun. You just don't believe them. They can't be true. Very carefully Dan Fraser put his suitcase down on the floor and straightened up again.

'The police,' said Joyce, swallowing hard, 'have been here since early this morning. They're not here now. They've taken her away to the mortuary. That's where she'll sleep tonight.'

Still Dan said nothing.

'Mr – Mr Edmund Ireton,' Joyce went on, 'has been here ever since it happened. So has Toby Curtis. So, fortunately, has a man named Dr Gideon Fell. Dr Fell's a bumbling old duffer, a very learned man or something. He's a friend of the police; he's kind; he's helped soften things. All the same, Dan, if you'd been here last night –'

'I couldn't get away. I told Brenda so.'

'Yes, I know all that talk about hard-working journalists. But if you'd only been here, Dan, it might not have happened at all.'

'Joyce, for God's sake!'

Then there was a silence in the bright, quiet room. A stricken look crept into Joyce's eyes.

'Dan, I'm sorry. I'm terribly sorry. I was feeling dreadful and so, I suppose, I had to take it out on the first person handy.'

'That's all right. But how did she die?' Then desperately he began to surmise. 'Wait, I've got it! She went out to swim early this morning, just as usual? She's been diving off those rocks on the headland again? And—'

'No,' said Joyce. 'She was strangled.'

'*Strangled?*'

What Joyce tried to say was 'murdered'. Her mouth shook and faltered round the syllables; she couldn't say them; her thoughts, it seemed, shied back and ran from the very word. But she looked at Dan steadily.

'Brenda went out to swim early this morning, yes.'

'Well?'

'At least, she must have. I didn't see her. I was still asleep in that back bedroom she always gives me. Anyway, she went down there in a red swimsuit and a white beach-robe.'

Automatically Dan's eyes moved over to an oil-painting above the fireplace. Painted by a famous RA, it showed a scene from classical antiquity; it was called 'The Lovers', and left little to the imagination. It had always been Brenda's favourite because the female figure in the picture looked so much like her.

'Well!' said Joyce, throwing out her hands. 'You know what Brenda always does. She takes off her beach-robe and spreads it out over King Arthur's Chair. She sits down in the chair and smokes a cigarette and looks out at the sea before she goes into the water.

'The beach-robe was still in that rock chair,' Joyce continued with an effort, 'when I came downstairs at half-past seven. But Brenda wasn't. She hadn't even put on her bathing-cap. Somebody had strangled her with that silk scarf she wore with the beach-robe. It was twisted so tightly into her neck they couldn't get it out. She was lying on the sand in front of the chair, on her back, in the red swimsuit, with her face black and swollen. You could see her clearly from the terrace.'

Dan glanced at the flesh tints of 'The Lovers', then quickly looked away.

Joyce, the cool and competent, was holding herself under restraint.

'I can only thank my lucky stars,' she burst out, 'I didn't run out there. I mean, from the flagstones of the lowest terrace out across the sand. They stopped me.'

'"They" stopped you? Who?'

'Mr Ireton and Toby. Or, rather, Mr Ireton did; Toby wouldn't have thought of it.'

'But—'

'Toby, you see, had come over here a little earlier. But he was at the back of the bungalow, practising with a .22 target rifle. I heard him once. Mr Ireton had just got there. All three of us walked out on the terrace at once. And saw her.'

'Listen, Joyce. What difference does it make whether or not you ran out across the sand? Why were you so lucky they stopped you?'

'Because if they hadn't, the police might have said I did it.'

'Did it?'

'Killed Brenda,' Joyce answered clearly. 'In all that stretch of sand, Dan, there weren't any footprints except Brenda's own.'

'Now hold on!' he protested. 'She – she was killed with that scarf of hers?'

'Oh, yes. The police and even Dr Fell don't doubt that.'

'Then how could anybody, anybody at all, go out across the sand and come back without leaving a footprint?'

'That's just it. The police don't know and they can't guess. That's why they're in a flat spin, and Dr Fell will be here again tonight.'

In her desperate attempt to speak lightly, as if all this didn't matter, Joyce failed. Her face was white. But again the expression of the dark-fringed eyes changed, and she hesitated.

'Dan—'

'Yes?'

'You do understand, don't you, why I was so upset when you came charging in and said what you did?'

'Yes, of course.'

'Whatever you had to tell me, or thought you had to tell me –'

'About – us?'

'About anything! You do see that you must forget it and not mention it again? Not ever?'

'I see why I can't mention it now. With Brenda dead, it wouldn't even be decent to think of it.' He could not keep his eyes off that mocking picture. 'But is the future dead too? If I happen to have been an idiot and thought I was head over heels gone on Brenda when all the time it was really—'

'*Dan!*'

There were five doors opening into the gaudy hall, which had too many mirrors. Joyce whirled round to look at every door, as if she feared an ambush behind each.

'For heaven's sake keep your voice down,' she begged. 'Practically every word that's said can be heard all over the house. I said never, and I meant it. If you'd spoken a week ago, even twenty-four hours ago, it might have been different. Do you think I didn't want you to? But now it's too late!'

'Why?'

'May *I* answer that question?' interrupted a new, dry, rather quizzical voice.

Dan had taken a step towards her, intensely conscious of her attractiveness. He stopped, burned with embarrassment, as one of the five doors opened.

Mr Edmund Ireton, shortish and thin and dandified in his middle-fifties, emerged with his usual briskness. There was not much grey in his polished black hair. His face was a benevolent satyr's.

'Forgive me,' he said.

Behind him towered Toby Curtis, heavy and handsome and fair-haired, in a bulky tweed jacket. Toby began to speak, but Mr Ireton's gesture silenced him before he could utter a sound.

'Forgive me,' he repeated. 'But what Joyce says is quite true. Every word can be overheard here, even with the rain pouring down. If you go on shouting and Dr Fell hears it, you will land that girl in serious danger.'

'Danger?' demanded Toby Curtis. He had to clear his throat. 'What danger could *Dan* get her into?'

Mr Ireton, immaculate in flannels and shirt and thin pull-over, stalked to the mantelpiece. He stared up hard at 'The Lovers' before turning round.

'The Psalmist tells us,' he said dryly, 'that all is vanity. Has none of you ever noticed – God forgive me for saying so – that Brenda's most outstanding trait was her vanity?'

His glance flashed towards Joyce, who abruptly turned away and pressed her hands over her face.

'Appalling vanity. Scratch that vanity deeply enough and our dearest Brenda would have committed murder.'

'Aren't you getting this backwards?' asked Dan. 'Brenda didn't commit any murder. It was Brenda —'

'Ah!' Mr Ireton pounced. 'And there might be a lesson in that, don't you think?'

'Look here, you're not saying she strangled herself with her own scarf?'

'No – but hear what I do say. Our Brenda, no doubt, had many passions and many fancies. But there was only one man she loved or ever wanted to marry. It was not Mr Dan Fraser.'

'Then who was it?' asked Toby.

'You.'

Toby's amazement was too genuine to be assumed. The colour drained out of his face. Once more he had to clear his throat.

'So help me,' he said, 'I never knew it! I never imagined –'

'No, of course you didn't,' Mr Ireton said even more dryly. A goatish amusement flashed across his face and was gone. 'Brenda, as a rule, could get any man she chose. So she turned Mr Fraser's head and became engaged to him. It was to sting you, Mr Curtis, to make you jealous. And you never noticed. While all the time Joyce Ray and Dan Fraser were eating their hearts out for each other; and *he* never noticed either.'

Edmund Ireton wheeled round.

'You may lament my bluntness, Mr Fraser. You may want to wring my neck, as I see you do. But can you deny one word I say?'

'No.' In honesty Dan could not deny it.

'Well! Then be very careful when you face the police, both of you, or they will see it too. Joyce already has a strong motive. She is Brenda's only relative, and inherits Brenda's money. If they learn she wanted Brenda's fiancé, they will have her in the dock for murder.'

'That's enough!' blurted Dan, who dared not look at Joyce. 'You've made it clear. All right, stop there!'

'Oh, I had intended to stop. If you are such fools that you won't help yourselves, I must help you. That's all.'

It was Toby Curtis who strode forward.

'Dan, don't let him bluff you!' Toby said. 'In the first place, they can't arrest anybody for this. You weren't here. I know —'

'I've heard about it, Toby.'

'Look,' insisted Toby. 'When the police finished measuring and photographing and taking casts of Brenda's footprints, I did some measuring myself.'

Edmund Ireton smiled. 'Are *you* attempting to solve this mystery, Mr Curtis?'

'I didn't say that.' Toby spoke coolly. 'But I might have a question or two for you. Why have you had your knife into me all day?'

'Frankly, Mr Curtis, because I envy you.'

'You – *what?*'

'So far as women are concerned, young man, I have not your advantages. *I* had no romantic boyhood on a veldt-farm in South Africa. I never learned to drive a span of oxen and flick a fly off the leader's ear with my whip. *I* was never taught to be a spectacular horseman and rifle shot.'

'Oh, turn it up!'

'"Turn it up?" Ah, I see. And was that the sinister question you had for me?'

'No. Not yet. You're too tricky.'

'My profoundest thanks.'

'Look, Dan,' Toby insisted. 'You've seen that rock formation they call King Arthur's Chair?'

'Toby, I've seen it fifty times,' Dan said. 'But I still don't understand –'

'And I don't understand,' suddenly interrupted Joyce, without turning round, 'why they made me sit there where Brenda had been sitting. It was horrible.'

'Oh, they were only reconstructing the crime.' Toby spoke rather grandly. 'But the question, Dan, is how anybody came near that chair without leaving a footprint?'

'Quite.'

'Nobody could have,' Toby said just as grandly. 'The murderer, for instance, couldn't have come from the direction of the sea. Why? Because the highest point at high tide, where the water might have blotted out footprints, is more than twenty feet in front of the chair. More than twenty feet!'

'Er – one moment,' said Mr Ireton, twitching up a finger.

'Surely Inspector Tregellis said the murderer must have crept up and caught her from the back? Before she knew it?'

'That won't do either. From the flagstones of the terrace to the back of the chair is at least twenty feet, too. Well, Dan? Do you see any way out of that one?'

Dan, not normally slow-witted, was so concentrating on Joyce that he could think of little else. She was cut off from him, drifting away from him, for ever out of reach just when he had found her. But he tried to think.

'Well ... could somebody have jumped there?'

'Ho!' scoffed Toby, who was himself a broad jumper and knew better. 'That was the first thing they thought of.'

'And that's out, too?'

'Definitely. An Olympic champion in good form might have done it, if he'd had any place for a running start and any place to land. But he hadn't. There was *no* mark in the sand. He couldn't have landed on the chair, strangled Brenda at his leisure, and then hopped back like a jumping bean. Now could he?'

'But somebody did it, Toby! It happened!'

'How?'

'I don't know.'

'You seem rather proud of this, Mr Curtis,' Edmund Ireton said smoothly.

'Proud?' exclaimed Toby, losing colour again.

'These romantic boyhoods—'

Toby did not lose his temper. But he had declared war.

'All right, gaffer. I've been very grateful for your hospitality, at that bungalow of yours, when we've come down here for weekends. All the same, you've been going on for hours about who I am and what I am. Who are *you!*'

'I beg your pardon?'

'For two or three years,' Toby said, 'you've been hanging about with us. Especially with Brenda and Joyce. Who are you? What are you?'

'I am an observer of life,' Mr Ireton answered tranquilly. 'A student of human nature. And – shall I say? – a courtesy uncle to both young ladies.'

'Is that all you were? To either of them?'

'Toby!' exclaimed Joyce, shocked out of her fear.

She whirled round, her gaze going instinctively to Dan, then back to Toby.

'Don't worry, old girl,' said Toby, waving his hand at her. 'This is no reflection on you.' He kept looking steadily at Mr Ireton.

'Continue,' Mr Ireton said politely.

'You claim Joyce is in danger. She isn't in any danger at all,' said Toby, 'as long as the police don't know how Brenda was strangled.'

'They will discover it, Mr Curtis. Be sure they will discover it!'

'You're trying to protect Joyce?'

'Naturally.'

'And that's why you warned Dan not to say he was in love with her?'

'Of course. What else?'

Toby straightened up, his hand inside the bulky tweed jacket. 'Then why didn't you take him outside, rain or no, and tell him on the quiet? Why did *you* shout out that Dan was in love with Joyce, and she was in love with him, and give 'em a motive for the whole house to hear?'

Edmund Ireton opened his mouth, and shut it again.

It was a blow under the guard, all the more unexpected because it came from Toby Curtis.

Mr Ireton stood motionless under the painting of 'The Lovers'. The expression of the pictured Brenda, elusive and mocking, no longer matched his own. Whereupon, while nerves were strained and still nobody spoke, Dan Fraser realised that there was a dead silence because the rain had stopped.

Small night-noises, the creak of woodwork or a drip of water from the eaves, intensified the stillness. Then they heard footsteps, as heavy as those of an elephant, slowly approaching behind another of the doors. The footfalls, heavy and slow and creaking, brought a note of doom.

Into the room, wheezing and leaning on a stick, lumbered a man so enormous that he had to manoeuvre himself sideways through the door.

His big mop of grey-streaked hair had tumbled over one ear. His eyeglasses, with a broad black ribbon, were stuck askew on his nose. His big face would ordinarily have been red and beaming, with chuckles animating several chins. Now it was only absent-minded, his bandit's moustache outthrust.

'Aha!' he said in a rumbling voice. He blinked at Dan with an air of refreshed interest. 'I think you must be Mr Fraser, the last of this rather curious weekend party? H'm. Yes. Your obedient servant, sir. I am Gideon Fell.'

Dr Fell wore a black cloak as big as a tent and carried a

shovel-hat in his other hand. He tried to bow and make a flourish with his stick, endangering all the furniture near him.

The others stood very still. Fear was as palpable as the scent after rain.

'Yes, I've heard of you,' said Dan. His voice rose in spite of himself. 'But you're rather far from home, aren't you? I suppose you had some – er – antiquarian interest in King Arthur's Chair?'

Still Dr Fell blinked at him. For a second it seemed that chuckles would jiggle his chins and waistcoat, but he only shook his head.

'Antiquarian interest? My dear sir!' Dr Fell wheezed gently. 'If there were any association with a semi-legendary King Arthur, it would be at Tintagel much farther south. No, I was here on holiday. This morning Inspector Tregellis fascinated me with the story of a fantastic murder. I returned tonight for my own reasons.'

Mr Ireton, at ease again, matched the other's courtesy. 'May I ask what these reasons were?'

'First, I wished to question the two maids. They have a room at the back, as Miss Ray has; and this afternoon, you may remember, they were still rather hysterical.'

'And that is all?'

'H'mf. Well, no.' Dr Fell scowled. 'Second, I wanted to detain all of you here for an hour or two. Third, I must make sure of the motive for this crime. And I am happy to say that I have made very sure.'

Joyce could not control herself. 'Then you did overhear everything!'

'Eh?'

'Every word that man said!'

Despite Dan's signals, Joyce nodded towards Mr Ireton and poured out the words. 'But I swear I hadn't anything to do with Brenda's death. What I told you today was perfectly true: I don't want her money and I won't touch it. As for my – my private affairs,' and Joyce's face flamed, 'everybody seems to know all about them except Dan and me. Please, please pay no attention to what that man has been saying.'

Dr Fell blinked at her in an astonishment which changed to vast distress.

'But, my dear young lady!' he rumbled. 'We never for a moment believed you did. No, no! Archons of Athens, no!' exclaimed Dr Fell, as though at incredible absurdity. 'As for what your friend Mr Ireton may have been saying, I did not hear it. I suspect it was only what he told me today, and it did supply the motive. But it was not your motive.'

'Please, is this true? You're not trying to trap me?'

'Do I really strike you,' Dr Fell asked gently, 'as being that sort of person? Nothing was more unlikely than that you killed your cousin, especially in the way she was killed.'

'Do you know how she was killed?'

'Oh, *that*,' grunted Dr Fell, waving the point away too. 'That was the simplest part of the whole business.'

He lumbered over, reflected in the mirrors, and put down stick and shovel-hat on a table. Afterwards he faced them with a mixture of distress and apology.

'It may surprise you,' he said, 'that an old scatterbrain like myself can observe anything at all. But I have an unfair advantage over the police. I began life as a schoolmaster: I have had more experience with habitual liars. Hang it all, think!'

'Of what?'

'The facts!' said Dr Fell, making a hideous face. 'According to the maids, Sonia and Dolly, Miss Brenda Lestrange went down to swim at ten minutes to seven this morning. Both Dolly and Sonia were awake, but did not get up. Some eight or ten minutes later, Mr Toby Curtis began practising with a target rifle some distance away behind the bungalow.'

'Don't look at me!' exclaimed Toby. 'That rifle has nothing to do with it. Brenda wasn't shot.'

'Sir,' said Dr Fell with much patience, 'I am aware of that.'

'Then what are you hinting at?'

'Sir,' said Dr Fell, 'you will oblige me if you too don't regard every question as a trap. I have a trap for the murderer, and the murderer alone. You fired a number of shots – the maids heard you and saw you.' He turned to Joyce. 'I believe you heard too?'

'I heard one shot,' answered the bewildered Joyce, 'as I told Dan. About seven o'clock, when I got up and dressed.'

'Did you look out of the windows?'

'No.'

'What happened to that rifle afterwards? Is it here now?'

'No,' Toby almost yelled. 'I took it back to Ireton's after we found Brenda. But if the rifle had nothing to do with it, and I had nothing to do with it, then what the hell's the point?'

Dr Fell did not reply for a moment. Then he made another hideous face. 'We know,' he rumbled, 'that Brenda Lestrange wore a beach-robe, a bathing-suit, and a heavy silk scarf knotted round her neck. Miss Ray?'

'Y-yes?'

'I am not precisely an authority on women's clothes,' said

Dr Fell. 'As a rule I should notice nothing odd unless I passed Madge Wildfire or Lady Godiva. I have seen men wear a scarf with a beach-robe, but is it customary for women to wear a scarf as well?'

There was a pause.

'No, of course it isn't,' said Joyce. 'I can't speak for everybody, but I never do. It was just one of Brenda's fancies. She always did.'

'Aha!' said Dr Fell. 'The murderer was counting on that.'

'On what?'

'On her known conduct. Let me show you rather a grisly picture of a murder.'

Dr Fell's eyes were squeezed shut. From inside his cloak and pocket he fished out an immense meerschaum pipe. Firmly under the impression that he had filled and lighted the pipe, he put the stem in his mouth and drew at it.

'Miss Lestrange,' he said, 'goes down to the beach. She takes off her robe. Remember that, it's very important. She spreads out the robe in King Arthur's Chair and sits down. She is still wearing the scarf, knotted tightly in a broad band round her neck. She is about the same height as you, Miss Ray. She is held there, at the height of her shoulders, by a curving rock formation deeply bedded in sand.'

Dr Fell paused and opened his eyes.

'The murderer, we believe, catches her from the back. She sees and hears nothing until she is seized. Intense pressure on the carotid arteries, here at either side of the neck under the chin, will strike her unconscious within seconds and dead within minutes. When her body is released, it should fall straight forward. Instead, what happens?'

To Dan, full of relief ever since danger had seemed to leave Joyce, it was as if a shutter had flown open in his brain.

'She was lying on her back,' Dan said. 'Joyce told me so. Brenda was lying flat on her back with her head towards the sea. And that means—'

'Yes?'

'It means she was twisted or spun round in some way when she fell. It has something to do with that infernal scarf – I've thought so from the first. Dr Fell! Was Brenda killed with the scarf?'

'In one sense, yes. In another sense, no.'

'You can't have it both ways! Either she was killed with the scarf, or she wasn't.'

'Not necessarily,' said Dr Fell.

'Then let's all retire to a loony bin,' Dan suggested, 'because nothing makes any sense at all. The murderer still couldn't have walked out there without leaving tracks. Finally, I agree with Toby: what's the point of the rifle? How does a .22 rifle figure in all this?'

'Because of its sound.'

Dr Fell took the pipe out of his mouth. Dan wondered why he had ever thought the learned doctor's eyes were vague. Magnified behind the glasses on the broad black ribbon, they were not vague at all.

'A .22 rifle,' he went on in his big voice, 'has a distinctive noise. Fired in the open air or anywhere else, it sounds exactly like the noise made by the real instrument used in this crime.'

'Real instrument? What noise?'

'The crack of a blacksnake whip,' replied Dr Fell.

Edmund Ireton, looking very tired and ten years older, went over and sat down in an easy chair. Toby Curtis took one step backwards, then another.

'In South Africa,' said Dr Fell, 'I have never seen the very long whip which drivers of long ox spans use. But in America I have seen the blacksnake whip, and it can be twenty-four feet long. You yourselves must have watched it used in a variety turn on the stage.'

Dr Fell pointed his pipe at them.

'Remember?' he asked. 'The user of the whip stands some distance away facing his girl-assistant. There is a vicious crack. The end of the whip coils two or three times round the girl's neck. She is not hurt. But she would be in difficulties if he pulled the whip towards him. She would be in grave danger if she were held back and could not move.

'Somebody planned a murder with a whip like that. He came here early in the morning. The whip, coiled round his waist, was hidden by a loose and bulky tweed jacket. Please observe the jacket Toby Curtis is wearing now.'

Toby's voice went high when he screeched out one word. It may have been protest, defiance, a jeer, or all three.

'Stop this!' cried Joyce, who had again turned away.

'Continue, I beg,' Mr Ireton said.

'In the dead hush of morning,' said Dr Fell, 'he could not hide the loud crack of the whip. But what could he do?'

'He could mask it,' said Edmund Ireton.

'Just that! He was always practising with a .22 rifle. So he fired several shots, behind the bungalow, to establish his presence. Afterwards nobody would notice when the crack of the whip – that single, isolated "shot" heard by Miss Ray – only seemed to come from behind the house.'

'Then, actually, he was——?'

'On the terrace, twenty feet behind a victim held immovable in the curve of a stone chair. The end of the whip coiled round the scarf. Miss Lestrange's breath was cut off instantly. Under the pull of a powerful arm she died in seconds.

'On the stage, you recall, a lift and twist dislodges the whip from the girl-assistant's neck. Toby Curtis had a harder task; the scarf was so embedded in her neck that she seemed to have been strangled with it. He *could* dislodge it. But only with a powerful whirl and lift of the arm which spun her up and round, to fall face upwards. The whip snaked back to him with no trace in the sand. Afterwards he had only to take the whip back to Mr Ireton's house, under pretext of returning the rifle. He had committed a murder which, in his vanity, he thought undetectable. That's all.'

'But it can't be all!' said Dan. 'Why should Toby have killed her? His motive —'

'His motive was offended vanity. Mr Edmund Ireton as good as told you so, I fancy. He had certainly hinted as much to me.'

Edmund Ireton rose shakily from the chair.

'I am no judge or executioner,' he said. 'I – I am detached from life. I only observe. If I guessed why this was done —'

'You could never speak straight out?' Dr Fell asked sardonically.

'No!'

'And yet that was the tragic irony of the whole affair. Miss Lestrange wanted Toby Curtis, as he wanted her. But, being a woman, her pretence of indifference and contempt was too good. He believed it. Scratch her vanity deeply enough and she would have committed murder. Scratch *his* vanity deeply enough —'

'Lies!'said Toby.

'Look at him, all of you!' said Dr Fell. 'Even when he's accused of murder, he can't take his eyes off a mirror.'

'Lies!'

'She laughed at him,' the big voice went on, 'and so she had to die. Brutally and senselessly he killed a girl who would have been his for the asking. That is what I meant by tragic irony.'

Toby had retreated across the room until his back bumped against a wall. Startled, he looked behind him; he had banged against another mirror.

'Lies!' he kept repeating. 'You can talk and talk and talk. But there's not a single damned thing you can prove!'

'Sir,' inquired Dr Fell, 'are you sure?'

'Yes!'

'I warned you,' said Dr Fell, 'that I returned tonight partly to detain all of you for an hour or so. It gave Inspector Tregellis time to search Mr Ireton's house, and the Inspector has since returned. I further warned you that I questioned the maids, Sonia and Dolly, who today were only incoherent. My dear sir, you underestimate your personal attractions.'

Now it was Joyce who seemed to understand. But she did not speak.

'Sonia, it seems,' and Dr Fell looked hard at Toby, 'has quite a fondness for you. When she heard that last isolated "shot" this morning, she looked out of the window again.

You weren't there. This was so strange that she ran out to the front terrace to discover where you were. She saw you.'

The door by which Dr Fell had entered was still open. His voice lifted and echoed through the hall.

'Come in, Sonia!' he called. 'After all, you are witness to the murder. You, Inspector, had better come in too.'

Toby Curtis blundered back, but there was no way out. There was only a brief glimpse of Sonia's swollen, tear-stained face. Past her marched a massive figure in uniform, carrying what he had found hidden in the other house.

Inspector Tregellis was reflected everywhere in the mirrors, with the long coils of the whip over his arm. And he seemed to be carrying not a whip but a coil of rope – gallows rope.

Chapter and Verse

Ngaio Marsh

When the telephone rang, Troy came in, sun-dazzled, from the cottage garden to answer it, hoping it would be a call from London.

'Oh,' said a strange voice uncertainly. 'May I speak to Superintendent Alleyn, if you please?'

'I'm sorry. He's away.'

'Oh, dear!' said the voice, crestfallen. 'Er – would that be – am I speaking to Mrs Alleyn?'

'Yes.'

'Oh. Yes. Well, it's Timothy Bates here, Mrs Alleyn. You don't know me,' the voice confessed wistfully, 'but I had the pleasure several years ago of meeting your husband. In New Zealand. And he did say that if I ever came home I was to get in touch, and when I heard quite by accident that you were here – well, I *was* excited. But, alas, no good after all.'

'I *am* sorry,' Troy said. 'He'll be back, I hope, on Sunday night. Perhaps—'

'Will he! Come, *that's* something! Because here I am at the Star and Garter, you see, and so—' The voice trailed away again.

'Yes, indeed. He'll be delighted,' Troy said, hoping that he would.

'I'm a bookman,' the voice confided. 'Old books, you know. He used to come into my shop. It was always such a pleasure.'

'But, of course!' Troy exclaimed. 'I remember perfectly now. He's often talked about it.'

'*Has* he? Has he, really! Well, you see, Mrs Alleyn, I'm here on business. Not to *sell* anything, please don't think that, but on a voyage of discovery; almost, one might say, of detection, and I think it might amuse him. He has such an eye for the curious. Not,' the voice hurriedly amended, 'in the trade sense. I mean curious in the sense of mysterious and unusual. But I mustn't bore you.'

Troy assured him that he was not boring her and indeed it was true. The voice was so much coloured by odd little overtones that she found herself quite drawn to its owner. 'I know where you are,' he was saying. 'Your house was pointed out to me.'

After that there was nothing to do but ask him to visit. He seemed to cheer up prodigiously. 'May I? May I, really? Now?'

'Why not?' Troy said. 'You'll be here in five minutes.' She heard a little crow of delight before he hung up the receiver.

He turned out to be exactly like his voice – a short,

middle-aged, bespectacled man, rather untidily dressed. As he came up the path she saw that with both arms he clutched to his stomach an enormous Bible. He was thrown into a fever over the difficulty of removing his cap.

'How ridiculous!' he exclaimed. 'Forgive me! One moment.' He laid his burden tenderly on a garden seat. 'There!' he cried. 'Now! How do you do!'

Troy took him indoors and gave him a drink. He chose sherry and sat in the window seat with his Bible beside him. 'You'll wonder,' he said, 'why I've appeared with this unusual piece of baggage. I *do* trust it arouses your curiosity.'

He went into a long excitable explanation. It appeared that the Bible was an old and rare one that he had picked up in a job lot of books in New Zealand. All this time he kept it under his square little hands as if it might open of its own accord and spoil his story.

'Because,' he said, 'the *really* exciting thing to me is *not* its undoubted authenticity but—' He made a conspiratorial face at Troy and suddenly opened the Bible. 'Look!' he invited.

He displayed the flyleaf. Troy saw that it was almost filled with entries in a minute, faded copperplate handwriting. 'The top,' Mr Bates cried. 'Top left-hand. Look at *that*.'

Troy read: *'Crabtree Farm at Little Copplestone in the County of Kent.* Why, it comes from our village!'

'Ah, ha! So it does. Now, the entries, my dear Mrs Alleyn. The entries.'

They were the recorded births and deaths of a family named Wagstaff, beginning in 1705 and ending in 1870 with the birth of William James Wagstaff. Here they broke off but were followed by three further entries, close together.

Stewart Shakespeare Hadet. Died: Tuesday, 5th April, 1779.
2nd Samuel 1.10.

Naomi Balbus Hadet. Died: Saturday, 13th August, 1779.
Jeremiah 50.24.

Peter Rook Hadet. Died: Monday, 12th September, 1779.
Ezekiel 7.6.

Troy looked up to find Mr Bates's gaze fixed on her. 'And what,' Mr Bates asked, 'my dear Mrs Alleyn, do you make of *that?*'

'Well,' she said cautiously, 'I know about Crabtree Farm. There's the farm itself, owned by Mr De'ath, and there's Crabtree House, belonging to Miss Hart, and – yes, I fancy I've heard they both belonged originally to a family named Wagstaff.'

'You are perfectly right. Now! What about the Hadets? What about *them?*'

'I've never heard of a family named Hadet in Little Copplestone. But –'

'Of course you haven't. For the very good reason that there never have been any Hadets in Little Copplestone.'

'Perhaps in New Zealand, then?'

'The dates, my dear Mrs Alleyn, the dates! New Zealand was not colonised in 1779. Look closer. Do you see the sequence of double dots – ditto marks – under the address? Meaning, of course, "also of Crabtree Farm at Little Copplestone in the County of Kent".'

'I suppose so.'

'Of course you do. And how right you are. Now! You

have noticed that throughout there are biblical references. For the Wagstaffs they are the usual pious offerings. You need not trouble yourself with them. But consult the text awarded to the three Hadets. Just you look *them* up! I've put markers.'

He threw himself back with an air of triumph and sipped his sherry. Troy turned over the heavy bulk of pages to the first marker. 'Second of Samuel, one, ten,' Mr Bates prompted, closing his eyes.

The verse had been faintly underlined.

'So I stood upon him,' Troy read, *'and slew him.'*

'That's Stewart Shakespeare Hadet's valedictory,' said Mr Bates. 'Next!'

The next was at the 50th chapter of Jeremiah, verse 24: '*I have laid a snare for thee and thou are taken.'*

Troy looked at Mr Bates. His eyes were still closed and he was smiling faintly.

'That was Naomi Balbus Hadet,' he said. 'Now for Peter Rook Hadet. Ezekiel, seven, six.'

The pages flopped back to the last marker.

'An end is come, the end is come: it watcheth for thee; behold it is come.'

Troy shut the Bible.

'How very unpleasant,' she said.

'And how very intriguing, don't you think?' And when she didn't answer, 'Quite up your husband's street, it seemed to me.'

'I'm afraid,' Troy said, 'that even Rory's investigations don't go back to 1779.'

'What a pity!' Mr Bates cried gaily.

'Do I gather that you conclude from all this that there was dirty work among the Hadets in 1779?'

'I don't know, but I'm dying to find out. *Dying* to. Thank you, I should enjoy another glass. Delicious!'

He had settled down so cosily and seemed to be enjoying himself so much that Troy was constrained to ask him to stay to lunch.

'Miss Hart's coming,' she said. 'She's the one who bought Crabtree House from the Wagstaffs. If there's any gossip to be picked up in Copplestone, Miss Hart's the one for it. She's coming about a painting she wants me to donate to the Harvest Festival raffle.'

Mr Bates was greatly excited. 'Who knows!' he cried. 'A Wagstaff in the hand may be worth two Hadets in the bush. I am your slave for ever, my dear Mrs Alleyn!'

Miss Hart was a lady of perhaps sixty-seven years. On meeting Mr Bates she seemed to imply that some explanation should be advanced for Troy receiving a gentleman caller in her husband's absence. When the Bible was produced, she immediately accepted it in this light, glanced with professional expertise at the inscriptions and fastened on the Wagstaffs.

'No doubt,' said Miss Hart, 'it was their family Bible and much good it did them. A most eccentric lot they were. Very unsound. Very unsound, indeed. Especially Old Jimmy.'

'Who,' Mr Bates asked greedily, 'was Old Jimmy?'

Miss Hart jabbed her forefinger at the last of the Wagstaff entries. 'William James Wagstaff. Born 1870. And died, although it doesn't say so, in April 1921. Nobody was left to complete the entry, of course. Unless you count the niece, which I don't. Baggage, if ever I saw one.'

'The niece?'

'Fanny Wagstaff. Orphan. Old Jimmy brought her up. Dragged would be the better word. Drunken old reprobate he was and he came to a drunkard's end. They said he beat her *and* I daresay she needed it.' Miss Hart lowered her voice to a whisper and confided in Troy. 'Not a *nice* girl. You know what I mean.'

Troy, feeling it was expected of her, nodded portentously.

'A drunken end, did you say?' prompted Mr Bates.

'Certainly. On a Saturday night after Market. Fell through the top landing stair rail in his nightshirt and split his skull on the flagstoned hall.'

'And your father bought it, then, after Old Jimmy died?' Troy ventured.

'Bought the house and garden. Richard De'ath took the farm. He'd been after it for years – wanted it to round off his own place. He and Old Jimmy were at daggers drawn over *that* business. And, of course, Richard being an atheist, over the Seven Seals.'

'I beg your pardon?' Mr Bates asked.

'Blasphemous!' Miss Hart shouted. 'That's what it was, rank blasphemy. It was a sect that Wagstaff founded. If the rector had known his business he'd have had him excommunicated for it.'

Miss Hart was prevented from elaborating this theory by the appearance at the window of an enormous woman, stuffily encased in black, with a face like a full moon.

'Anybody at home?' the newcomer playfully chanted. 'Telegram for a lucky girl! Come and get it!'

It was Mrs Simpson, the village postmistress. Miss Hart said, 'Well, *really!*' and gave an acid laugh.

'Sorry, I'm sure,' said Mrs Simpson, staring at the Bible which lay under her nose on the window seat. 'I didn't realise there was company. Thought I'd pop it in as I was passing.'

Troy read the telegram while Mrs Simpson, panting, sank heavily on the window ledge and eyed Mr Bates, who had drawn back in confusion. 'I'm no good in the heat,' she told him. 'Slays me.'

'Thank you so much, Mrs Simpson,' Troy said. 'No answer.'

'Righty-ho. Cheerie-bye,' said Mrs Simpson and with another stare at Mr Bates and the Bible, and a derisive grin at Miss Hart, she waddled away.

'It's from Rory,' Troy said. 'He'll be home on Sunday evening.'

'As that woman will no doubt inform the village,' Miss Hart pronounced. 'A busybody of the first water and ought to be taught her place. Did you ever!'

She fulminated throughout luncheon and it was with difficulty that Troy and Mr Bates persuaded her to finish her story of the last of the Wagstaffs. It appeared that Old Jimmy had died intestate, his niece succeeding. She had at once announced her intention of selling everything and had left the district to pursue, Miss Hart suggested, a life of freedom, no doubt in London or even in Paris. Miss Hart wouldn't, and didn't want to, know. On the subject of the Hadets, however, she was uninformed and showed no inclination to look up the marked Bible references attached to them.

After luncheon Troy showed Miss Hart three of her paintings, any one of which would have commanded a high price at an exhibition of contemporary art, and Miss Hart chose the one that, in her own phrase, really did look like something. She insisted that Troy and Mr Bates accompany her to the parish hall where Mr Bates would meet the rector, an authority on village folklore. Troy in person must hand over her painting to be raffled.

Troy would have declined this honour if Mr Bates had not retired behind Miss Hart and made a series of beseeching gestures and grimaces. They set out therefore in Miss Hart's car which was crammed with vegetables for the Harvest Festival decorations.

'And if the woman Simpson thinks she's going to hog the lectern with *her* pumpkins,' said Miss Hart, 'she's in for a shock. Hah!'

St Cuthbert's was an ancient parish church round whose flanks the tiny village nestled. Its tower, an immensely high one, was said to be unique. Nearby was the parish hall where Miss Hart pulled up with a masterful jerk.

Troy and Mr Bates helped her unload some of her lesser marrows to be offered for sale within. They were observed by a truculent-looking man in tweeds who grinned at Miss Hart. 'Burnt offerings,' he jeered, 'for the tribal gods, I perceive.' It was Mr Richard De'ath, the atheist. Miss Hart cut him dead and led the way into the hall.

Here they found the rector, with a crimson-faced elderly man and a clutch of ladies engaged in preparing for the morrow's sale.

The rector was a thin gentle person, obviously frightened of Miss Hart and timidly delighted by Troy. On being shown the Bible he became excited and dived at once into the story of Old Jimmy Wagstaff.

'Intemperate, I'm afraid, in everything,' sighed the rector. 'Indeed, it would not be too much to say that he both preached and drank hellfire. He *did* preach, on Saturday nights at the crossroads outside the Star and Garter. Drunken, blasphemous nonsense it was and although he used to talk about his followers, the only one he could claim was his niece, Fanny, who was probably too much under his thumb to refuse him.'

'Edward Pilbrow,' Miss Hart announced, jerking her head at the elderly man who had come quite close to them. 'Drowned him with his bell. They had a fight over it. Deaf as a post,' she added, catching sight of Mr Bates's startled expression. 'He's the verger now. *And* the town crier.'

'What!' Mr Bates exclaimed.

'Oh, yes,' the rector explained. 'The village is endowed with a town crier.' He went over to Mr Pilbrow, who at once cupped his hand round his ear. The rector yelled into it.

'When did you start crying, Edward?'

'Twenty-ninth September, 'twenty-one,' Mr Pilbrow roared back.

'I thought so.'

There was something in their manner that made it difficult to remember, Troy thought, that they were talking about events that were almost fifty years back in the past. Even the year 1779 evidently seemed to them to be not so long ago, but, alas, none of them knew of any Hadets.

'By all means,' the rector invited Mr Bates, 'consult the church records, but I can assure you – no Hadets. Never any Hadets.'

Troy saw an expression of extreme obstinacy settle round Mr Bates's mouth.

The rector invited him to look at the church and as they both seemed to expect Troy to tag along, she did so. In the lane they once more encountered Mr Richard De'ath out of whose pocket protruded a paper-wrapped bottle. He touched his cap to Troy and glared at the rector, who turned pink and said, 'Afternoon, De'ath,' and hurried on.

Mr Bates whispered imploringly to Troy, *'Would you mind? I *do* so want to have a word—' and she was obliged to introduce him. It was not a successful encounter. Mr Bates no sooner broached the topic of his Bible, which he still carried, than Mr De'ath burst into an alcoholic diatribe against superstition, and on the mention of Old Jimmy Wagstaff, worked himself up into such a state of reminiscent fury that Mr Bates was glad to hurry away with Troy.

They overtook the rector in the churchyard, now bathed in the golden opulence of an already westering sun.

'There they all lie,' the rector said, waving a fatherly hand at the company of headstones. 'All your Wagstaffs, right back to the sixteenth century. But no Hadets, Mr Bates, I assure you.'

They stood looking up at the spire. Pigeons flew in and out of a balcony far above their heads. At their feet was a little flagged area edged by a low coping. Mr Bates stepped forward and the rector laid a hand on his arm.

'Not there,' he said. 'Do you mind?'

'Don't!' bellowed Mr Pilbrow from the rear. 'Don't you set foot on them bloody stones, Mister.'

Mr Bates backed away.

'Edward's not swearing,' the rector mildly explained. 'He is to be taken, alas, literally. A sad and dreadful story, Mr Bates.'

'Indeed?' Mr Bates asked eagerly.

'Indeed, yes. Some time ago, in the very year we have been discussing – 1921, you know – one of our girls, a very beautiful girl she was, named Ruth Wall, fell from the balcony of the tower and was, of course, killed. She used to go up there to feed the pigeons and it was thought that in leaning over the low balustrade she overbalanced.'

'Ah!' Mr Pilbrow roared with considerable relish, evidently guessing the purport of the rector's speech. 'Terrible, terrible! And 'er sweetheart after 'er, too. Terrible!'

'Oh, no!' Troy protested.

The rector made a dabbing gesture to subdue Mr Pilbrow. 'I wish he wouldn't,' he said. 'Yes. It was a few days later. A lad called Simon Castle. They were to be married. People said it must be suicide but – it may have been wrong of me – I couldn't bring myself – in short, he lies beside her over there. If you would care to look.'

For a minute or two they stood before the headstones.

'Ruth Wall. Spinster of this Parish. 1903–1921. *I will extend peace to her like a river.*'

'Simon Castle. Bachelor of this Parish. 1900–1921. *And God shall wipe away all tears from their eyes.*'

The afternoon having by now worn on, and the others having excused themselves, Mr Bates remained alone in the churchyard, clutching his Bible and staring at the head-stones. The light of the hunter's zeal still gleamed in his eyes.

Troy didn't see Mr Bates again until Sunday night service when, on her way up the aisle, she passed him, sitting in the rearmost pew. She was amused to observe that his gigantic Bible was under the seat.

'*We plough the fields,*' sang the choir, '*and scatter—*' Mrs Simpson roared away on the organ, the smell of assorted greengrocery rising like some humble incense. Everybody in Little Copplestone except Mr Richard De'ath was there for the Harvest Festival. At last the rector stepped over Miss Hart's biggest pumpkin and ascended the pulpit, Edward Pilbrow switched off all the lights except one and they settled down for the sermon.

'A sower went forth to sow,' announced the rector. He spoke simply and well but somehow Troy's attention wandered. She found herself wondering where, through the centuries, the succeeding generations of Wagstaffs had sat until Old Jimmy took to his freakish practices; and whether Ruth Wall and Simon Castle, poor things, had shared the same hymn book and held hands during the sermon; and whether, after all, Stewart Shakespeare Hadet and Peter Rook Hadet had not, in 1779, occupied some dark corner of the church and been unaccountably forgotten.

Here we are, Troy thought drowsily, and there, outside in the churchyard, are all the others going back and back— She saw a girl, bright in the evening sunlight, reach from a balcony towards a multitude of wings. She was falling

– dreadfully – into nothingness. Troy woke with a sickening jerk.

'– on stony ground,' the rector was saying. Troy listened guiltily to the rest of the sermon.

Mr Bates emerged on the balcony. He laid his Bible on the coping and looked at the moonlit tree tops and the church-yard so dreadfully far below. He heard someone coming up the stairway. Torchlight danced on the door jamb.

'You were quick,' said the visitor.

'I am all eagerness and, I confess, puzzlement.'

'It had to be here, on the spot. If you *really* want to find out—'

'But I do, I do!'

'We haven't much time. You've brought the Bible?'

'You particularly asked—'

'If you open it at Ezekiel, chapter twelve. I'll shine my torch.'

Mr Bates opened the Bible.

'The thirteenth verse. There!'

Mr Bates leaned forward. The Bible tipped and moved.

'Look out!' the voice urged.

Mr Bates was scarcely aware of the thrust. He felt the page tear as the book sank under his hands. The last thing he heard was the beating of a multitude of wings.

'– and forevermore,' said the rector in a changed voice, facing east. The congregation got to its feet. He announced the last hymn. Mrs Simpson made a preliminary rumble and Troy groped in her pocket for the collection plate.

Presently they all filed out into the autumnal moonlight.

It was coldish in the churchyard. People stood about in groups. One or two had already moved through the lychgate. Troy heard a voice, which she recognised as that of Mr De'ath. 'I suppose,' it jeered, 'you all know you've been assisting at a fertility rite.'

'Drunk as usual, Dick De'ath,' somebody returned without rancour. There was a general laugh.

They had all begun to move away when, from the shadows at the base of the church tower, there arose a great cry. They stood, transfixed, turned towards the voice.

Out of the shadows came the rector in his cassock. When Troy saw his face she thought he must be ill and went to him.

'No, no!' he said. 'Not a woman! Edward! Where's Edward Pilbrow?'

Behind him, at the foot of the tower, was a pool of darkness; but Troy, having come closer, could see within it a figure, broken like a puppet on the flagstones. An eddy of night air stole round the church and fluttered a page of the giant Bible that lay pinned beneath the head.

It was nine o'clock when Troy heard the car pull up outside the cottage. She saw her husband coming up the path and ran to meet him, as if they had been parted for months.

He said, 'This is mighty gratifying!' And then, 'Hullo, my love. What's the matter?'

As she tumbled out her story, filled with relief at telling him, a large man with uncommonly bright eyes came up behind them.

'Listen to this, Fox,' Roderick Alleyn said. 'We're in demand, it seems.' He put his arm through Troy's and closed his hand round hers. 'Let's go indoors, shall we? Here's Fox, darling, come for a nice bucolic rest. Can we give him a bed?'

Troy pulled herself together and greeted Inspector Fox. Presently she was able to give them a coherent account of the evening's tragedy. When she had finished, Alleyn said, 'Poor little Bates. He was a nice little bloke.' He put his hand on Troy's. 'You need a drink,' he said, 'and so, by the way, do we.'

While he was getting the drinks he asked quite casually, 'You've had a shock and a beastly one at that, but there's something else, isn't there?'

'Yes,' Troy swallowed hard, 'there is. They're all saying it's an accident.'

'Yes?'

'And, Rory, I don't think it is.'

Mr Fox cleared his throat. 'Fancy,' he said.

'Suicide?' Alleyn suggested, bringing her drink to her.

'No. Certainly not.'

'A bit of rough stuff, then?'

'You sound as if you're asking about the sort of weather we've been having.'

'Well, darling, you don't expect Fox and me to go into hysterics. Why not an accident?'

'He knew all about the other accidents, he *knew* it was dangerous. And then the oddness of it, Rory. To leave the Harvest Festival service and climb the tower in the dark, carrying that enormous Bible!'

'And he was hellbent on tracing these Hadets?'

'Yes. He kept saying you'd be interested. He actually brought a copy of the entries for you.'

'Have you got it?'

She found it for him. 'The selected texts,' he said, 'are pretty rum, aren't they, Br'er Fox?' and handed it over.

'Very vindictive,' said Mr Fox.

'Mr Bates thought it was in your line,' Troy said.

'The devil he did! What's been done about this?'

'The village policeman was in the church. They sent for the doctor. And – well, you see, Mr Bates had talked a lot about you and they hope you'll be able to tell them something about him – whom they should get in touch with and so on.'

'Have they moved him?'

'They weren't going to until the doctor had seen him.'

Alleyn pulled his wife's ear and looked at Fox. 'Do you fancy a stroll through the village, Foxkin?'

'There's a lovely moon,' Fox said bitterly and got to his feet.

The moon was high in the heavens when they came to the base of the tower and it shone on a group of four men – the rector, Richard De'ath, Edward Pilbrow, and Sergeant Botting, the village constable. When they saw Alleyn and Fox, they separated and revealed a fifth, who was kneeling by the body of Timothy Bates.

'Kind of you to come,' the rector said, shaking hands with Alleyn. 'And a great relief to all of us.'

Their manner indicated that Alleyn's arrival would remove a sense of personal responsibility. 'If you'd like to have a look—?' the doctor said.

The broken body lay huddled on its side. The head rested

on the open Bible. The right hand, rigid in cadaveric spasm, clutched a torn page. Alleyn knelt and Fox came closer with the torch. At the top of the page Alleyn saw the word Ezekiel and a little farther down, Chapter 12.

Using the tip of his finger Alleyn straightened the page. 'Look,' he said, and pointed to the thirteenth verse. "*My net also will I spread upon him and he shall be taken in my snare.*"'

The words had been faintly underlined in mauve.

Alleyn stood up and looked round the circle of faces.

'Well,' the doctor said, 'we'd better see about moving him.'

Alleyn said, 'I don't think he should be moved just yet.'

'Not!' the rector cried out. 'But surely – to leave him like this – I mean, after this terrible accident—'

'It has yet to be proved,' Alleyn said, 'that it was an accident.'

There was a sharp sound from Richard De'ath.

'– and I fancy,' Alleyn went on, glancing at De'ath, 'that it's going to take quite a lot of proving.'

After that, events, as Fox observed with resignation, took the course that was to be expected. The local Superintendent said that under the circumstances it would be silly not to ask Alleyn to carry on, the Chief Constable agreed, and appropriate instructions came through from Scotland Yard. The rest of the night was spent in routine procedure. The body having been photographed and the Bible set aside for fingerprinting, both were removed and arrangements put in hand for the inquest.

At dawn Alleyn and Fox climbed the tower. The winding

stair brought them to an extremely narrow doorway through which they saw the countryside lying vaporous in the faint light. Fox was about to go through to the balcony when Alleyn stopped him and pointed to the door jambs. They were covered with a growth of stonecrop.

About three feet from the floor this had been brushed off over a space of perhaps four inches and fragments of the microscopic plant hung from the scars. From among these, on either side, Alleyn removed morsels of dark coloured thread. 'And here,' he sighed, 'as sure as fate, we go again. O Lord, O Lord!'

They stepped through to the balcony and there was a sudden whirr and beating of wings as a company of pigeons flew out of the tower. The balcony was narrow and the balustrade indeed very low. 'If there's any looking over,' Alleyn said, 'you, my dear Foxkin, may do it.'

Nevertheless he leaned over the balustrade and presently knelt beside it. 'Look at this. Bates rested the open Bible here – blow me down flat if he didn't! There's a powder of leather where it scraped on the stone and a fragment where it tore. It must have been moved – outward. Now, why, *why?*'

'Shoved it accidentally with his knees, then made a grab and overbalanced?'

'But why put the open Bible there? To read by moonlight? *My net also will I spread upon him and he shall be taken in my snare.* Are you going to tell me he underlined it and then dived overboard?'

'I'm not going to tell you anything,' Fox grunted and then: 'That old chap Edward Pilbrow's down below swabbing the stones. He looks like a beetle.'

'Let him look like a rhinoceros if he wants to, but for the love of Mike don't leer over the edge – you give me the willies. Here, let's pick this stuff up before it blows away.'

They salvaged the scraps of leather and put them in an envelope. Since there was nothing more to do, they went down and out through the vestry and so home to breakfast.

'Darling,' Alleyn told his wife, 'you've landed us with a snorter.'

'Then you *do* think—?'

'There's a certain degree of fishiness. Now, see here, wouldn't *somebody* have noticed little Bates get up and go out? I know he sat all alone on the back bench, but wasn't there *someone?*'

'The rector?'

'No. I asked him. Too intent on his sermon, it seems.'

'Mrs Simpson? If she looks through her little red curtain she faces the nave.'

'We'd better call on her, Fox. I'll take the opportunity to send a couple of cables to New Zealand. She's fat, jolly, keeps the shop-cum-post office, and is supposed to read all the postcards. Just your cup of tea. You're dynamite with postmistresses. Away we go.'

Mrs Simpson sat behind her counter doing a crossword puzzle and refreshing herself with liquorice. She welcomed Alleyn with enthusiasm. He introduced Fox and then he retired to a corner to write out his cables.

'What a catastrophe!' Mrs Simpson said, plunging straight into the tragedy. 'Shocking! As nice a little gentleman as you'd wish to meet, Mr Fox. Typical New Zealander. Pick him a mile away and a friend of Mr Alleyn's, I'm told, and if I've said it once I've said it a hundred times, Mr Fox, they ought to have put something up to prevent it. Wire netting or a bit of ironwork; but, no, they let it go on from year to year and now see what's happened – history repeating itself and giving the village a bad name. Terrible!'

Fox bought a packet of tobacco from Mrs Simpson and paid her a number of compliments on the layout of her shop, modulating from there into an appreciation of the village. He said that one always found such pleasant company in small communities. Mrs Simpson was impressed and offered him a piece of liquorice.

'As for pleasant company,' she chuckled, 'that's as may be, though by and large I suppose I mustn't grumble. I'm a cockney and a stranger here myself, Mr Fox. Only twenty-four years and that doesn't go for anything with this lot.'

'Ah,' Fox said, 'then you wouldn't recollect the former tragedies. Though to be sure,' he added, 'you wouldn't do that in any case, being much too young, if you'll excuse the liberty, Mrs Simpson.'

After this classic opening Alleyn was not surprised to hear Mrs Simpson embark on a retrospective survey of life in Little Copplestone. She was particularly lively on Miss Hart, who, she hinted, had had her eye on Mr Richard De'ath for many a long day.

'As far back as when Old Jimmy Wagstaff died, which was why she was so set on getting the next door house; but Mr De'ath never looked at anybody except Ruth Wall, and her head-over-heels in love with young Castle, which together with her falling to her destruction when feeding pigeons led

Mr De'ath to forsake religion and take to drink, which he has done something cruel ever since.

'They do say he's got a terrible temper, Mr Fox, and it's well known he give Old Jimmy Wagstaff a thrashing on account of straying cattle and threatened young Castle, saying if he couldn't have Ruth, nobody else would, but fair's fair and personally I've never seen him anything but nice-mannered, drunk or sober. Speak as you find's my motto and always has been, but these old maids, when they take a fancy they get it pitiful hard. You wouldn't know a word of nine letters meaning "pale-faced lure like a sprat in a fishy story", would you?'

Fox was speechless, but Alleyn, emerging with his cables, suggested 'whitebait'.

'Correct!' shouted Mrs Simpson. 'Fits like a glove. Although it's not a bit like a sprat and a quarter the size. Cheating, I call it. Still, it fits.' She licked her indelible pencil and triumphantly added it to her crossword.

They managed to lead her back to Timothy Bates. Fox, professing a passionate interest in organ music, was able to extract from her that when the rector began his sermon she had in fact dimly observed someone move out of the back bench and through the doors. 'He must have walked round the church and in through the vestry and little did I think he was going to his death,' Mrs Simpson said with considerable relish and a sigh like an earthquake.

'You didn't happen to hear him in the vestry?' Fox ventured, but it appeared that the door from the vestry into the organ loft was shut and Mrs Simpson, having settled herself to enjoy the sermon with, as she shamelessly admitted, a bag of chocolates, was not in a position to notice.

Alleyn gave her his two cables: the first to Timothy Bates's partner in New Zealand and the second to one of his own colleagues in that country asking for any available information about relatives of the late William James Wagstaff of Little Copplestone, Kent, possibly resident in New Zealand after 1921, and of any persons of the name of Peter Rook Hadet or Naomi Balbus Hadet.

Mrs Simpson agitatedly checked over the cables, professional etiquette and burning curiosity struggling together in her enormous bosom. She restrained herself, however, merely observing that an event of this sort set you thinking, didn't it?

'And no doubt,' Alleyn said as they walked up the lane, 'she'll be telling her customers that the next stop's bloodhounds and manacles.'

'Quite a tidy armful of lady, isn't she, Mr Alleyn?' Fox calmly rejoined.

The inquest was at 10:20 in the smoking room of the Star and Garter. With half an hour in hand, Alleyn and Fox visited the churchyard. Alleyn gave particular attention to the headstones of Old Jimmy Wagstaff, Ruth Wall and Simon Castle. 'No mention of the month or day,' he said. And after a moment: 'I wonder. We must ask the rector.'

'No need to ask the rector,' said a voice behind them. It was Miss Hart. She must have come soundlessly across the soft turf. Her air was truculent. 'Though why,' she said, 'it should be of interest, I'm sure I don't know. Ruth Wall died on 13 August 1921. It was a Saturday.'

'You've a remarkable memory,' Alleyn observed.

'Not as good as it sounds. That Saturday afternoon I came to do the flowers in the church. I found her and I'm not likely ever to forget it. Young Castle went the same way almost a month later. September twelfth. In my opinion there was never a more glaring case of suicide. I believe,' Miss Hart said harshly, 'in facing facts.'

'She was a beautiful girl, wasn't she?'

'I'm no judge of beauty. She set the men by the ears. *He* was a fine-looking young fellow. Fanny Wagstaff did her best to get *him*.'

'Had Ruth Wall,' Alleyn asked, 'other admirers?'

Miss Hart didn't answer and he turned to her. Her face was blotted with an unlovely flush. 'She ruined two men's lives, if you want to know. Castle and Richard De'ath,' said Miss Hart. She turned on her heel and without another word marched away.

'September twelfth,' Alleyn murmured. 'That would be a Monday, Br'er Fox.'

'So it would,' Fox agreed, after a short calculation, 'so it would. Quite a coincidence.'

'Or not, as the case may be. I'm going to take a gamble on this one. Come on.'

They left the churchyard and walked down the lane, overtaking Edward Pilbrow on the way. He was wearing his town crier's coat and hat and carrying his bell by the clapper. He manifested great excitement when he saw them.

'Hey!' he shouted, 'what's this I hear? Murder's the game, is it? What a go! Come on, gents, let's have it. Did 'e fall or was 'e pushed? Hor, hor, hor! Come on.'

'Not until after the inquest,' Alleyn shouted.

'Do we get a look at the body?'

'Shut up,' Mr Fox bellowed suddenly.

'I got to know, haven't I? It'll be the smartest bit of crying I ever done, this will! I reckon I might get on the telly with this. "Town crier tells old world village death stalks the churchyard." Hor, hor, hor!'

'Let us,' Alleyn whispered, 'leave this horrible old man.'

They quickened their stride and arrived at the pub, to be met with covert glances and dead silence.

The smoking room was crowded for the inquest. Everybody was there, including Mrs Simpson who sat in the back row with her candies and her crossword puzzle. It went through very quickly. The rector deposed to finding the body. Richard De'ath, sober and less truculent than usual, was questioned as to his sojourn outside the churchyard and said he'd noticed nothing unusual apart from hearing a disturbance among the pigeons roosting in the balcony. From where he stood, he said, he couldn't see the face of the tower.

An open verdict was recorded.

Alleyn had invited the rector, Miss Hart, Mrs Simpson, Richard De'ath, and, reluctantly, Edward Pilbrow, to join him in the Bar-Parlour and had arranged with the landlord that nobody else would be admitted. The Public Bar, as a result, drove a roaring trade.

When they had all been served and the hatch closed, Alleyn walked into the middle of the room and raised his hand. It was the slightest of gestures but it secured their attention.

He said, 'I think you must all realise that we are not satisfied this was an accident. The evidence against accident has been collected piecemeal from the persons in this room and I am going to put it before you. If I go wrong I want you to correct me. I ask you to do this with absolute frankness, even if you are obliged to implicate someone who you would say was the last person in the world to be capable of a crime of violence.'

He waited. Pilbrow, who had come very close, had his ear cupped in his hand. The rector looked vaguely horrified. Richard De'ath suddenly gulped down his double whisky. Miss Hart coughed over her lemonade and Mrs Simpson avidly popped a peppermint cream in her mouth and took a swig of her port and raspberry.

Alleyn nodded to Fox, who laid Mr Bates's Bible, open at the flyleaf, on the table before him.

'The case,' Alleyn said, 'hinges on this book. You have all seen the entries. I remind you of the recorded deaths in 1779 of the three Hadets – Stewart Shakespeare, Naomi Balbus and Peter Rook. To each of these is attached a biblical text suggesting that they met their death by violence. There have never been any Hadets in this village and the days of the week are wrong for the given dates. They are right, however, for the year 1921 and *they fit the deaths*, all by falling from a height, of William Wagstaff, Ruth Wall and Simon Castle.

'By analogy the Christian names agree. William suggests Shakespeare. Naomi – Ruth; Balbus – a wall. Simon – Peter; and a Rook is a Castle in chess. And Hadet,' Alleyn said without emphasis, 'is an anagram of Death.'

'Balderdash!' Miss Hart cried out in an unrecognisable voice.

'No, it's not,' said Mrs Simpson. 'It's jolly good crossword stuff.'

'Wicked balderdash. Richard!'

De'ath said, 'Be quiet. Let him go on.'

'We believe,' Alleyn said, 'that these three people met their deaths by one hand. Motive is a secondary consideration, but it is present in several instances, predominantly in one. Who had cause to wish the death of these three people? Someone whom old Wagstaff had bullied and to whom he had left his money and who killed him for it. Someone who was infatuated with Simon Castle and bitterly jealous of Ruth Wall. Someone who hoped, as an heiress, to win Castle for herself and who, failing, was determined nobody else should have him. Wagstaff's orphaned niece – Fanny Wagstaff.'

There were cries of relief from all but one of his hearers. He went on. 'Fanny Wagstaff sold everything, disappeared, and was never heard of again in the village. But twenty-four years later she returned, and has remained here ever since.'

A glass crashed to the floor and a chair overturned as the vast bulk of the postmistress rose to confront him.

'Lies! *Lies!*' screamed Mrs Simpson.

'Did you sell everything again, before leaving New Zealand?' he asked as Fox moved forward. 'Including the Bible, Miss Wagstaff?'

'But,' Troy said, 'how could you be so sure?'

'She was the only one who could leave her place in the church unobserved. She was the only one fat enough to rub her hips against the narrow door jambs. She uses an indelible pencil. We presume she arranged to meet Bates on the balcony, giving a cock-and-bull promise to tell him something nobody else knew about the Hadets. She indicated the text with her pencil, gave the Bible a shove, and, as he leaned out to grab it, tipped him over the edge.

'In talking about 1921 she forgot herself and described the events as if she had been there. She called Bates a typical New Zealander but gave herself out to be a Londoner. She said whitebait are only a quarter of the size of sprats. New Zealand whitebait are – English whitebait are about the same size.

'And as we've now discovered, she didn't send my cables. Of course she thought poor little Bates was hot on her tracks, especially when she learned that he'd come here to see me. She's got the kind of crossword-puzzle mind that would think up the biblical clues, and would get no end of a kick in writing them in. She's overwhelmingly conceited and vindictive.'

'Still—'

'I know. Not good enough if we'd played the waiting game. But good enough to try shock tactics. We caught her off her guard and she cracked up.'

'Not,' Mr Fox said, 'a nice type of woman.'

Alleyn strolled to the gate and looked up the lane to the church. The spire shone golden in the evening sun.

'The rector,' Alleyn said, 'tells me he's going to do something about the balcony.'

'Mrs Simpson, née Wagstaff,' Fox remarked, 'suggested wire netting.'

'And she ought to know,' Alleyn said and turned back to the cottage.

The Mysterious Visitor

R. Austin Freeman

'So,' said Thorndyke, looking at me reflectively, 'you are a full-blown medical practitioner with a practice of your own. How the years slip by! It seems but the other day that you were a student, gaping at me from the front bench of the lecture theatre.'

'Did I gape?' I asked incredulously.

'I use the word metaphorically,' said he, 'to denote ostentatious attention. You always took my lectures very seriously. May I ask if you have ever found them of use in your practice?'

'I can't say that I have ever had any very thrilling medico-legal experiences since that extraordinary cremation case that you investigated – the case of Septimus Maddock, you know. But that reminds me that there is a little matter that I meant to speak to you about. It is of no interest, but I just wanted your advice, though it isn't even my business, strictly speaking. It concerns a patient of mine, a man named Crofton, who has disappeared rather unaccountably.'

'And do you call that a case of no medico-legal interest?' demanded Thorndyke.

'Oh, there's nothing in it. He just went away for a holiday and he hasn't communicated with his friends very recently. That is all. What makes me a little uneasy is that there is a departure from his usual habits – he is generally a fairly regular correspondent – that seems a little significant in view of his personality. He is markedly neurotic and his family history is by no means what one would wish.'

'That is an admirable thumb-nail sketch, Jardine,' said Thorndyke; 'but it lacks detail. Let us have a full-size picture.'

'Very well,' said I, 'but you mustn't let me bore you. To begin with Crofton: he is a nervous, anxious, worrying sort of fellow, everlastingly fussing about money affairs, and latterly this tendency has been getting worse. He fairly got the jumps about his financial position; felt that he was steadily drifting into bankruptcy and couldn't get the subject out of his mind. It was all bunkum. I am more or less a friend of the family, and I know that there was nothing to worry about. Mrs Crofton assured me that, although they were a trifle hard up, they could rub along quite safely.

'As he seemed to be getting the hump worse and worse, I advised him to go away for a change and stay in a boarding-house where he would see some fresh faces. Instead of that, he elected to go down to a bungalow that he has at Seasalter, near Whitstable, and lets out in the season. He proposed to stay by himself and spend his time in sea-bathing and country walks. I wasn't very keen on this, for solitude was the last thing that he wanted. There was a strong family history of melancholia and some unpleasant rumours of suicide. I didn't like his being alone at all. However, another friend of the family, Mrs Crofton's brother, in fact, a chap named Ambrose, offered to go down and spend a weekend with him to give him a start, and afterwards to run down for an afternoon whenever he was able. So off he went with Ambrose on Friday, 16 June, and for a time all went well. He seemed to be improving in health and spirits and wrote to his wife regularly two or three times a week. Ambrose went down as often as he could to cheer him up, and the last time brought back the news that Crofton thought of moving on to Margate for a further change. So, of course, he didn't go down to the bungalow again.

'Well, in due course, a letter came from Margate; it had been written at the bungalow, but the postmark was Margate and bore the same date – 16 July – as the letter itself. I have it with me. Mrs Crofton sent it for me to see and I haven't returned it yet. But there is nothing of interest in it beyond the statement that he was going on to Margate by the next train and would write again when he had found rooms there. That was the last that was heard of him. He never wrote and nothing is known of his movements excepting that he left Seasalter and arrived at Margate. This is the letter.'

I handed it to Thorndyke, who glanced at the postmark and then laid it on the table for examination later. 'Have any inquiries been made?' he asked.

'Yes. His photograph has been sent to the Margate police, but, of course – well, you know what Margate is like in July. Thousands of strangers coming and going every day. It is hopeless to look for him in that crowd; and it is quite possible that he isn't there now. But his disappearance is most inopportune, for a big legacy has just fallen in, and, naturally, Mrs Crofton is frantically anxious to let him know. It is a matter of about thirty thousand pounds.'

'Was this legacy expected?' asked Thorndyke.

'No. The Croftons knew nothing about it. They didn't know that the old lady – Miss Shuler – had made a will or that she had very much to leave; and they didn't know that she was likely to die, or even that she was ill. Which is rather odd; for she was ill for a month or two, and, as she suffered from a malignant abdominal tumour, it was known that she couldn't recover.'

'When did she die?'

'On 13 July.'

Thorndyke raised his eyebrows. 'Just three days before the date of this letter,' he remarked; 'so that, if he should never reappear, this letter will be the sole evidence that he survived her. It is an important document. It may come to represent a value of thirty thousand pounds.'

'It isn't really so important as it looks,' said I. 'Miss Shuler's will provides that if Crofton should die before the testatrix, the legacy should go to his wife. So whether he is alive or not, the legacy is quite safe. But we must hope that he is alive, though I must confess to some little anxiety on his account.'

Thorndyke reflected awhile on this statement. Presently he asked:

'Do you know if Crofton has made a will?'

'Yes, he has,' I replied; 'quite recently. I was one of the

witnesses and I read it through at Crofton's request. It was full of the usual legal verbiage, but it might have been stated in a dozen words. He leaves practically everything to his wife, but instead of saying so it enumerates the property item by item.'

'It was drafted, I suppose, by the solicitor?'

'Yes; another friend of the family named Jobson, and he is the executor and residuary legatee.'

Thorndyke nodded and again became deeply reflective. Still meditating, he took up the letter, and as he inspected it, I watched him curiously and not without a certain secret amusement. First he looked over the envelope, back and front. Then he took from his pocket a powerful Coddington lens and with this examined the flap and the postmark. Next, he drew out the letter, held it up to the light, then read it through and finally examined various parts of the writing through his lens.

'Well,' I asked, with an irreverent grin, 'I should think you have extracted the last grain of meaning from it.'

He smiled as he put away his lens and handed the letter back to me.

'As this may have to be produced in proof of survival,' said he, 'it better be put in a place of safety. I notice that he speaks of returning later to the bungalow. I take it that it has been ascertained that he did not return there?'

'I don't think so. You see, they have been waiting for him to write. You think that someone ought—'

I paused; for it began to be borne in on me that Thorndyke was taking a somewhat gloomy view of the case.

'My dear Jardine,' said he. 'I am merely following your

158

own suggestion. Here is a man with an inherited tendency to melancholia and suicide who has suddenly disappeared. He went away from an empty house and announced his intention of returning to it later. As that house is the only known locality in which he could be sought, it is obvious that it ought to have been examined. And even if he never came back there, the house might contain some clues to his present whereabouts.'

This last sentence put an idea into my mind which I was a little shy of broaching. What was a clue to Thorndyke might be perfectly meaningless to an ordinary person. I recalled his amazing interpretations of the most commonplace facts in the mysterious Maddock case and the idea took fuller possession. At length I said tentatively:

'I would go down myself if I felt competent. Tomorrow is Saturday and I could get a colleague to look after my practice; there isn't much doing just now. But when you speak of clues, and when I remember what a duffer I was last time – I wish it were possible for you to have a look at the place.'

To my surprise, he assented almost with enthusiasm. 'Why not?' said he. 'It is a weekend. We could put up at the bungalow, I suppose, and have a little gipsy holiday. And there are undoubtedly points of interest in the case. Let us go down tomorrow. We can lunch in the train and have the afternoon before us. You had better get a key from Mrs Crofton, or, if she hasn't got one, an authority to visit the house. We may want that if we have to enter without a key. And we go alone, of course.'

I assented joyfully. Not that I had any expectations as to what we might learn from our inspection. But something in

Thorndyke's manner gave me the impression that he had extracted from my account of the case some significance that was not apparent to me.

The bungalow stood on a space of rough ground a little way behind the sea-wall, along which we walked towards it from Whitstable, passing on our way a shipbuilder's yard and a slipway, on which a collier brigantine was hauled up for repairs. There were one or two other bungalows adjacent, but a considerable distance apart, and we looked at them as we approached to make out the names painted on the gates.

'That will probably be the one,' said Thorndyke, indicating a small building enclosed within a wooden fence and provided, like the others, with a bathing hut, just above high-water mark. Its solitary, deserted aspect and lowered blinds supported his opinion and when we reached the gate, the name 'Middlewick' painted on it settled the matter.

'The next question is,' said I, 'how the deuce are we going to get in? The gate is locked, and there is no bell. Is it worth while to hammer at the fence?'

'I wouldn't do that,' replied Thorndyke. 'The place is pretty certainly empty or the gate wouldn't be locked. We shall have to climb over unless there is a back gate unlocked, so the less noise we make the better.'

We walked round the enclosure, but there was no other gate, nor was there any tree or other cover to disguise our rather suspicious proceedings. 'There's no help for it, Jardine,' said Thorndyke, 'so here goes.' He put his green canvas suitcase on the ground, grasped the top of the fence with both hands and went over like a harlequin. I picked up the case and handed it over to him, and, having taken a quick glance round, followed my leader.

'Well,' I said, 'here we are. And now, how are we going to get into the house?'

'We shall have to pick a lock if there is no door open, or else go in by a window. Let us take a look round.'

We walked round the house to the back door, but found it not only locked but bolted top and bottom, as Thorndyke ascertained with his knife-blade. The windows were all case-ments and all fastened with their catches.

'The front door will be the best,' said Thorndyke. 'It can't be bolted unless he got out by the chimney, and I think my "smoker's companion" will be able to cope with an ordinary door-lock. It looked like a common builder's fitting.'

As he spoke, we returned to the front of the house and he produced the 'smoker's companion' from his pocket (I don't know what kind of smoker it was designed to accompany). The lock was apparently a simple affair, for the second trial with the 'companion' shot back the bolt, and when I turned the handle, the door opened. As a precaution, I called out to inquire if there was anybody within, and then, as there was no answer, we entered, walking straight into the living-room, as there was no hall or lobby.

A couple of paces from the threshold we halted to look round the room, and on me the aspect of the place produced a vague sense of discomfort. Though it was early in a bright afternoon, the room was almost completely dark, for not only were the blinds lowered, but the curtains were drawn as well.

'It looks,' said I, peering about the dim and gloomy

apartment with sun-dazzled eyes, 'as if he had gone away at night. He wouldn't have drawn the curtains in the daytime.'

'One would think not,' Thorndyke agreed; 'but it doesn't follow.' He stepped to the front window and drawing back the curtains pulled up the blind, revealing a half-curtain of green serge over the lower part of the window. As the bright daylight flooded the room, he stood with his back to the window looking about with deep attention, letting his eyes travel slowly over the walls, the furniture, and especially the floor. Presently he stooped to pick up a short match-end which lay just under the table opposite the door, and as he looked at it thoughtfully, he pointed to a couple of spots of candle grease on the linoleum near the table. Then he glanced at the mantelpiece and from that to an ash-bowl on the table.

'These are only trifling discrepancies,' said he, 'but they are worth noting. You see,' he continued in response to my look of inquiry, 'that this room is severely trim and orderly. Everything seems to be in its place. The matchbox, for instance, has its fixed receptacle above the mantelpiece, and there is a bowl for the burnt matches, regularly used, as its contents show. Yet here is a burnt match thrown on the floor, although the bowl is on the table quite handy. And the match, you notice, is not of the same kind as those in the box over the mantelpiece, which is a large Bryant and May, or as the burnt matches in the bowl which have evidently come from it. But if you look in the bowl,' he continued, picking it up, 'you will see two burnt matches of this same kind – apparently the small size Bryant and May – one burnt quite short and one only half burnt. The suggestion is fairly obvious, but, as I say, there is a slight discrepancy.'

'I don't know,' said I, 'that either the suggestion or the discrepancy is very obvious to me.'

He walked over to the mantelpiece and took the matchbox from its case.

'You see,' said he, opening it, 'that this box is nearly full. It has an appointed place and it was in that place. We find a small match, burnt right out, under the table opposite the door, and two more in the bowl under the hanging lamp. A reasonable inference is that someone came in in the dark and struck a match as he entered. That match must have come from a box that he brought with him in his pocket. It burnt out and he struck another, which also burnt out while he was raising the chimney of the lamp, and he struck a third to light the lamp. But if that person was Crofton, why did he need to strike a match to light the room when the matchbox was in its usual place; and why did he throw the match-end on the floor?'

'You mean that the suggestion is that the person was not Crofton; and I think you are right. Crofton doesn't carry matches in his pocket. He uses wax vestas and carries them in a silver case.'

'It might possibly have been Ambrose,' Thorndyke suggested.

'I don't think so,' said I. 'Ambrose uses a petrol lighter.'

Thorndyke nodded. 'There may be nothing in it,' said he, 'but it offers a suggestion. Shall we look over the rest of the premises?'

He paused for a moment to glance at a small key-board on the wall on which one or two keys were hanging, each distinguished by a little ivory label and by the name written underneath the peg; then he opened a door in the corner of the room. As this led into the kitchen, he closed it and opened an adjoining one which gave access to a bedroom.

'This is probably the extra bedroom,' he remarked as we entered. 'The blinds have not been drawn down and there is a general air of trimness that suggests a tidy up of an unoccupied room. And the bed looks as if it had been out of use.'

After an attentive look round, he returned to the living-room and crossed to the remaining door. As he opened it, we looked into a nearly dark room, both the windows being covered by thick serge curtains.

'Well,' he observed, when he had drawn back the curtains and raised the blinds, 'there is nothing painfully tidy here. That is a very roughly made bed, and the blanket is outside the counterpane.'

He looked critically about the room and especially at the bedside table.

'Here are some more discrepancies,' said he. 'There are two candlesticks, in one of which the candle has burnt itself right out, leaving a fragment of wick. There are five burnt matches in it, two large ones from the box by its side, and three small ones, of which two are mere stumps. The second candle is very much guttered', and I think' – he lifted it out of the socket – 'yes, it has been used out of the candlestick. You see that the grease has run down right to the bottom and there is a distinct impression of a thumb – apparently a left thumb – made while the grease was warm. Then you notice the mark on the table of a tumbler which had contained some liquid that was not water, but there is no tumbler. However, it may be an old mark, though it looks fresh.'

'It is hardly like Crofton to leave an old mark on the table,' said I. 'He is a regular old maid. We had better see if the tumbler is in the kitchen.'

'Yes,' agreed Thorndyke. 'But I wonder what he was doing with that candle. Apparently he took it out of doors, as there is a spot on the floor of the living-room; and you see that there are one or two spots on the floor here.' He walked over to a chest of drawers near the door and was looking into a drawer which he had pulled out, and which I could see was full of clothes, when I observed a faint smile spreading over his face. 'Come round here, Jardine,' he said in a low voice, 'and take a peep through the crack of the door.'

I walked round, and, applying my eye to the crack, looked across the living-room at the end window. Above the half-curtain I could distinguish the unmistakable top of a constabulary helmet.

'Listen,' said Thorndyke. 'They are in force.'

As he spoke, there came from the neighbourhood of the kitchen a furtive scraping sound, suggestive of a pocket-knife persuading a window-catch. It was followed by the sound of an opening window and then of a stealthy entry. Finally, the kitchen door opened softly, someone tip-toed across the living-room and a burly police-sergeant appeared framed in the bedroom doorway.

'Good afternoon, Sergeant,' said Thorndyke, with a genial smile.

'Yes, that's all very well,' was the response, 'but the question is, who might you be, and what might you be doing in this house?'

Thorndyke briefly explained our business, and, when we

had presented our cards and Mrs Crofton's written authority, the sergeant's professional stiffness vanished like magic.

'It's all right, Tomkins,' he sang out to an invisible myrmidon. 'You had better shut the window and go out by the front door. You must excuse me, gentlemen,' he added; 'but the tenant of the next bungalow cycled down and gave us the tip. He watched you through his glasses and saw you pick the front-door lock. It did look a bit queer, you must admit.'

Thorndyke admitted it freely with a faint chuckle, and we walked across the living-room to the kitchen. Here, the sergeant's presence seemed to inhibit comments, but I noticed that my colleague cast a significant glance at a frying-pan that rested on a Primus stove. The congealed fat in it presented another 'discrepancy'; for I could hardly imagine the fastidious Crofton going away and leaving it in that condition.

Noting that there was no unwashed tumbler in evidence, I followed my friend back to the living-room, where he paused with his eye on the key-board.

'Well,' remarked the sergeant, 'if he ever did come back here, it's pretty clear that he isn't here now. You've been all over the premises, I think?'

'All excepting the bathing-hut,' replied Thorndyke; and, as he spoke, he lifted the key so labelled from its hook.

The sergeant laughed softly. 'He's not very likely to have taken up his quarters there,' said he. 'Still, there's nothing like being thorough. But you notice that the key of the front door and that of the gate have both been taken away, so we can assume that he has taken himself away too.'

'That is a reasonable inference,' Thorndyke admitted; 'but we may as well make our survey complete.'

With this he led the way out into the garden and to the gate, where he unblushingly produced the 'smoker's companion' and insinuated its prongs into the keyhole.

'Well, I'm sure!' exclaimed the sergeant as the lock clicked and the gate opened. 'That's a funny sort of tool; and you seem quite handy with it, too. Might I have a look at it?'

He looked at it so very long and attentively, when Thorndyke handed it to him, that I suspected him of an intention to infringe the patent. By the time he had finished his inspection we were at the bottom of the bank below the sea-wall and Thorndyke had inserted the key into the lock of the bathing-hut. As the sergeant returned the 'companion' Thorndyke took it and pocketed it; then he turned the key and pushed the door open; and the officer started back with a shout of amazement.

It was certainly a grim spectacle that we looked in on. The hut was a small building about six feet square, devoid of any furniture or fittings excepting one or two pegs high up the wall. The single, unglazed window was closely shuttered and on the bare floor in the farther corner a man was sitting, leaning back into the corner, with his head dropped forward on his breast. The man was undoubtedly Arthur Crofton. That much I could say with certainty, notwithstanding the horrible changes wrought by death and the lapse of time. 'But,' I added when I had identified the body, 'I should have said that he had been dead more than a fortnight. He must have come straight back from Margate and done this. And that will probably be the missing tumbler,' I concluded, pointing to one that stood on the floor close to the right hand of the corpse.

'No doubt,' replied Thorndyke, somewhat abstractedly. He had been looking critically about the interior of the hut, and now remarked: 'I wonder why he did not shoot the bolt instead of locking himself in; and what has become of the key? He must have taken it out of the lock and put it in his pocket.'

He looked interrogatively at the sergeant, who having no option but to take the hint, advanced with an expression of horrified disgust and proceeded very gingerly to explore the dead man's clothing.

'Ah!' he exclaimed at length, 'here we are.' He drew from the waistcoat pocket a key with a small ivory label attached to it. 'Yes, this is the one. You see, it is marked "Bathing Hut".'

He handed it to Thorndyke, who looked at it attentively, and even with an appearance of surprise, and then, producing an indelible pencil from his pocket, wrote on the label, 'Found on body.'

'The first thing,' said he, 'is to ascertain if it fits the lock.'

'Why, it must,' said the sergeant, 'if he locked himself in with it.'

'Undoubtedly,' Thorndyke agreed, 'but that is the point. It doesn't look quite similar to the other one.'

He drew out the key which we had brought from the house and gave it to me to hold. Then he tried the key from the dead man's pocket; but it not only did not fit, it would not even enter the keyhole. The sceptical indifference faded suddenly from the sergeant's face. He took the key from Thorndyke, and having tried it with the same result, stood up and stared, round-eyed, at my colleague.

'Well!' he exclaimed. 'This is a facer! It's the wrong key!'

'There may be another key on the body,' said Thorndyke. 'It isn't likely, but you had better make sure.'

The sergeant showed no reluctance this time. He searched the dead man's pockets thoroughly and produced a bunch of keys. But they were all quite small keys, none of them in the least resembling that of the hut door. Nor, I noticed, did they include those of the bungalow door or the garden gate. Once more the officer drew himself up and stared at Thorndyke.

'There's something rather fishy about this affair,' said he.

'There is,' Thorndyke agreed. 'The door was certainly locked; and as it was not locked from within, it must have been locked from without. Then that key – the wrong key – was presumably put in the dead man's pocket by some other person. And there are some other suspicious facts. A tumbler has disappeared from the bedside table, and there is a tumbler here. You notice one or two spots of candle grease on the floor here, and it looks as if a candle had been stood in that corner near the door. There is no candle here now; but in the bedroom there is a candle which has been carried without a candlestick and which, by the way, bears an excellent impression of a thumb. The first thing to do will be to take the deceased's finger-prints. Would you mind fetching my case from the bedroom, Jardine?'

I ran back to the house (not unobserved by the gentleman in the next bungalow) and, catching up the case, carried it down to the hut. When I arrived there I found Thorndyke holding the tumbler delicately in his gloved left hand while he examined it against the light with the aid of his lens. He handed the latter to me and observed:

'If you look at this carefully, Jardine, you will see a very interesting thing. There are the prints of two different thumbs – both left thumbs, and therefore of different persons. You will remember that the tumbler stood by the right hand of the body and that the table, which bore the mark of a tumbler, was at the left-hand side of the bed.'

When I had examined the thumb-prints he placed the tumbler carefully on the floor and opened his 'research-case', which was fitted as a sort of portable laboratory. From this he took a little brass box containing an ink tube, a tiny roller and some small cards, and, using the box-lid as an inking-plate, he proceeded methodically to take the dead man's fingerprints, writing the particulars on each card.

'I don't quite see what you want with Crofton's finger-prints,' said I. 'The other man's would be more to the point.'

'Undoubtedly,' Thorndyke replied. 'But we have to prove that they are another man's – that they are not Crofton's. And there is that print on the candle. That is a very important point to settle; and as we have finished here, we had better go and settle it at once.'

He closed his case, and, taking up the tumbler with his gloved hand, led the way back to the house, the sergeant following when he locked the door. We proceeded direct to the bedroom, where Thorndyke took the candle from its socket and, with the aid of his lens, compared it carefully with the two thumb-prints on the card, and then with the tumbler.

'It is perfectly clear,' said he. 'This is a mark of a left thumb. It is totally unlike Crofton's and it appears to be identical with the strange thumb-print on the tumbler. From which it seems to follow that the stranger took the candle from this room to the hut and brought it back. But he probably blew it out before leaving the house and lit it again in the hut.'

The sergeant and I examined the cards, the candle and the tumbler, and then the former asked:

'I suppose you have no idea whose thumb-print that might be? You don't know, for instance, of anyone who might have had any motive for making away with Mr Crofton?'

'That,' replied Thorndyke, 'is rather a question for the coroner's jury.'

'So it is,' the sergeant agreed. 'But there won't be much question about their verdict. It is a pretty clear case of wilful murder.'

To this Thorndyke made no reply excepting to give some directions as to the safekeeping of the candle and tumbler; and our proposed 'gipsy holiday' being now evidently impossible, we took our leave of the sergeant – who already had our cards – and wended back to the station.

'I suppose,' said I, 'we shall have to break the news to Mrs Crofton.'

'That is hardly our business,' he replied. 'We can leave that to the solicitor or to Ambrose. If you know the lawyer's address, you might send him a telegram, arranging a meeting at eight o'clock tonight. Give no particulars. Just say "Crofton found", but mark the telegram "urgent" so that he will keep the appointment.'

On reaching the station, I sent off the telegram, and very soon afterwards the London train was signalled. It turned out to be a slow train, which gave us ample time to discuss the case and me ample time for reflection. And, in fact, I reflected a good deal; for there was a rather uncomfortable question in my mind – the very question that the sergeant had raised and that Thorndyke had obviously evaded.

Was there anyone who might have had a motive for making away with Crofton? It was an awkward question when one remembered the great legacy that had just fallen in and the terms of Miss Shuler's will; which expressly provided that, if Crofton died before his wife, the legacy should go to her. Now Ambrose was the wife's brother; and Ambrose had been in the bungalow alone with Crofton, and nobody else was known to have been there at all. I meditated on these facts uncomfortably and would have liked to put the case to Thorndyke; but his reticence, his evasion of the sergeant's question and his decision to communicate with the solicitor rather than with the family, showed pretty clearly what was in his mind and that he did not wish to discuss the matter.

Promptly at eight o'clock, having dined at a restaurant, we presented ourselves at the solicitor's house and were shown into the study, where we found Mr Jobson seated at a writing-table. He looked at Thorndyke with some surprise, and when the introductions had been made, said somewhat dryly:

'We may take it that Dr Thorndyke is in some way connected with our rather confidential business?'

'Certainly,' I replied. 'That is why he is here.'

Jobson nodded. 'And how is Crofton?' he asked, 'and where did you dig him up?'

'I am sorry to say,' I replied, 'that he is dead. It is a dreadful affair. We found his body locked in the bathing-hut. He was sitting in a corner with a tumbler on the floor by his side.'

'Horrible! horrible!' exclaimed the solicitor. 'He ought never to have gone there alone. I said so at the time. And it is most unfortunate on account of the insurance, though that is not a large amount. Still the suicide clause, you know—'

'I doubt whether the insurance will be affected,' said Thorndyke. 'The coroner's finding will almost certainly be wilful murder.'

Jobson was thunderstruck. In a moment his face grew livid and he gazed at Thorndyke with an expression of horrified amazement.

'Murder!' he repeated incredulously. 'But you said he was locked in the hut. Surely that is clear proof of suicide.'

'He hadn't locked himself in, you know. There was no key inside.'

'Ah!' The solicitor spoke almost in a tone of relief. 'But, perhaps – did you examine his pockets?'

'Yes, and we found a key labelled "Bathing Hut". But it was the wrong key. It wouldn't go into the lock. There is no doubt whatever that the door was locked from the outside.'

'Good God!' exclaimed Jobson, in a faint voice. 'It does look suspicious. But still, I can't believe – it seems quite incredible.'

'That may be,' said Thorndyke, 'but it is all perfectly clear. There is evidence that a stranger entered the bungalow at night and that the affair took place in the bedroom. From thence the stranger carried the body down to the hut and he also took a tumbler and a candle from the bedside table. By the light of the candle – which was stood on the floor of the hut in a corner – he arranged the body, having put into its pocket a key from the board in the living-room. Then he locked the hut, went back to the house, put the key on its peg and the candle in its candlestick. Then he locked up the house and the garden gate and took the keys away with him.'

The solicitor listened to this recital in speechless amazement. At length he asked:

'How long ago do you suppose this happened?'

'Apparently on the night of the fifteenth of this month,' was the reply.

'But,' objected Jobson, 'he wrote home on the sixteenth.'

'He wrote,' said Thorndyke, 'on the sixth. Somebody put a one in front of the six and posted the letter at Margate on the sixteenth. I shall give evidence to that effect at the inquest.'

I was becoming somewhat mystified. Thorndyke's dry, stern manner – so different from his usual suavity – and the solicitor's uncalled-for agitation, seemed to hint at something more than met the eye. I watched Jobson as he lit a cigarette – with a small Bryant and May match, which he threw on the floor –and listened expectantly for his next question. At length he asked:

'Was there any sort of – er – clue as to who this stranger might be?'

'The man who will be charged with the murder? Oh, yes. The police have the means of identifying him with absolute certainty.'

'That is, if they can find him,' said Jobson.

'Naturally. But when all the very remarkable facts have transpired at the inquest, that individual will probably come pretty clearly into view.'

Jobson continued to smoke furiously with his eyes fixed

on the floor as if he were thinking hard. Presently he asked, without looking up:

'Supposing they do find this man. What then? What evidence is there that he murdered Crofton?'

'You mean direct evidence?' said Thorndyke. 'I can't say, as I did not examine the body; but the circumstantial evidence that I have given you would be enough to convict unless there were some convincing explanation other than murder. And I may say,' he added, 'that if the suspected person has a plausible explanation to offer, he would be well advised to produce it before he is charged. A voluntary statement has a good deal more weight than the same statement made by a prisoner in answer to a charge.'

There was an interval of silence, in which I looked in bewilderment from Thorndyke's stern visage to the pale face of the solicitor. At length the latter rose abruptly, and, after one or two quick strides up and down the room, halted by the fireplace, and, still avoiding Thorndyke's eye, said, somewhat brusquely, though in a low, husky voice:

'I will tell you how it happened. I went down to Seasalter, as you said, on the night of the fifteenth, on the chance of finding Crofton at the bungalow. I wanted to tell him of Miss Shuler's death and of the provisions of her will.'

'You had some private information on that subject, I presume?' said Thorndyke.

'Yes. My cousin was her solicitor and he kept me informed about the will.'

'And about the state of her health?'

'Yes. Well, when I arrived at the bungalow, it was in darkness. The gate and the front door were unlocked, so I entered, calling out Crofton's name. As no one answered, I struck a match and lit the lamp. Then I went into the bedroom and struck a match there; and by its light I could see Crofton lying on the bed, quite still. I spoke to him, but he did not answer or move. Then I lighted a candle on his table; and now I could see what I had already guessed, that he was dead, and that he had been dead some time – probably more than a week.

'It was an awful shock to find a dead man in this solitary house, and my first impulse was to rush out and give the alarm. But when I went into the living-room, I happened to see a letter lying on the writing-table and noticed that it was in his own handwriting and addressed to his wife. Unfortunately, I had the curiosity to take it out of the unsealed envelope and read it. It was dated the sixth and stated his intention of going to Margate for a time and then coming back to the bungalow.

'Now, the reading of that letter exposed me to an enormous temptation. By simply putting a one in front of the six and thus altering the date from the sixth to the sixteenth and posting the letter at Margate, I stood to gain thirty thousand pounds. I saw that at a glance. But I did not decide immediately to do it. I pulled down all the blinds, drew the curtains and locked up the house while I thought it over. There seemed to be practically no risk, unless someone should come to the bungalow and notice that the state of the body did not agree with the altered date on the letter. I went back and looked at the dead man. There was a burnt-out candle by his side and a tumbler containing the dried-up remains of some brown liquid. He had evidently poisoned himself. Then it occurred to me that, if I put the body and the tumbler in some place where they were not likely to be found for some time, the discrepancy between the condition of the body and the date of the letter would not be noticed.

'For some time I could think of no suitable place, but at last I remembered the bathing-hut. No one would look there for him. If they came to the bungalow and didn't find him there, they would merely conclude that he had not come back from Margate. I took the candle and the key from the key-board and went down to the hut; but there was a key in the door already, so I brought the other key back and put it in Crofton's pocket, never dreaming that it might not be the duplicate. Of course, I ought to have tried it in the door.

'Well, you know the rest. I took the body down, about two in the morning, locked up the hut, brought away the key and hung it on the board, took the counterpane off the bed, as it had some marks on it, and re-made the bed with the blanket outside. In the morning I took the train to Margate, posted the letter, after altering the date, and threw the gate-key and that of the front door into the sea.

'That is what really happened. You may not believe me; but I think you will as you have seen the body and will realise that I had no motive for killing Crofton before the fifteenth, whereas Crofton evidently died before that date.'

'I would not say "evidently",' said Thorndyke; 'but, as the date of his death is the vital point in your defence, you would be wise to notify the coroner of the importance of the issue.'

'I don't understand this case,' I said, as we walked

homewards (I was spending the evening with Thorndyke). 'You seemed to smell a rat from the very first. And I don't see how you spotted Jobson. It is a mystery to me.'

'It wouldn't be if you were a lawyer,' he replied. 'The case against Jobson was contained in what you told me at our first interview. You yourself commented on the peculiarity of the will that he drafted for Crofton. The intention of the latter was to leave all his property to his wife. But instead of saying so, the will specified each item of property, and appointed a residuary legatee, which was Jobson himself. This might have appeared like mere legal verbiage; but when Miss Shuler's legacy was announced, the transaction took on a rather different aspect. For this legacy was not among the items specified in the will. Therefore it did not go to Mrs Crofton. It would be included in the residue of the estate and would go to the residuary legatee – Jobson.'

'The deuce it would!' I exclaimed.

'Certainly, until Crofton revoked his will or made a fresh one. This was rather suspicious. It suggested that Jobson had private information as to Miss Shuler's will and had drafted Crofton's will in accordance with it; and as she died of malignant disease, her doctor must have known for some time that she was dying and it looked as if Jobson had information on that point, too. Now the position of affairs that you described to me was this: Crofton, a possible suicide, had disappeared and had made no fresh will.

'Miss Shuler died on the thirteenth, leaving thirty thousand pounds to Crofton, if he survived her, or if he did not, then to Mrs Crofton. The important question then was whether Crofton was alive or dead; and if he was dead, whether he had died before or after the thirteenth. For if he died before the thirteenth the legacy went to Mrs Crofton, but if he died after that date the legacy went to Jobson.

'Then you showed me that extraordinarily opportune letter dated the sixteenth. Now, seeing that that date was worth thirty thousand pounds to Jobson, I naturally scrutinised it narrowly. The letter was written with ordinary blue-black ink. But this ink, even in the open, takes about a fortnight to blacken completely. In a closed envelope it takes considerably longer. On examining this date through a lens, the one was very perceptibly bluer than the six. It had therefore been added later. But for what reason? And by whom?

'The only possible reason was that Crofton was dead and had died before the thirteenth. The only person who had any motive for making the alteration was Jobson. Therefore, when we started for Seasalter I already felt sure that Crofton was dead and that the letter had been posted at Margate by Jobson. I had further no doubt that Crofton's body was concealed somewhere on the premises of the bungalow. All that I had to do was to verify those conclusions.'

'Then you believe that Jobson has told us the truth?'

'Yes. But I suspect that he went down there with the deliberate intention of making away with Crofton before he could make a fresh will. The finding of Crofton's body must have been a fearful disappointment, but I must admit that he showed considerable resource in dealing with the situation; and he failed only by the merest chance. I think his defence against the murder charge will be admitted; but, of course, it will involve a plea of guilty to the charge of fraud in connection with the legacy.'

Thorndyke's forecast turned out to be correct. Jobson was acquitted of the murder of Arthur Crofton, but is at present 'doing time' in respect of the forged letter and the rest of his too-ingenious scheme.

A Case in Camera

Edmund Crispin

Detective Inspector Humbleby, of New Scotland Yard, had been induced by his wife to spend the first week of his summer's leave with his wife's sister, and his wife's sister's husband, in Munsingham, and was correspondingly aggrieved.

Munsingham, large and sooty, seemed to him not at all the place for recreation and jollity; moreover, his wife's sister's husband, by name Pollitt, was, like himself, a policeman, being superintendent of the Munsingham City CID, so that inevitably shop would be talked.

On the second day of the visit, however, Humbleby's grievances were erased from his mind by the revelation of a serious crisis in his brother-in-law's affairs.

'I'm going to be retired,' said Pollitt abruptly that evening, over tankards in the pub. 'I haven't got round to telling Marion about it yet.'

Humbleby was staring at him in amazement. 'Retired? But you're not nearly at retirement age yet. Why on earth—'

'Because I've got across the chief constable,' said Pollitt. 'He wanted a case to be considered closed – with perfectly good reason, I must say – and I wanted it kept open. I did keep it open, too, for a week or so – against his orders. Several of my men were tied up with it when they ought to have been doing other things.

'I didn't have the least excuse. I was going on instinct, and the fact that a couple of witnesses were just a bit too consistent in their stories to be true ... If I *did* possess definite evidence that the facts in this case aren't what they seem, I could put it up to the Watch Committee, and I'm pretty sure they'd uphold me. In fact, it wouldn't come to that; the CC'd withdraw. But definite evidence is just what's lacking – so ...' And Pollitt shrugged resignedly.

'M'm,' said Humbleby. 'Just what is this case?'

'Well, if you don't mind coming along to my office tomorrow morning, and having a look at the dossier ...'

And the basic facts of the case, Humbleby found, were in themselves simple enough.

A month previously, on 27 June, between 10:30 and 11:00 in the morning (the evidence as to these times being positive and irrefragable), a fifty-year-old woman, a Mrs Whittington, had been murdered in the kitchen of her home on the outskirts of the town.

The weapon – a heavy iron poker, with which Mrs Whittington had been struck violently on the back of the head – was found, wiped clean of fingerprints, nearby. The back door was open, and it was evident that the murder had followed, or been followed by, a certain amount of pilfering.

Mrs Whittington's husband, Leslie Whittington, a man younger and a good deal better-looking than his wife, held the post of chief engineer in the machinetool manufacturing firm of Heathers and Bardgett, whose factory was some ten minutes' walk from the Whittington home.

On the morning in question Whittington had been, as usual on weekdays, in his office at the factory. And the only respect in which, from his point of view, this particular morning had differed from any other was that he had been visited by a reporter, a girl, who worked for the most important of the Munsingham local newspapers. This girl, by name Sheila Pratt, was doing a series on the managers and technicians of Munsingham industry, and Whittington, an important man in his line, represented her current assignment.

She had arrived at Whittington's office shortly before 10:30 and had left again three-quarters of an hour later. During this period Whittington's secretary had, on Whittington's own instructions, told callers, and people who telephoned, that Whittington was out, thereby ensuring that the interview remained undisturbed.

Moreover, there was a fire-escape running down past Whittington's office window to a little-frequented yard.

As a matter of course, Pollitt had set in train the routine of investigating whether some previous association could have existed between Whittington and Sheila Pratt. Their own assertion was that until the interview they had been complete strangers to one another; but Mrs Whittington, Pollitt had learned, was not the divorcing sort – and the pilfering could easily have been a blind.

Before any results could be obtained from this investigation, however, there had occurred that development which had resulted in the chief constable's ordering the file on the case to be closed. Two days after the murder, a notorious young thug called Miller was run over and killed by a lorry on the by-pass road, and in his pocket were found several small pieces of jewellery looted from Mrs Whittington's bedroom at the time of her death.

'There were witnesses, too,' said Pollitt, 'who'd seen Miller hanging about near the Whittington house on the morning Mrs W was done in. So it was reasonable enough to put the blame on him, and just leave it at that. Of course, Miller could quite well have come along and pinched the stuff *after* the murder was committed, but the CC thought that in the absence of any evidence against the husband that was stretching it a bit far, and one sees his point of view.'

'One does,' Humbleby agreed. 'And I must admit, Charlie, that at the moment I still don't quite see yours.'

'I know, I know,' said Pollitt, disgruntled. 'But I still maintain that those two – Whittington and the Pratt girl – had their story far too pat. I took them both through it several times – separately, and with all sorts of camouflage stuff about unimportant detail –and neither of them ever put a foot wrong. Look.' He thrust a sheaf of typescript at Humbleby. 'Here are their various statements. *You* have a look at them.'

'M'm,' said Humbleby, nearly an hour later. 'Yes … Look, Charlie, the girl's statements all contain stuff about the

camera she brought with her to the interview. "Tripod …
three seconds' exposure" – all that. Do you happen to have
copies of the pictures she took?'

'She only kept one,' said Pollitt. 'But I've got a blow-up
print of that, all right.' He produced it and handed it across.
'It's a good picture, isn't it?'

It was unusually sharp and clear, showing Whittington
at his desk with the desk clock very properly registering ten
minutes to eleven.

'But there's nothing in it that's any help, that I can see,'
Pollitt went on. 'The clothes are right. The—'

'Just a minute,' Humbleby interrupted sharply. He had
reverted from the photograph to the signed statements of
Sheila Pratt, and was frowning in perplexity. 'It's possible
that – I say, Charlie, is this girl an experienced photographer
– a professional, I mean?'

Pollitt shook his head. 'No, she's just a beginner. I understand she's only bought her camera quite recently. But why—'

'And this factory,' said Humbleby. 'Is there a lot of heavy
machinery? A lot of noise and vibration?'

'Yes, there is. What are you getting at?'

'A couple more questions and you'll see it for yourself. Is
Whittington's office somewhere *over* the factory? Can you
feel the vibration *there?*'

'You can. But I still don't understand—'

'You will, Charlie. Because here's the really critical query.
*Were those machines running continuously during the whole of
the time Sheila Pratt was in Whittington's office?*'

And with that, Pollitt realised. 'Tripod,' he muttered.
Then his voice rose. 'Time-exposure … Wait.' He grabbed

the telephone, asked for a number, asked for a name, put his question, listened, thanked his informant, and rang off. 'Yes, they were running,' he said triumphantly. 'They were running all right.'

And Humbleby chuckled. He flicked the photograph with his forefinger. 'So that very obviously this beautifully clear picture wasn't taken at the time when Sheila Pratt and Whittington allege it was taken – because tripod plus time-exposure plus vibration would inevitably have resulted in blurring … I imagine they must have faked it up one evening, after the factory had stopped work; and the girl was too inexperienced in photography to realise the difference that that would make in the finished product …'

'Well, Charlie, will your chief like it, do you think?'

Pollitt grinned. 'He won't like it at all. But give the devil his due, he'll swallow it all right.' He hesitated. 'So that solves my own personal problem – and I needn't tell you how grateful I am … But as to whether we can get a prosecution out of it—'

They never did. 'And really, it was a good thing,' said Pollitt two years later in London, when he and his wife were returning the Humblebys' visit, and the conversation had turned to the topic of Whittington and his fate. 'Because if the DPP had allowed it to be taken to court, the chances are he'd have been acquitted in spite of the lies and in spite of the information we dug out about the surreptitious meetings between him and the Pratt girl in the eighteen months before the murder.

'And if he *had been* acquitted – well, he wouldn't have needed to worry about the possibility of his new wife giving him away, would he? And he wouldn't have set about stopping her mouth in that clumsy, panicky fashion ...'

'And they wouldn't be hanging him for it at Pentonville at nine o'clock tomorrow morning ... What a bit of luck, eh?'

The Fever Tree

Ruth Rendell

Where malaria is, there grows the fever tree.

It has the feathery fern-like leaves, fresh green and tender, that are common to so many trees in tropical regions. Its shape is graceful with an air of youth, of immaturity, as if every fever tree is waiting to grow up. But the most distinctive thing about it is the colour of its bark, which is the yellow of an unripe lemon. The fever trees stand out from among the rest because of their slender yellow trunks.

Ford knew what the tree was called and he could recognise it but he didn't know what its botanical name was. Nor had he ever heard why it was called the fever tree, whether the tribesmen used its leaves or bark or fruit as a specific against malaria or if it simply took its name from its warning presence wherever the malaria-carrying mosquito was. The sight of it in Ntsukunyane seemed to promote a fever in his blood.

An African in khaki shorts and shirt lifted up the bar for them so that their car could pass through the opening in the wire fence. Inside it looked no different from outside, the same bush, still, silent, unstirred by wind, stretching away on either side. Ford, driving the two miles along the tarmac road to the reception hut, thought of how it would be if he turned his head and saw Marguerite in the passenger seat beside him. It was an illusion he dared not have and was allowed to keep for perhaps a minute. Tricia shattered it. She began to belabour him with schoolgirl questions, uttered in a bright and desperate voice.

Another African, in a fancier, more decorated uniform, took their booking voucher and checked it against a ledger. You had to pay weeks in advance for the privilege of staying here. Ford had booked the day after he had said goodbye to Marguerite and returned, for ever, to Tricia.

'My wife wants to know the area of Ntsukunyane,' he said.

'Four million acres.'

Ford gave the appropriate whistle. 'Do we have a chance of seeing leopard?'

The man shrugged, smiled. 'Who knows? You may be lucky. You're here a whole week, so you should see lion, elephant, hippo, cheetah maybe. But the leopard is nocturnal and you must be back in camp by six p.m.' He looked at his watch. 'I advise you to get on now, sir, if you're to make Thaba before they close the gates.'

Ford got back into the car. It was nearly four. The sun of Africa, a living presence, a personal god, burned through a net of haze. There was no wind. Tricia, in a pale yellow sun dress with frills, had hung her arm outside the open window and the fair downy skin was glowing red. He told her what the man had said and he told her about the notice pinned inside the hut: *It is strictly forbidden to bring firearms into the game reserve, to feed the animals, to exceed the speed limit, to litter.*

'And most of all you mustn't get out of the car,' said Ford.

'What, not ever?' said Tricia, making her pale blue eyes round and naive and marble-like.

'That's what it says.'

She pulled a face. 'Silly old rules!'

'They have to have them,' he said.

In here as in the outside world. It is strictly forbidden to fall in love, to love your wife, to try and begin anew. He glanced at Tricia to see if the same thoughts were passing through her mind. Her face wore its arch expression, winsome.

'A prize,' she said, 'for the first one to see an animal.'

'All right.' He had agreed to this reconciliation, to bring her on this holiday, this second honeymoon, and now he must try. He must work at it. It wasn't just going to happen as love had sprung between him and Marguerite, unsought and untried for. 'Who's going to award it?' he said.

'You are if it's me and I am if it's you. And if it's me I'd like a presey from the camp shop. A very nice pricey presey.'

Ford was the winner. He saw a single zebra come out from among the thorn trees on the right-hand side, then a small herd.

'Do I get a present from the shop?' he asked.

He could sense rather than see her shake her head with calculated coyness. 'A kiss,' she said and pressed warm dry lips against his cheek.

It made him shiver a little. He slowed down for the zebra to cross the road. The thorn bushes had spines on them two inches long. By the roadside grew a species of wild zinnia with tiny flowers, coral red, and these made red drifts among the coarse pale grass. In the bush were red ant hills with tall peaks like towers on a castle in a fairy story. It was thirty miles to Thaba.

He drove on just within the speed limit, ignoring Tricia as far as he could whenever she asked him to slow down. They weren't going to see one of the big predators, anyway, not this afternoon, he was certain of that, only impala and zebra and maybe a giraffe. On business trips in the past he'd taken time off to go to Serengeti and Kruger and he knew.

He got the binoculars out for Tricia and adjusted them and hooked them round her neck, for he hadn't forgotten the binoculars and cameras she had dropped and smashed in the past through failing to do that, and her tears afterwards. The car wasn't air-conditioned and the heat lay heavy and still between them. Ahead of them, as they drove westwards, the sun was sinking in a dull yellow glare. The sweat flowed out of Ford's armpits and between his shoulder blades, soaking his already wet shirt and laying a cold sticky film on his skin.

A stone pyramid with arrows on it, set in the middle of a junction of roads, pointed the way to Thaba, to the main camp at Waka-suthu and to Hippo Bridge over the Suthu River. On top of it a baboon sat with her grey fluffy infant on her knees. Tricia yearned for it, stretching out her arms. She had never had a child. The baboon began picking fleas out of its baby's scalp. Tricia gave a little nervous scream, half disgusted, half joyful. Ford drove down the road to Thaba and in through the entrance to the camp ten minutes before they closed the gates for the night.

The dark comes down fast in Africa. Dusk is of short duration and no sooner have you noticed it than it is gone and night has fallen. In the few moments of dusk pale things glimmer brightly and birds murmur. In the camp at Thaba were a restaurant and a shop, round huts with thatched roofs, and wooden chalets with porches. Ford and Tricia had been assigned a chalet on the northern perimeter, and from their porch, across an expanse of turf and beyond the high wire fence, you could see the Suthu River flowing smoothly and silently between banks of tall reeds.

Dusk had just come as they walked up the wooden steps, Ford carrying their cases. It was then that he saw the fever trees, two of them, their ferny leaves bleached to grey by the twilight but their trunks a sharper, stronger yellow than in the day.

'Just as well we took our anti-malaria pills,' said Ford as he pushed open the door. When the light was switched on he could see two mosquitos on the opposite wall. '*Anopheles* is the malaria carrier, but unfortunately they don't announce whether they're *anopheles* or not.'

Twin beds, a table, lamps, an air conditioner, a fridge, a door, standing open, to lavatory and shower. Tricia dropped her makeup case, without which she went nowhere, on to the bed by the window. The light wasn't very bright. None of the lights in the camp were because the electricity came from a generator. They were a small colony of humans in a world that belonged to the animals, a reversal of the usual order of

192

things. From the window you could see other chalets, other dim lights, other parked cars.

Tricia talked to the two mosquitos.

'Is your name Anna Phyllis? No, darling, you're quite safe. She says she's Mary Jane and her husband's John Henry.'

Ford managed to smile. He had accepted and grown used to Tricia's facetiousness until he had encountered Marguerite's wit. He shoved his case, without unpacking it, into the cupboard and went to have a shower.

Tricia stood on the porch, listening to the cicadas, thousands of them. It had gone pitch-dark while she was hanging up her dresses and the sky was punctured all over with bright stars.

She had got Ford back from that woman and now she had to keep him. She had lost some weight and bought a lot of new clothes and had highlights put in her hair. Men had always made her feel frightened, starting with her father when she was a child. It was then, when a child, that she had purposely begun *playing* the child with its cajolements and its winning little ways. She had noticed that her father was kinder and more forbearing towards little girls than towards her mother. Ford had married a little girl, clinging and winsome, and had liked it well enough till he met a grown woman.

Tricia knew all that, but now she knew no better how to keep him than by the old methods, as weary and stale to her as she guessed they might be to him. Standing there on the porch, she half wished she were alone and didn't have to have a husband, didn't, for the sake of convention and pride, support and society, have to hold on tight to him. She listened wistfully for a lion to roar out there in the bush beyond the fence, but there was no sound except the cicadas.

Ford came out in a towelling robe. 'What did you do with the mosquito stuff? The spray?'

Frightened at once, she said, 'I don't know.'

'What d'you mean, you don't know? You must know. I gave you the aerosol at the hotel and said to put it in that makeup case of yours.'

She opened the case although she knew the mosquito stuff wasn't there. Of course it wasn't there. She could see it on the bathroom shelf in the hotel, left behind because it was too bulky. She bit her lip, looked sideways at Ford. 'We can get some more at the shop.'

'Tricia, the shop closes at seven and it's now ten past.'

'We can get some in the morning.'

'Mosquitos happen to be most active at night.' He rummaged with his hands among the bottles and jars in the case. 'Look at all this useless rubbish. "Skin cleanser", "pearlised foundation", "moisturiser" – like some young model girl. I suppose it didn't occur to you to bring the anti-mosquito spray and leave the "pearlised foundation" behind.'

Her lip trembled. She could feel herself, almost involuntarily, rounding her eyes, forming her mouth into the shape of lisping. 'We did 'member to take our pills.'

'That won't stop the damn things biting.' He went back into the shower and slammed the door.

Marguerite wouldn't have forgotten to bring that aerosol. Tricia knew he was thinking of Marguerite again, that his head was full of her, that she had entered his thoughts powerfully and insistently on the long drive to Thaba. She began to cry. The tears went on running out of her eyes and wouldn't stop, so she changed her dress while she cried and the tears came through the powder she put on her face.

They had dinner in the restaurant. Tricia, in pink flowered crepe, was the only dressed-up woman there, and while once she would have fancied that the other diners looked at her in admiration, now she thought it must be with derision. She ate her small piece of overcooked hake and her large piece of overcooked, bread-crumbed veal, and watched the red weals from mosquito bites coming up on Ford's arms.

There were no lights on in the camp but those which shone from the windows of the main building and from the chalets. Gradually the lights went out and it became very dark. In spite of his mosquito bites, Ford fell asleep at once but the noise of the air conditioning kept Tricia awake. At eleven she switched it off and opened the window. Then she did sleep but she awoke again at four, lay awake for half an hour, got up, put on her clothes, and went out.

It was still dark but the darkness was lifting as if the thickest veil of it had been withdrawn. A heavy dew lay on the grass. As she passed under the merula tree, laden with small green apricot-shaped fruits, a flock of bats flew out from its branches and circled her head. If Ford had been with her she would have screamed and clung to him but because she was alone she kept silent. The camp and the bush beyond the fence were full of sound. The sounds brought to Tricia's mind the paintings of Hieronymus Bosch, imps and demons and dreadful homunculi which, if they had uttered, might have made noises like these, gruntings and soft whistles and chirps and little thin squeals.

She walked about, waiting for the dawn, expecting it to come with drama. But it was only a grey pallor in the sky, a paleness between parting black clouds, and the feeling of let-down frightened her as if it were a symbol or an omen of something more significant in her life than the coming of morning.

Ford woke up, unable at first to open his eyes for the swelling from mosquito bites. There were mosquitos like threads of thistledown on the walls, all over the walls. He got up and staggered, half blind, out of the bedroom and let the water from the shower run on his eyes. Tricia came and stared at his face, giggling nervously and biting her lip.

The camp gates opened at five thirty and the cars began their exodus. Tricia had never passed a driving test and Ford couldn't see, so they went to the restaurant for breakfast instead. When the shop opened, Ford bought two kinds of mosquito repellent, and impatiently, because he could no longer bear her apologies and her pleading eyes, a necklace of ivory beads for Tricia and a skirt with giraffes printed on it. At nine o'clock, when the swelling round Ford's eyes had subsided a little, they set off in the car, taking the road for Hippo Bridge.

The day was humid and thickly hot. Ford had counted the number of mosquito bites he had had and the total was twenty-four. It was hard to believe that two little tablets of quinine would be proof against twenty-four bites, some of which must certainly have been inflicted by *anopheles*. Hadn't he seen the two fever trees when they arrived last night? Now he drove the car slowly and doggedly, hardly speaking, his swollen eyes concealed behind sunglasses.

By the Suthu River and then by a water hole he stopped and they watched. But they saw nothing come to the water's edge unless you counted the log which at last disappeared, thus proving itself to have been a crocodile. It was too late in the morning to see much apart from the marabou storks which stood one-legged, still and hunched, in a clearing or on the gaunt branch of a tree. Through binoculars Ford stared at the bush which stretched in unbroken, apparently untenanted, sameness to the blue ridge of mountains on the far horizon.

There could be no real fever from the mosquito bites. If malaria were to come it wouldn't be yet. But Ford, sitting in the car beside Tricia, nevertheless felt something like a delirium of fever. It came perhaps from the gross irritation of the whole surface of his body, from the tender burning of his skin and from his inability to move without setting up fresh torment. It affected his mind too, so that each time he looked at Tricia a kind of panic rose in him. Why had he done it? Why had he gone back to her? Was he mad? His eyes and his head throbbed as if his temperature were raised. Tricia's pink jeans were too tight for her and the frills on her white voile blouse ridiculous. With the aid of the binoculars she had found a family of small grey monkeys in the branches of a peepul tree and she was cooing at them out of the window. Presently she opened the car door, held it just open, and turned to look at him the way a child looks at her father when he has forbidden something she nevertheless longs and means to do.

They hadn't had sight of a big cat or an elephant, they hadn't even seen a jackal. Ford lifted his shoulders.

'Okay. But if a ranger comes along and catches you we'll be in deep trouble.'

She got out of the car, leaving the door open. The grass which began at the roadside and covered the bush as far as the eye could see was long and coarse. It came up above Tricia's knees. A lioness or a cheetah lying in it would have been entirely concealed. Ford picked up the binoculars and looked the other way to avoid watching Tricia who had once again forgotten to put the camera strap round her neck. She was making overtures to the monkeys who shrank away from her, embracing each other and burying heads in shoulders, like menaced refugees in a sentimental painting.

Ford moved the glasses slowly. About a hundred yards from where a small herd of buck grazed uneasily, he saw the two cat faces close together, the bodies nestled together, the spotted backs. Cheetah. It came into his mind how he had heard that they were the fastest animals on earth.

He ought to call to Tricia and get her back at once into the car. He didn't call. Through the glasses he watched the big cats that reclined there so gracefully, satiated, at rest, yet with open eyes. Marguerite would have liked them; she loved cats, she had a Burmese, as lithe and slim and poised as one of these wild creatures.

Tricia got back into the car, exclaiming about how sweet the monkeys were. He started the car and drove off without saying anything to her about the cheetahs.

Later, at about five in the afternoon, she wanted to get out of the car again and he didn't stop her. She walked up and down the road, talking to mongooses. In something over an hour it would be dark. Ford imagined starting up the car and driving back to the camp without her. Leopards were nocturnal hunters, waiting till dark.

The swelling around his eyes had almost subsided now but his arms and hands ached from the stiffness of the bites. The mongooses fled into the grass as Tricia approached, whispering to them, hands outstretched. A car with four men in it was coming along from the Hippo Bridge direction. It slowed down and the driver put his head out. His face was brick-red, thick-featured, his hair corrugated blond, and his voice had the squashed vowel accent of the white man born in Africa.

'The lady shouldn't be out on the road like that.'

'I know,' Ford said. 'I've told her.'

'Excuse me, d'you know you're doing a very dangerous thing, leaving your car?' The voice had a hectoring boom. Tricia blushed. She bridled, smiled, bit her lip, though she was in fact very afraid of this man who was looking at her as if he despised her, as if she disgusted him. When he got back to camp, would he betray her?

'Promise you won't tell on me?' she faltered, her head on one side.

The man gave an exclamation of anger and withdrew his head. The car moved forward. Tricia gave a skip and a jump into the passenger seat beside Ford. They had under an hour to get back to Thaba and Ford followed the car with the four men in it.

At dinner they sat at adjoining tables. Tricia wondered how many people they had told, for she fancied that some of the diners looked at her with curiosity or antagonism. The man with fair curly hair they called Eric boasted loudly of what he and his companions had seen that day, a whole pride of lions, two rhinoceros, hyena, and the rare sable antelope.

'You can't expect to see much down that Hippo Bridge road, you know,' he said to Ford. 'All the game's up at Sotingwe. You take the Sotingwe road first thing tomorrow and I'll guarantee you lions.' He didn't address Tricia, he didn't even look at her. Ten years before, men in restaurants had turned their heads to look at her and though she had feared them, she had basked, trembling, in their gaze. Walking across the grass, back to their chalet, she held on to Ford's arm.

'For God's sake, mind my mosquito bites,' said Ford.

He lay awake a long while in the single bed a foot away from Tricia's, thinking about the leopard out there beyond the fence that hunted by night. The leopard would move along the branch of a tree and drop upon prey. Lionesses hunted in the early morning and brought the kill to their mate and the cubs. Ford had seen all that sort of thing on television. How cheetahs hunted he didn't know except that they were very swift. An angry elephant would lean on a car and crush it or smash a windshield with a blow from its foot.

It was too dark for him to see Tricia but he knew she was awake, lying still, sometimes holding her breath. He heard her breath released in an exhalation, a sigh, that was audible above the rattle of the air conditioner.

Years ago he had tried to teach her to drive. They said a husband should never try to teach his wife, he would have no patience with her and make no allowances. Tricia's progress had never been maintained, she had always been liable to do silly reckless things and then he had shouted at her. She took a driving test and failed and said this was because the examiner had bullied her. Tricia seemed to think no one should ever raise his voice to her, and at one glance from her all men should fall slaves at her feet.

He would have liked her to be able to take a turn at driving. There was no doubt you missed a lot when you had to concentrate on the road. But it was no use suggesting it. Theirs was one of the first cars in the line to leave the gates at five thirty, to slip out beyond the fence into the grey dawn, the still bush. At the stone pyramid, on which a family of baboons sat clustered, Ford took the road for Sotingwe.

A couple of miles up they came upon the lions. Eric and his friends were already there, leaning out of the car windows with cameras. The lions, two full-grown lionesses, two lioness cubs and a lion cub with his mane beginning to sprout, were lying on the roadway. Ford stopped and parked the car on the opposite side to Eric.

'Didn't I say you'd be lucky up here?' Eric called to Tricia. 'Not got any ideas about getting out and investigating, I hope.'

Tricia didn't answer him or look at him. She looked at the lions. The sun was coming up, radiating the sky with a pinkish-orange glow, and a little breeze fluttered all the pale green, fern-like leaves. The larger of the adult lionesses, bored rather than alarmed by Eric's elaborate photographic equipment, got up slowly and strolled into the bush, in among the long dry grass and the red zinnias. The cubs followed her, the other lioness followed her. Through his binoculars Ford watched them stalk with proud lifted heads, walking, even the little ones, in a graceful, measured, controlled way. There were no impala anywhere, no giraffe, no wildebeest. The world here belonged to the lions.

All the game was gathered at Sotingwe, near the water hole. An elephant with ears like punkahs was powdering himself with red earth blown through his trunk. Tricia got out of the car to photograph the elephant and Ford didn't try to stop her. He scratched his mosquito bites which had passed the burning and entered the itchy stage.

Once more Tricia had neglected to pass the camera strap around her neck. She made her way down to the water's edge and stood at a safe distance – was it a safe distance? Was any distance safe in here? – looking at a crocodile. Ford thought, without really explaining to himself or even understanding what he meant, that it was the wrong time of day, it was too early. They went back to Thaba for breakfast.

At breakfast and again at lunch Eric was very full of what he had seen. He had taken the dirt road that ran down from Sotingwe to Suthu Bridge and there, up in a tree near the water, had been a leopard. Malcolm had spotted it first, stretched out asleep on a branch, a long way off but quite easy to see through field glasses.

'Massive great fella with your authentic square-type spots,' said Eric, smoking a cigar.

Tricia, of course, wanted to go to Suthu Bridge, so Ford took the dirt road after they had had their siesta. Malcolm described exactly where he had seen the leopard which might, for all he knew, still be sleeping on its branch.

'About half a mile up from the bridge. You look over on your left and there's a sort of clearing with one of those trees with yellow trunks in it. This chap was on a branch on the right side of the clearing.'

The dirt road was a track of crimson earth between green verges. Ford found the clearing with the single fever tree but the leopard had gone. He drove slowly down to the bridge that spanned the sluggish green river. When he switched off the engine it was silent and utterly still, the air hot and close, nothing moving but the mosquitos that danced in their haphazard yet regular measure above the surface of the water.

Tricia was getting out of the car as a matter of course now. This time she didn't even trouble to give him the coy glance that asked permission. She was wearing a red and white striped sundress with straps that were too narrow and a skirt that was too tight. She ran down to the water's edge, took off a sandal, and dipped in a daring foot. She laughed and twirled her feet, dabbling the dry round stones with water drops. Ford thought how he had loved this sort of thing when he had first met her, and now he was going to have to bear it for the rest of his life. He broke into a sweat as if his temperature had suddenly risen.

She was prancing about on the stones and in the water, holding up her skirt. There were no animals to be seen. All afternoon they had seen nothing but impala, and the sun was moving down now, beginning to colour the hazy pastel sky. Tricia, on the opposite bank, broke another Ntsukunyane rule and picked daisies, tucking one behind each ear. With a flower between her teeth like a Spanish dancer, she swayed her hips and smiled.

Ford turned the ignition key and started the car. It would be dark in just an hour and long before that they would have closed the gates at Thaba. He moved the car forward, reversed, making what Tricia, no doubt, would call a three-point turn. Facing towards Thaba now, he put the shift into drive, his foot on the accelerator, and took a deep breath as the sweat trickled between his shoulder blades. The heat made mirages on the road and out of them a car was coming. Ford stopped and switched off the engine. It wasn't Eric's car but one belonging to a couple of young Americans on holiday. The boy raised his hand in a salute at Ford.

Ford called out to Tricia, 'Come on or we'll be late.'

She got into the car, dropping her flowers on to the roadway. Ford had been going to leave her there, that was how much he wanted to be rid of her. Her body began to shake and she clasped her hands tightly together so that he couldn't see. He had been going to drive away and leave her there to the darkness and the lions, the leopard that hunted by night. He had been driving away, only the Americans' car had come along.

She was silent, thinking about it. The Americans turned back soon after they did and followed them up the dirt road. Impala stood around the solitary fever tree, listening perhaps to inaudible sounds or scenting invisible danger. The sky was smoky yellow with sunset. Tricia thought about what Ford must have intended to do – drive back to camp just before they closed the gates, watch the darkness come down, knowing she was out there, say not a word of her absence to anyone – and who would miss her? Eric? Malcolm? Ford wouldn't have gone to the restaurant and in the morning when they opened the gates he would have driven away.

No need even to check out at Ntsukunyane where you paid weeks in advance.

The perfect murder. Who would search for her, not knowing there was need for search? And if her bones were found? One set of bones, human, impala, waterbuck, looks very much like another when the jackals have been at them and the vultures. And when he reached home he would have said he had left her for Marguerite ...

He was nicer to her that evening, gentler. Because he was afraid she had guessed or might guess the truth of what had happened at Sotingwe?

'We said we'd have champagne one night. How about now? No time like the present.'

'If you like,' Tricia said.

She felt sick all the time, she had no appetite. Ford toasted them in champagne.

'To us!'

He ordered the whole gamut of the menu, soup, fish, Wiener schnitzel, crème brûlée. She picked at her food, thinking how he had meant to kill her. She would never be safe now, for having failed once he would try again. Not the same method perhaps but some other. How was she to know he hadn't already tried? Perhaps, for instance, he had substituted aspirin for those quinine tablets, or when they were back at the hotel in Mombasa he might try to drown her. She would never be safe unless she left him.

Which was what he wanted, which would be the next best thing to her death. Lying awake in the night, she thought of what leaving him would mean – going back to live with her mother while he went to Marguerite. He wasn't asleep either.

She could hear the sound of his irregular wakeful breathing. She heard the bed creak as he moved in it restlessly, the air conditioner grinding, the whine of a mosquito.

Now, if she hadn't already been killed, she might be wandering out there in the bush, in terror in the dark, afraid to take a step but afraid to remain still, fearful of every sound yet not knowing which sound most to fear. There was no moon. She had taken note of that before she came to bed and had seen in her diary that tomorrow the moon would be new. The sky had been overcast at nightfall and now it was pitch-dark. The leopard could see perhaps by the light of the stars or with an inner instinctive eye more sure than simple vision, and would drop silently from its branch to sink its teeth into the lifted throat.

The mosquito that had whined stung Ford in several places on his face and neck and on his left foot. He had forgotten to use the repellent the night before. Early in the morning, at dawn, he got up and dressed and went for a walk round the camp. There was no one about but one of the African staff, hosing down a guest's car. Squeaks and shufflings came from the bush beyond the fence.

Had he really meant to rid himself of Tricia by throwing her, as one might say, to the lions? For a mad moment, he supposed, because fever had got into his blood, poison into his veins. She knew, he could tell that. In a way it might be all to the good, her knowing; it would show her how hopeless the marriage was that she was trying to preserve.

The swellings on his foot, though covered by his sock, were making the instep bulge through the sandal. His foot felt stiff and burning and he became aware that he was limping slightly. Supporting himself against the trunk of a fever tree, his skin against its cool, dampish, yellow bark, he took off his sandal and felt his swollen foot tenderly with his fingertips. Mosquitos never touched Tricia; they seemed to shirk contact with her pale dry flesh.

She was up when he hobbled in; she was sitting on her bed, painting her fingernails. How could he live with a woman who painted her fingernails in a game reserve?

They didn't go out till nine. On the road to Waka-suthu, Eric's car met them, coming back.

'There's nothing down there for miles, you're wasting your time.'

'Okay,' said Ford. 'Thanks.'

'Sotingwe's the place. Did you see the leopard yesterday?' Ford shook his head. 'Oh, well, we can't all be lucky.'

Elephants were playing in the river at Hippo Bridge, spraying each other with water and nudging heavy shoulders. Ford thought that was going to be the high spot of the morning until they came upon the kill. They didn't really see it. The kill had taken place some hours before, but the lioness and her cubs were still picking at the carcass, at a blood-blackened rib cage.

They sat in the car and watched. After a while the lions left the carcass and walked away in file through the grass, but the little jackals were already gathered, a pack of them, posted behind trees. Ford came back that way at four and by then the vultures had moved in, picking the bones.

It was a hot day of merciless sunshine, the sky blue and perfectly clear. Ford's foot was swollen to twice its normal size. He noticed that Tricia hadn't left the car that day, nor had she spoken girlishly to him or giggled or given him a roguish kiss. She thought he had been trying to kill her, a preposterous notion really. The truth was he had only been giving her a fright, teaching her how stupid it was to flout the rules and leave the car. Why should he kill her, anyway? He could leave her, he *would* leave her and once they were back in Mombasa he would tell her so. The thought of it made him turn to her and smile. He had stopped by the clearing where the fever tree stood, yellow of bark, delicate and fern-like of leaf, in the sunshine like a young sapling in springtime.

'Why don't you get out any more?'

She faltered, 'There's nothing to see.'

'No?'

He had spotted the porcupine with his naked eye but he handed her the binoculars. She looked and she laughed with pleasure. That was the way she used to laugh when she was young, not from amusement but delight. He shut his eyes.

'Oh, the sweetie porky-pine!'

She reached on to the back seat for the camera. And then she hesitated. He could see the fear, the caution, in her eyes. Silently he took the key out of the ignition and held it out to her on the palm of his hand. She flushed. He stared at her, enjoying her discomfiture, indignant that she should suspect him of such baseness.

She hesitated but she took the key. She picked up the camera and opened the car door, holding the key on its fob in her left hand and the camera in her right. He noticed she hadn't passed the strap of the camera, his treasured Pentax, round her neck. For the thousandth time he could have told her but he lacked the heart to speak. His swollen foot throbbed and he thought of the long days at Ntsukunyane that remained to them. Marguerite seemed infinitely far away, farther even than at the other side of the world where she was.

He knew Tricia was going to drop the camera some fifteen seconds before she did so. It was because she had the key in her other hand. If the strap had been round her neck it wouldn't have mattered. He knew how it was when you held something in each hand and lost your grip or your footing. You had no sense then, in that instant, of which of the objects was valuable and mattered and which did not. Tricia held on to the key and dropped the camera. The better to photograph the porcupine, she had mounted on to the twisted roots of a tree, roots that looked as hard as a flight of stone steps.

She gave a little cry. At the sounds of the crash and the cry the porcupine erected its quills. Ford jumped out of the car, wincing when he put his foot to the ground, hobbling through the grass to Tricia who stood as if petrified with fear of him. The camera, the pieces of camera, had fallen among the gnarled, stone-like tree roots. He dropped on to his knees, shouting at her, cursing her.

Tricia began to run. She ran back to the car and pushed the key into the ignition, the car was pointing in the direction of Thaba and the clock on the dashboard shelf said five thirty-five. Ford came limping back waving his arms at her, his hands full of broken pieces of camera. She looked away and put her foot hard down on the accelerator.

The sky was clear orange with sunset, black bars of the coming night lying on the horizon. She found she could drive when she had to, even though she couldn't pass a test.

A mile along the road she met the American couple. The boy put his head out.

'Anything worth going down there for?'

'Not a thing,' said Tricia. 'You'd be wasting your time.'

The boy turned his car round and followed her back. It was two minutes to six when they entered Thaba, the last cars to do so, and the gates were closed behind them.

Parking Space

Simon Brett

'Your wife tells me you're going to take up shooting,' said Alex Paton, during a lull in the dinner party conversation.

Kevin Hooson-Smith flashed a look of annoyance at his wife, Avril, but smiled casually and responded, 'Well, thought it might be rather fun. You know, at some point. When I've got time for a proper weekend hobby. Old Andersen keeps us at it so hard at the moment, I think that may be a few years hence.'

He laughed heartily to dissipate the subject, but Alex Paton wasn't going to let it go. 'But Avril said you'd actually bought a shotgun.'

'Well …' Kevin shrugged uncomfortably. 'Useful thing to have. You know, if the opportunity came up for a bit of shooting, one wouldn't want to say, No, sorry, no can do, no gun.' He laughed again, hoping the others would join in. Surely he'd got the words right. If Alex Paton or Philip

Wilkinson had said that, the other would certainly have laughed. But they didn't, so he had to continue. 'You shoot at all, Alex?'

'Not much these days. Pop off the occasional rabbit if I go down to the country to see Mother. Father left me his pair of Purdey's, which aren't bad. What make was the gun you got, Kevin?'

'Oh, I forget the name. Foreign.'

'Dear, dear. Some evil continental pop-gun.' They all laughed at that.

'Absolutely,' said Kevin. At least he'd got that right. 'More wine, Alex?'

'Thank you.'

'It's a seventy-one – Pommard.'

'I noticed.'

Kevin busied himself with dispensing wine to his guests, but Alex was still not deflected from the subject. 'Avril said she thought you were going off shooting this weekend …'

'Oh, I don't know. Maybe. Will you have a little more, Elizabeth? Fine. No, I saw something about one of these weekend teaching courses, you know, in shooting … We all have to learn some time, don't we?' Kevin laughed again.

'Oh yes,' Alex agreed. 'If we don't already know.'

Philip Wilkinson came kindly into the pause. 'You know, anyone who's keen on shooting ought to chat up that new girl who's just started cooking the directors' lunches. Davina Whatsername …'

'Entick,' Kevin supplied.

'Yes. Her old man's Sir Richard Entick.'

Alex Paton was impressed. 'Really? I hadn't made that connection. Well, he's got some of the best shooting in the country. Yes, keep on chatting her up, Kevin.'

Kevin laughed again, but again alone. They were silent, though there was quite a lot of noise from the cutlery. Avril hoped the steak wasn't too tough. She had done it exactly as the cordon bleu monthly part-work had said. Well, except that had said *best* grilling steak, but the best was so expensive. The stuff she had got had been expensive enough. She was sure it was all right.

Maybe they weren't talking because they were too busy eating. Enjoying it. The other two wives hadn't said much all evening. Maybe the wives of stockbrokers from Andersen Small weren't expected to say anything. Well, she wasn't going to be totally silent and submissive. Particularly with an empty wine glass. 'Hey, Kev, you missed me out on your rounds. Could I have a bit more wine?'

Kevin somewhat ungraciously pushed the wine bottle towards her.

'Kev,' Alex Paton repeated. 'That's rather an attractive coining.'

Kevin was immediately on the defensive. Though he smiled, Avril recognised the tension in his jaw muscles. 'Actually, the name Kevin is quite old. Came across something about it the other day. Means "handsome birth". There was a St Kevin way back in the sixth century. A hermit, I think. In Ireland.'

'Ah,' murmured Alex Paton. 'In Ireland.'

They all laughed at that, though neither Kevin nor Avril could have said exactly why. Emboldened by his success, Alex Paton went on, 'And tell me, what about Hooson-Smith? Does that name go back to the sixth century?'

After the laugh that greeted that one, they were all silent again. Kevin didn't start any new topic of conversation, so Avril decided it was her duty as hostess to speak. The sound of a car at the front of the house provided her cue.

'I bet that's our next door neighbour moving his car. You know, he's really strange. Very petty. He gets terribly upset if he can't park his car exactly outside his front door. And I mean exactly. We have known him to get up at three in the morning and move it, if he hears someone moving theirs and leaving a space. I mean, isn't that ridiculous? It's no trouble just to walk a couple of yards, but he always wants to be exactly outside. I hope we never get as petty as that.'

They were all looking at her. She didn't know why. Maybe she had spoken rather louder than usual. She felt relaxed by the wine. It had been a long day. All the usual vexations of the children and tidying the house and then, on top of that, cooking this dinner party. Kevin insisted that everything had to be just so for his colleagues from Andersen Small. She didn't really see why. It was not as if they had ever been invited to them. And the wives didn't seem real, just exquisitely painted clothes-horses, not real women who you could have a good natter with.

Alex Paton broke the pause and responded to her speech. 'Yes, well, fortunately that's a problem we don't have to cope with. We are blessed with a rather quaint, old-fashioned device called a garage.'

After the laugh, Philip Wilkinson started talking about the

intention of Andersen Small to open an office in Manila, and the attention moved away from Avril.

Only Kevin was still looking at her. She seemed to see him through a swimmy haze. And there was no love in his expression.

'I don't like to leave the washing-up till the morning, Kev.'

'Well, do it now, if you feel that strongly about it.' He was already out of his suit and unbuttoning the silk shirt that had been a special offer in the *Observer*. 'All I know is, it's after one and I have a heavy day tomorrow. I have a long costing meeting with Andersen first thing.'

'I've got a lot to do tomorrow too.'

'Having coffee with some other under-employed woman, then tea with someone else.'

'No, not that. I've hardly met anyone since we've been in Dulwich. Not like it was in Willesden.'

'Equally the people here are rather different than those there were in Willesden. Better for the boys to grow up with.' Kevin was now down to his underpants. He turned away from her to take them off, as if ashamed.

'But the boys don't grow up with them. They spend all their time travelling back and forth to that bloody private school and don't seem to make any friends.'

'Don't say "bloody". It makes you sound more Northern than ever.'

'Well, I am bloody Northern, aren't I?'

'There's no need to rub everyone's face in it all the time, though, is there?'

'Anyway, I'm no more Northern than you are. I just

haven't tarted up my vowels and started talking in a phoney accent that all my posh friends laugh at.'

'They do not laugh at me!' Kevin was dangerously near the edge of violence.

Avril bit back her rejoinder. No, calm down. She hadn't wanted the evening to end like this. She lingered in front of the dressing table, unwilling to start removing her make-up. It had used to be a signal between them. Well, more than a signal. She would start to remove her make-up and he would say, 'Come on, time enough for that. We've got more important things to do', and pull her down on to the bed. Now he rarely seemed to think they had more important things to do. Now, she felt, he wouldn't notice if she never even put on any make-up.

He was in his pyjamas and under the duvet, his back unanswerably turned to her side of the bed. (Why a duvet? She hated it. She loved the secure strapped-in feeling of sheets and blankets, the tight little cocoon their bed had been back in the flat in Willesden.)

Then she remembered their new chore. 'Have you potted James?'

'No.'

'But I thought we'd agreed you'd do it.'

'You may have agreed that. I haven't agreed anything. Anyway, it's ridiculous, a child of six needing to be potted.'

'If he isn't, he wets the bed.'

'If he is, he still seems to wet it. It's ridiculous.'

'It's only since he's been at that new school.'

'I don't see what that has to do with it.'

'It has everything to do with it. He hates it there. He hates how all the other boys make fun of him, hates how they imitate his accent.'

'Perhaps that'll teach him to improve his accent.'

'What, you want another phoney voice in the family?'

'Avril! shut up, shut up, shut up!' He was sitting up in bed, his face red with fury.

Avril again retreated and went and potted James. When she came back, Kevin was pretending to be asleep. The rigidity of his body showed he wasn't really. She knew his mind was working, rehearsing tiny humiliations, planning revenges, planning more success. He worked hard to make himself what he wanted to be.

She sat down at the dressing table and picked up a new jar of cream to remove her make-up. But she didn't open it. Somehow she felt something might still happen; he might get out of bed and put his arms round her. 'Kevin ...'

The totality of his silence again gave the lie to his appearance of sleep.

'Kev, did you mean that about not going away this weekend?'

'No, I'm going.'

'On this shooting course?'

'Yes.'

'But you told Alex you might not.'

'Because it wasn't his business. I was bloody annoyed at you for starting talking about shooting anyway.'

'But you only bought the gun this week. And they seemed to know about it. I thought at last there was a common subject we could all talk about.'

'Well, you were wrong. In future, stick to talking about

cooking or children or the next door neighbour's car. And, for Christ's sake, let me go to sleep!'

'So you're definitely going this weekend?'

'Yes.'

'Taking the car?'

'Yes. Why do you ask?'

'I was thinking, if you weren't here, I could take the kids up to see Mum.'

'All the way to Rochdale?'

'It'd be a break. She'd love to see them. And now you've taken over the fourth bedroom, it's very difficult for her to come and stay down here.'

'I need a study. But even more than that I need sleep.'

'We could go up to Rochdale by train.'

'What? Do you have any idea how much fares are these days?'

'I'd just like to see Mum. She's getting on and she was pretty knocked out by that bout of 'flu.'

'If you can afford it out of the housekeeping, then go by all means.'

'You know I can't. You'd have to pay.'

'Well, I can't afford to.'

'You can afford brand new shotguns and shooting courses and bottles of wine and—'

'Avril!' Kevin sat up again in bed. This time he was icy cool, even more potentially violent than he had been when he was shouting. 'I make all the money that comes into this household, so will you please leave it to me to decide how it should be spent. From an early age I have tried to better myself and I intend to continue to do that. When I die, the boys will be left in a much better position than where I started. I know what I'm doing.'

Avril sighed. 'It depends on your definition of "better". From where I'm sitting, everything seems to be a lot worse than it ever was.'

'I'm sorry, Avril. If you can't appreciate the improvements that I have brought into our lives, then I'm afraid there is no point in continuing this rather fruitless discussion.'

'Right.' Avril opened the jar of cream. 'Right, I am now going to remove my make-up.'

'Fine.' Kevin looked curiously at the jar. 'What's that stuff? It's new.'

'It's called rejuvenating cream.'

'Left it a bit late, haven't you?' he said and turned back into the duvet.

By eight o'clock on the Saturday night Avril was exhausted. The boys were so highly-strung at the moment. They were so tensely on their best behaviour at the new school that the release of the weekend made them manically high-spirited and quarrelsome. Kevin's absence didn't make things any easier. Though Avril often resented, or even laughed at, his performance as the stern Victorian *paterfamilias*, it did curb the boys' worst excesses. Without him there, and having made no friends in the area, the boys put all their emotional pressure on to their mother. She had to be playleader, entertainer, referee and caterer.

By eight o'clock, when she had finally dragged them away from the television and got them into bed, largely by brute force, she was absolutely drained. She collapsed on the sofa in the sitting-room and once again everything seemed to swim before her eyes.

A pall of depression draped itself over her. She tried to lift it by using her mother's eternal remedy, counting her blessings. She could hear her mother's voice, with its warm Lancastrian vowels, saying, 'Now come on, our Avril, cheer up. Remember, there's always someone worse off than yourself. You just count your blessings, young lady.'

She felt a terrible lonely nostalgia and an urge to ring her mother immediately. But no, Mum needed her help now; she mustn't ring and burden the old lady with her troubles. That was giving in.

No, come on, our Avril, count your blessings.

Right, for a start, nice house, two lovely boys, husband very successful, making far more money than any of the other boys from Rochdale you might have married. Okay, marriage going through a sticky patch at the moment, but that was only to be expected from time to time. Kevin's was an exacting job, and it was only to be expected that some of the tension he felt should be released at home. It was her job as a wife to make that home an attractive place for him to return to and relax in.

And if he needed to get out sometimes on his own, she mustn't make a fuss. This shooting weekend would probably do him a lot of good. Do them both a lot of good, give them a break from the claustrophobia of marriage.

And he'd been so excited about the gun. He seemed to have spent all his spare time that week cleaning it and oiling it, fiddling with all the little pads and brushes that he had bought with it. And this weekend was his chance to show it off. It was no different from James's desire to take his new Action Man to school on his birthday.

And at least it wasn't a woman. Let him fiddle with guns to his heart's content, so long as he wasn't fiddling with another woman. True, he hadn't been fiddling with her much recently, but that again was just a phase. It'd get better.

She started to feel more confident. Good God, they hadn't kept the marriage going from Rochdale, through all his time at college, the squalid flat in Willesden, his awful job in ICI, bringing up small children, all that pressure and aggravation, for it to fall apart now.

No, it'd be all right.

Good old Mum. It always worked. Count your blessings and you'll feel better. Come on, they breed them tough in Rochdale. Pick yourself up, get yourself a drink and cook yourself some supper.

The sherry bottle was empty.

Oh no. She couldn't really go out to the off-licence and leave the boys alone in the house. They'd never wake, but … No, she couldn't. Anyway, come to think of it, she hadn't got any cash. The housekeeping didn't seem to go far these days, and with that dinner party in the middle of the week, there was nothing left.

Damn. She could really use a drink.

On the other hand … Upstairs in Kevin's study there was a whole huge rack full of wine. All those bottles that involved so much correspondence with what he called his 'shipper' and so much consultation of books on wine appreciation and tables of good years and …

Yes, Kevin could certainly spare her a bottle of wine. A

221

small recompense for her letting him go off for the weekend on his own. She wouldn't take one of his most precious ones, not one of the dinner party specials, just something modest and warming.

His study was unlike the rest of the house. It was the spare bedroom, but he had moved the bed out and had the room decorated in dark green. There was an old (well, reproduction) desk and leather chairs. It sought to capture the look of a gentleman's club.

The boys were never allowed inside. Avril was discouraged from entering except to clean. The difference in décor seemed symbolic of a greater difference, as if the room had declared U.D.I, from the rest of the house.

The wine-rack covered one whole wall. The range was extensive. Kevin approached the purchase of wine as he did everything else, with punctilious attention to detail and a desire to do the correct thing.

Avril chose a bottle of 1977 Côtes du Rhône, which surely couldn't be too important. Anyway, he owed her at least that.

There was a corkscrew on his desk, so she opened it straight away. The presence of the corkscrew suggested that Kevin himself drank the occasional bottle up there, which in turn suggested that somewhere he must have glasses.

She opened the cupboard by the window. She didn't notice whether there were any glasses. Something else took her attention.

Standing upright in the cupboard, with all its cleaning materials ranged neatly beside it, was Kevin's new shotgun.

Avril swayed for a moment. This dizziness was getting

worse. She supported herself against the window frame and looked out into the road.

Parked exactly in front of their house was a silver-grey Volkswagen Golf.

It was the Monday evening before she got a chance to confront him. He had arrived back late on the Sunday and Monday morning was the usual scrum of forcing breakfast into her three men and rushing the boys through heavy traffic to their distant private school.

All day she phrased and rephrased what she was going to say to him, and when the opportunity came, she was determined not to shirk it. He had bought some sherry and poured her a drink, a perfunctory politeness which he performed automatically every evening before retiring upstairs with his brief-case to work until told that his supper was ready.

She took the glass, and, before he could get out his 'Just going up to do a bit of work', said, 'I see you didn't take your shotgun away with you for your shooting weekend.'

He looked first surprised, then very annoyed. 'You've been up rooting round my study.' When he was angry, his voice lapsed back into Lancastrian. The 'u' in 'study' sounded as in 'stood'.

'I went up there.'

'Well, I wish you bloody wouldn't! I've got a lot of important papers up there and I don't like the thought of getting them all out of order.'

But she wasn't going to be deflected so easily. 'Stop changing the subject. I want to know why you didn't take your precious brand-new shotgun with you when you went off on this shooting weekend.'

He smiled patronisingly. 'Oh really, Avril. You don't know the first thing about shooting. It isn't just something you can step straight into. You have to learn a lot of theoretical stuff first – you know, safety drill and so on. You don't start handling guns straight away. I knew that, so I left the gun this time.'

'This time? You mean there will be more weekends?'

'Oh yes. As I say, it's not something you can pick up overnight.'

She looked downcast. He put his arms round her. 'Why don't we go upstairs?'

She looked up into his eyes gratefully.

The phone rang.

'You get it. It's bound to be for you. Join me upstairs.' And he went up.

After the phone-call, she found him in the study rather than the bedroom, but she was too upset to register his change of intention. 'It was Mrs Eady.'

'Mrs Eady?'

'Who lives next door to Mum. Kev, Mum's had a stroke.'

'Oh no. Is she ... I mean, how is she?'

'Mrs Eady says it wasn't a bad one, but I don't know what that means. I'll have to go up there.'

'I suppose so.'

'Straight away. I'll have to. Can I take the car?'

'It's not going to be very convenient. I've got one or—'

'Kev ...'

He crumbled in the face of this appeal. 'Of course. Are you really going to go straight off?'

'I must. I can't just leave her.'

'What about the boys?'

'You can manage for a couple of days.'

'But getting them to school? If you've got the car ...'

'Oh God, yes. Look, there's Mrs Bentley. Lives round in Parsons Road. Her son goes to the school. I'm sure she'd take them too.'

'How well do you know her?'

'Hardly at all. But this is an emergency.'

'Will you ring her?'

'No, you do it, Kev. I've got to dash.' She started looking round the room for a holdall to take with her.

'I think it'd be better if you rang, Avril. Avril. What are you looking at, Avril?'

It was nearly dark, but the study curtains were still open. The light from a street-lamp shone on the silver top of the Volkswagen Golf.

'That car. It's the third day it's been parked outside.'

'So what? Lots of people park round here. It's near the station.'

'But that car hasn't moved for three days.'

'Perhaps someone's left it while they go on holiday.'

'I don't think so.'

'Well, what do you think?'

'I don't know, Kev.' Abruptly she moved from the window. 'I must go.'

The cars on the Ml kept blurring, losing their shape and

becoming little blobs of colour. Avril clenched her jaw and tensed the muscles round her eyes, fighting to keep them open. In three nights she couldn't have had more than half an hour's sleep. Driving through Monday night and then the worry about Mum.

The fact that the stroke had been so slight and Mum had seemed so little affected by it only made things worse. The incident became a divine admonition. It's nothing this time, but next time it could be serious, and there's you living over two hundred miles away.

Not that Mum had said that. She wouldn't. She was temperamentally incapable of using any sort of emotional blackmail. But Avril's mind supplied the pressure.

No, Mum had been remarkably cheerful. She fully expected to die soon and regarded this mild stroke as an unexpected bonus, a remission. And she was delighted to see Avril, though very apologetic at having 'dragged her all this way'.

Mum would be all right. Even if she were taken seriously ill, there would be no problem. She was surrounded by friends. Mrs Eady kept an eye on her and there were lots more ready at a moment's notice to perform any small service that might be required. That was what really upset Avril, the knowledge that her mother didn't need her. That, and the warmth that she encountered in her home town. The world of ever-open back doors and ever-topped-up teapots contrasted painfully with the frosty genteel anonymity of Dulwich.

And yet they'd all seemed impressed by her life, not envious, but respectful, as if she and Kevin were somehow their ambassadors in a more sophisticated world.

She'd met Tony Platt in the supermarket. Tony Platt, who

she'd gone out with for nearly a year and even considered marrying. And there he was, looking just the same except balding, and with three kids. Three bouncing kids with cheerful, squabbling Lancastrian voices and not an inhibition between them.

Tony had been pleased to see her. Friendly and slow, as he'd always been. 'Heard you were living down in the Smoke. Sorry we lost touch. You married Kevin Smith, didn't you?'

And he'd said she was looking grand, and she knew it wasn't true. She knew that strain reflected itself immediately in her face, pulling it down, etching deep lines in her skin. And make-up no longer seemed to smooth out the lines, but rather to highlight them. Still, if she could get some sleep, maybe she'd start to feel better. Yes, when she got home she'd get some sleep. Kevin had rung through each day and assured her that everything was all right.

The cars around her started to lose their outlines again. Must concentrate. Keep going. Only another seventy miles.

A car overtook her, fast, and then cut in in front of her. Too close. Far too close. She had to brake.

She focused on the car.

It was a silver-grey Volkswagen Golf.

I see, trying to get me now, she thought. Right, I'll show them.

She flattened her foot on the accelerator. They wouldn't get away with trying to frighten her.

Her car moved closer and closer to the large-windowed back of the Golf. It speeded up, but it couldn't get away from her. She was gaining.

Suddenly the Golf, pressed for space, swung out to overtake a lorry in front. Avril snatched her steering wheel to the right too.

There was a furious hooting and a scream of brakes as the Range Rover overtaking her had to slam on everything to avoid collision.

There was no collision. Avril swung back to the left and her car slowed down with a crunch on the hard shoulder. As she rubbed her swimming eyes, she could hear the voice of the Range Rover's driver ringing round her head. 'You bloody fool! What the hell do you think you're doing?'

The car was still parked outside when she got back to the house. The silver-grey Volkswagen Golf.

Its number-plate was different from the one on the motorway, but she wasn't necessarily fooled by that. She still felt the bonnet to see if the engine was warm and listened for the tick of contracting metal. But there was nothing. It seemed that the car had not been used recently.

Inside the house was absolutely quiet. It was nearly half-past six. The boys should be back from school. She swayed with exhaustion as she stood in the hall.

No, must resist the temptation to go to bed. Must find where the boys were. Probably with Kevin. Perhaps he'd left work early to fetch them from school. Even Andersen Small must recognise emergencies.

Must be with Kevin. Nowhere else they could be. Unless they were with that Mrs Bentley. Anyway, better ring her to thank her for taking them to school.

'Oh, Mrs Hooson-Smith, I must say I'm very relieved

you've rung. I was beginning to wonder if I was going to have to look after your sons for the rest of my life.'

'I'm so sorry. I thought you wouldn't mind just taking them to and from school. My mother's been ill and—'

'No, I didn't mind that at all, but I must confess having them to stay for the past three days has been a bit of a strain.'

'I'm so sorry. I didn't know.'

'Your husband had to go away on business.'

'Oh no.'

'So on Tuesday afternoon I was faced with the alternatives of putting them up or turning them out on to the streets. I must say, I do regard it as something of an imposition. It's not as if they're even special friends of Nigel.'

'I had no idea. I'm so grateful. I do hope they behaved themselves.'

'To an extent. Of course, people have different standards. About a lot of things.'

'Oh dear. Did my husband warn you about James's bed-wetting?'

'No, he didn't.'

It was quarter past eight. The boys were finally in bed, though not asleep. Still arguing fiercely. They were upset and confused, and, as usual, expressed their confusion by fighting.

Avril fell on to her bed without taking any of her clothes off. Just sleep, sleep.

The phone rang. She answered it blearily.

'It's Philip Wilkinson. Is Kevin there?'

'No, he's away on business. I don't know when he'll be back.'

'He's not away on business. I saw him in the office this morning. Then he went off after lunch.'

'Then I've no idea where he is. All I know is that he's been away on business for the last three days.'

'He hasn't.'

'What?'

'He's been in the office for the last few days. On and off. A bit distracted, but he's been there.'

'Oh. Well, I'm sorry, we've got our wires crossed somehow. As I say, I have no idea where he is. I'm absolutely shagged out and I'm going to sleep.'

She put the phone down and lay back on the bed. But, in spite of her exhaustion, sleep didn't come. Her mind had started working.

Kevin came back about half-past eleven. She heard the front door, then his footsteps up the stairs. But he didn't come straight into the bedroom as usual. She heard him going into the bathroom, where he seemed to be going through some fairly extensive washing and teeth-cleaning.

Eventually he came into the bedroom. 'Oh, I thought you'd be asleep.'

'As you see, I'm not.'

'No. How's your Mum?'

'Better.'

'Good.' He reached for his pyjamas. 'Oh, I'm tired out.'

'Kevin, what do you mean by leaving the boys with Mrs Bentley?'

'I had to do something. I was called away on business.'

'You weren't.'

'What do you mean?'

'That smoothie Philip Wilkinson rang to speak to you. In the course of conversation, he revealed that you have not been away on business for the past three days.'

'Ah.' Kevin put his pyjamas down again. Slowly he started to put his clothes back on. As he did so, he spoke. Flatly, without emotion. 'Right, in that case I'd better tell you. You'd have to know soon, anyway. The fact is, I have fallen in love with someone else.'

'What, you mean another woman?'

'Yes. I have spent most of the past week with her.'

'Most of the past week? The shooting weekend ...'

'There was no shooting weekend.'

'But how could you? What about me?'

'I don't think there's much left between us now, Avril.'

'Who is she?'

'Her name's Davina Entick. She works at Andersen Small.'

Avril started laughing. 'Oh God, Kevin, you're predictable. Clawing your grubby way up the social ladder. First you got the voice, then you got the job and the house. Then you looked around and you thought, what haven't I got? The right woman. I need a matching woman to make a set with my shotgun and my wine-rack and all my other phoney status-symbols. So you start sniffing round some little feather-headed debutante.

'Well, let me tell you, Kevin Smith, it won't work. Okay, maybe you managed to get into bed with her. A man can usually manage that if he's sufficiently determined, and you've never lacked determination, Kevin Smith. But that's all you'll get out of her. You can't screw your way into the upper classes. You've always been as common as dirt, Kevin Smith. And about as wholesome.'

He knotted his silk tie. 'I didn't expect you to understand. I'm sure you've forgotten what love feels like.'

'If I have, it's only because I've been living with you for the past fourteen years.'

'I'm going now.'

'Oh, back to the little lovenest in Mayfair?'

'Fulham, actually.'

'Oh, Fulham – what a let-down. Couldn't you find a nice upper-class dolly-bird with the right address? Never mind, maybe you can trade them in at Harrods. Fix yourself up with a nice shop-soiled Duke's daughter, how about that?'

Kevin still spoke quietly. 'I'm leaving, Avril. I won't come back, except to pick up my things.'

'Oh yes, pick up your things.' She rose from the bed and went across to the chest of drawers. 'Why not take your things with you now? I'm sure Davina won't want to soil her pretty little hands with washing sweaty shirts and horrid stained Y-fronts, will she?' As she spoke, she opened the drawers and started throwing clothes at Kevin. 'Here, have your things. Have your clean shirts, and your socks, and your Y-fronts, and your vests, and your handkerchiefs and your bloody Aran sweaters and ...'

Quite suddenly, she collapsed on the floor crying.

Kevin, who had stood still while all his clothes were flung at him, looked down at her contemptuously. 'And you wonder why I'm leaving you.'

She heard the car start. But when she looked out of the window, it was out of sight. All she could see, through the distorting film of her eyes, parked exactly outside the house, was the silver-grey Volkswagen Golf.

'Mummy, why have you drawn the curtains?'

'It's nearly night-time, James.'

'But it's not dark. It's summer.'

'Look, if I want to draw the curtains in my own house, I will bloody well draw them.'

'But you must have a reason.'

Oh yes, Avril had a reason. But not one she could tell. You can't tell your six-year-old son that you've drawn the front curtains because you can't bear another second looking at the car parked outside your house. You can't tell anyone that sort of thing. It doesn't make sense.

So, as usual, answer by going on to the attack. 'Anyway, it's time you were in bed. Go on, upstairs.'

'Am I going to have a bath?'

'No, you can have one tomorrow night.'

'You said that last night.'

'Look, I have not got the energy to give you a bath tonight. Now GO UPSTAIRS!'

'Can't I wait till Christopher comes home?'

'No. You go to bed.' Avril didn't want to think where her ten-year-old son was. Mrs Bentley, who had very grudgingly picked up James from school, had brought back some message about Christopher's being off with some friends and making his own way home on the bus. Avril knew she should be worried about him, but her mind was so full of other anxieties that that problem would have to join the queue and be dealt with when its time came.

A new thought came into her head. A new thought, calming like a sedative injection. Yes, of course, that was the answer. She'd just have to go out and check. Then it would be easy. Just get James into bed and she could go. He'd be all right for a few minutes.

'Go on, James, upstairs, or I'll get really cross.'

Her younger son looked stubborn and petulant, just like his father when he didn't get his own way. With an appalling shock, Avril realised that she could never be free of Kevin. She could remove his belongings, fumigate the house of his influence, even move somewhere else, but the boys would always be with her. Two little facsimiles of their father, two little memento moris.

'I need some clean pyjamas,' objected James. 'I haven't got any clean pyjamas in my drawer, because you haven't done any washing.'

Now she had no control over her anger. 'And you know why you need clean pyjamas every night, don't you? Because you wet your bloody bed like a six-month-old baby!'

She knew she shouldn't have said it. She knew all the child psychology books said shouting at them only made the problem worse. And, when she saw James's face disintegrate into tears, she knew how much she had hurt him. She was his defender. His father had told him off about it, but she was always the one who intervened, made light of it, said it'd soon be all right. And now she had turned against him.

At least it got him out of the room. He did go upstairs. Maybe, when all this was over, she'd have time to rebuild her relationship with her children. Now she was just too tired. It was the Thursday. Kevin had gone the previous Friday. Nearly a week ago. And still she had hardly slept at all. She lay back on the sofa. Strangely, she felt relaxed. Maybe now sleep would come.

But no, of course. Her good thought. Yes, her good peace-bringing thought. Yes, she must do that.

She stood up. The whole room seemed to sway insubstantially around her.

She went into the hall, then out of the front door. She averted her eyes from the thing parked in front of the house and set off briskly up the road.

A five-minute walk brought her to her objective. It was where she had remembered it would be, in the middle of the council estate.

It was an old Citroën DS. The tyres were flat and the back window smashed. Aerosols had passed comment on its bodywork.

But what she was looking for was affixed to the windscreen. It was a notice from the Council, saying that the car was dangerous rubbish and would have to be moved. She noted down the details of the department responsible.

Back outside the house, she forced herself to look at the car. It hadn't moved. It was in exactly the same position. Resin from a tree above it had dropped on to the bodywork and dust had stuck to this, dulling the silver-grey sheen.

But it was still a new car. This year's model. Some residual logic in her mind told her that no Council was going to come and tow this away as dangerous rubbish.

For a moment she wanted to cry. But then everything became clear.

She wondered why she hadn't seen it earlier. Yes, of course. The car had arrived on the supposed shooting weekend. The smart new car had arrived just at the time Kevin had gone off with his smart new girlfriend. At last she understood why she felt threatened by it.

She was so absorbed that she didn't hear the police car draw up behind her. It was only when the officer who got out of it spoke to her directly that she came back to life.

'Mrs Hooson-Smith?'

'Yes.'

'I've brought your son Christopher back. I'm afraid he was caught shop-lifting from the supermarket.'

Avril sat by the window in Kevin's study, looking down at the silver-grey Volkswagen Golf. Now she knew who it belonged to she could face it.

It was Saturday. People walked up and down the road loaded with shopping or planks and paint pots for the weekend's Do-It-Yourself. She had sent the boys out. She didn't know where they had gone. Probably the park. The policeman had said she must keep an eye on them, particularly Christopher until his appearance in the Juvenile Court on the Tuesday. But she couldn't yet. Not till all this was over.

It was sunny and very hot. But she didn't open the window. Her dressing-gown was hot, but she couldn't be bothered to take it off, still less to get dressed. A sickly smell of urine wafted from James's room, but she was too distracted to go and change his wet sheets. Even to close the study door and shut out the smell.

She had to watch the car.

The phone rang.

It was a dislocating intrusion. Like someone forgetting their lines in the middle of a good play, a reminder of another reality.

She lifted the receiver gingerly. 'Hello.'

'It's Kevin.'

He sounded businesslike. This was the way she had heard him speak into the phone on the rare occasions when she'd gone up to Andersen Small to meet him and had to wait in his office.

'Oh.' She hadn't expected ever to hear from him again. He was a part of her life that she no longer thought about. It was strange to be reminded that he was still alive. He had no place in the weightless, transitional world she now inhabited.

'How are things, Avril?'

She didn't answer. She couldn't cope with the philosophical ramifications of the question.

'Listen, I've been thinking. I want to get things cut and dried.'

Unaccountably she giggled. 'You always did, Kevin.'

'What I mean is, I want a divorce. I want to marry Davina.'

'And does she want to marry you?'

'I haven't asked her yet, not in so many words. I wanted to get our end sorted out first, to feel free …'

'Free,' she echoed colourlessly.

He ignored the interruption. 'Then I'll speak to Davina. It'll be all right. We have an understanding.'

'I'm sure you have.' Suddenly anger animated Avril's lethargy. 'It'll be easy enough for her to have an understanding of you. All she has to understand is selfishness and petty-mindedness and social-climbing. And I'm sure, from your point of view, she takes no understanding at all. You can't understand something when there's nothing there to understand.'

'There's no need to be abusive. Particularly about someone you haven't met. Davina is in fact a highly intelligent girl.'

Avril didn't think this assertion worthy of comment.

'Anyway, all I'm saying is that I will be starting proceedings for divorce, and it's going to be easier all round if you don't create any problems over it. I'll see that you and the boys are well looked after financially. By the way, how are the boys?'

'Fine,' she replied. Why bother to tell him otherwise?

'Anyway, I'll be round at some point to pick up my things. I hope we'll be able to meet without too much awkwardness. We're both grown-up people and I hope we'll be able to deal with this whole business in a civilised, adult manner.'

Avril put the phone down.

A civilised, adult manner. She laughed.

Pick up my things. She laughed further.

If, of course, you have any things to pick up.

She took a bottle out of the wine-rack and threw it against the opposite wall. It shattered satisfyingly.

She did the same with another bottle. And another and another, until the whole rack was empty.

It was enjoyable. She looked round for further destruction.

She opened the cupboard by the window.

And there it was. Of course. The brand-new shotgun.

Kevin had a book about shotguns on his desk. Good old Kevin. Never go into anything without buying lots of books to show you how to do it. Do your homework, you don't want to look a fool.

The book made it easy to load the gun and showed how to release the safety-catch. Avril slipped a cartridge into each barrel from Kevin's unopened box.

Then she opened the window a little and continued watching the silver-grey Volkswagen Golf parked outside.

It was early Sunday morning. Eight o'clock maybe. She had seen it get light a couple of hours earlier. All night she had watched the car outside. It would be terrible not to be there when they arrived.

She didn't know where the boys were. She vaguely recollected their coming back at lunchtime on the Saturday. But they had found there was no lunch prepared and had gone out again. She thought they had said something about spending the night in the park, but she couldn't be sure. It had been difficult to take in what they said. Her dizziness and the mobility of everything that surrounded her seemed to have grown. It was as if her head had levitated and floated above her body in some transparent viscous pool.

But she knew she would be all right. Her body would hold up as long as was necessary.

The phone rang. This time its intrusion didn't seem so incongruous. It now took on the ambivalence of everything else she saw and heard. It might be real, it might not. It didn't matter much one way or the other.

She answered it. As she did so, she thought to herself, 'If it's real, then I'm answering it. If it's not, then I'm not.' That was very funny, and she giggled into the receiver.

'Hello, is that Avril?'

'Yes. Almost definitely.' She giggled again.

'It's Mrs Eady.'

'Ah, Mrs Eady.'

'It's about your Mum, Avril. I'm afraid she's had another stroke. Doctor's with her now.'

'Ah.'

'And I'm afraid this one's more serious. Doctor says he doesn't think she'll last long.'

'Ah.'

'Look, Avril, can you come up? I mean, she's still alive now, but I don't know how long it'll be. They're going to take her into hospital and … Avril, are you still there?'

'Oh yes,' said Avril wisely.

'Can you come up?'

'Come up?'

'To Rochdale.'

'Oh no, I'm very busy.'

'But it's your Mum. I mean, she can still recognise me and—'

'No, I'm sorry. I can't do anything till they come.' She put the phone down.

It was nearly eleven o'clock when the girl arrived. She came up the road carrying two suitcases.

It was the suitcases that alerted Avril. Kevin had got a nerve. To send the girl to pick up his things. A bloody nerve.

The girl walked up the road slowly, giving Avril plenty of time to look at her. No, she wasn't that pretty. Not even as young as she'd expected. Looked about her age. Very brown, though, very tanned.

Avril knew she would stop by the car and, sure enough, she did. The two cases were put down, and the girl fumbled in her handbag for car-keys. I see, she'd load up with Kevin's things and then drive off in the car.

Avril could see everything very clearly now. The world around her had stabililised, in fact she could see it in sharper detail than usual. She sighted along the barrels of the shotgun.

The girl had found her key and was bending to open the car door. Avril felt the trigger with her finger. Just one trigger. Kevin wouldn't approve of waste. Just one cartridge would do it.

She squeezed the trigger.

She was totally unprepared for the recoil, which knocked her off her chair. But when she picked herself up and looked out of the window, she saw she had succeeded.

The girl seemed to be kneeling against the side of the car. Her back was a mass of red. The side windows were holed and frosted and there were small holes in the silver-grey bodywork of the Volkswagen Golf.

Kevin arrived in his car a moment later and parked behind the Golf. He was in a furious temper.

Davina had turned down his proposal. Not only that, she had laughed at him when he made it. She had let him know in no uncertain terms that at the moment she had no thoughts of marriage and was only looking for good sex. She had added as riders that, if she had been looking for a husband, she would have looked some way beyond him, and that she was beginning to have grave doubts about the quality of the sex he provided.

So he was coming home with his tail between his legs. Avril, he knew, would welcome him. She had no alternative.

As he got out of the car, he couldn't help noticing the bloody mess beside the Golf. He stared at the body with his back to his house.

So it was the back of his head that received the main blast of the second barrel of his new shotgun. Some more holes appeared in the bodywork of the silver-grey Volkswagen Golf.

The Detective-Inspector watched the police car drive off. 'Well, she seemed to go docilely enough, Sergeant.'

'Yes, sir. The only thing she seemed worried about was that the Golf would definitely get towed away. Said it was in her parking space. I assured her it would, and she seemed quite happy.'

'Strange. I mean, not her shooting the husband. Apparently he'd left her and gone off with some other woman, so there's a motive there. But the other woman she shot ... completely random.'

'She's not hubby's girlfriend?'

'Oh, Sergeant, wouldn't that be nice and neat.' The Detective Inspector smiled. 'No, we've identified her from things in her handbag. Passport, airline ticket stubs – very well-documented. Just come back from a fortnight's package holiday in Sardinia.'

'No connection with this family at all?'

The Detective-Inspector shook his head. 'Not yet. I personally don't think we'll probably ever find one. I think that poor woman's only offence was to use someone else's parking space.'

Death in the Sun

Michael Innes

The villa stood on a remote Cornish cape. Its flat roof commanded a magnificent view, but was not itself commanded from anywhere. So it was a good spot either for sunbathing, or for suicide of a civilised and untroublesome sort. George Elwin appeared to have put it to both uses successively. His dead body lay on the roof, bronzed and stark naked – or stark naked except for a wrist watch. The gun lay beside him. His face was a mess.

'I don't usually bring my weekend guests to view this kind of thing.' The Chief Constable had glanced in honest apology at Appleby. 'But you're a professional, after all.'

'Fair enough.' Appleby gazed down dispassionately at the corpse. 'What kind of a chap was this Elwin?'

'Wealthy, for a start. But – as you can see – retaining some unassuming tastes.' The Chief Constable had pointed to the watch, which was an expensive one, but on a simple leather strap. 'Poor devil!' he added softly. 'Think, Appleby, of taking a revolver and doing that to yourself.'

'Mayn't somebody have murdered him? A thief? This is an out-of-the-way place, and you say he lived here in solitude, working on his financial schemes, for weeks at a time. Anybody might come and go.'

'True enough. But there's £5,000 in notes in a drawer downstairs. An unlocked drawer, heaven help us! And Elwin's fingerprints are on the gun – the fellow I sent along this morning established that. So there's no mystery, I'm afraid. And another thing: George Elwin had a history.'

'You mean, he'd tried to kill himself before?'

'Just that. He was a hypochondriac, and always taking drugs. And he suffered from periodic fits of melancholy. Last year, it seems, he took an enormous dose of barbiturate – and was discovered just in time, naked like this in a lonely cove. He seems to have had a fancy for death in the sun.'

'I think I'd prefer it to death in the dark.' As he said this, Appleby knelt beside the body. Gently, he turned over the left hand and removed the wrist watch. It was still going. On its back the initials *G E* were engraved in the gold. Equally gently, Appleby returned the watch to the wrist, and buckled the strap. For a moment he paused, frowning.

'Do you know,' he said, 'I'd rather like to have a look at his bedroom.'

The bedroom confirmed the impression made by the watch. The furnishings were simple, but the simplicity was of the kind that costs money. Appleby opened a wardrobe and looked at the clothes. He removed a couple of suits and studied them with care. He returned one, and laid the other on the bed.

'Just what did you mean,' he asked, 'by saying that Elwin was always taking drugs?'

'Ambiguous expression nowadays, I agree. He kept doctoring himself – messing around with medicines. Just take a glance into that corner-cupboard. Regular chemist's shop.'

The cupboard was certainly crammed with medicine bottles and pill boxes. Appleby took rather more than a glance. He started a systematic examination.

'Proprietary stuffs,' he said. 'But they mostly carry their pharmaceutical name as well. What's tetracycline for, would you suppose? Ah, it's an antibiotic. The poor chap was afraid of infections. Do you know? You could work out all his fears and phobias from this cupboard.'

'A curious thought,' the Chief Constable said grimly.

'Various antihistamines – no doubt he went in for allergies in a big way. Benzocaine, dexamphetamine, sulphafurazole – terrible mouthfuls they are.'

'In every sense, I'd suppose.'

'Quite so. A suntan preparation. But look, barbiturates again. He could have gone out that way if he'd wanted to. There's enough to kill an elephant, and Elwin's not all that bulky. Endless analgesics. You can bet he was always expecting pain.' Appleby closed the cupboard door, and glanced round the rest of the room. 'By the way, how do you propose to have the body identified at the inquest?'

'Identified?' The Chief Constable stared.

'Just a thought. His dentist, perhaps?'

'As a matter of fact, that wouldn't work. The police

surgeon examined his mouth this morning. Teeth perfect –
Elwin probably hadn't been to a dentist since he was a child.
But, of course, the matter's merely formal, since there can't
be any doubt of his identity. I didn't know him well, but I
recognise him myself, more or less – even with his face like
that.'

'I see. By the way, how does one bury a naked corpse?
Still naked? It seems disrespectful. In a shroud? No longer
fashionable. Perhaps just in a nice business suit.' Appleby
turned to the bed. 'I think we'll dress George Elwin that
way now.'

'My dear fellow!'

'Just rummage in those drawers, would you?' Appleby
was inexorable. 'Underclothes and a shirt, but you needn't
bother about socks or a tie.'

Ten minutes later the body, still supine on the roof, was
almost fully clothed. The two men looked down at it
sombrely.

'Yes,' the Chief Constable said slowly. 'I see what you
had in mind.'

'I think we need some information about George Elwin's
connections. And about his relatives, in particular. What do
you know about that yourself?'

'Not much.' The Chief Constable took a restless turn up
and down the flat roof. 'He had a brother named Arnold
Elwin. Rather a bad-hat brother, or at least a shiftless one,
living mostly in Canada, but turning up from time to time to
cash in on his brother George's increasing wealth.'

'Arnold would be about the same age as George?'

'That's my impression. They may have been twins, for that matter.' The Chief Constable broke off. 'In heaven's name, Appleby, what put this hoary old piece of melodrama in your head?'

'Look at this.' Appleby was again kneeling by the body. Again he turned over the left hand so that the strap of the wrist watch was revealed. 'What do you see on the leather, a third of an inch outward from the present position of the buckle?'

'A depression.' The Chief Constable was precise. 'A narrow and discoloured depression, parallel with the line of the buckle itself.'

'Exactly. And what does that suggest?'

'That the watch really belongs to another man – someone with a slightly thicker wrist.'

'And those clothes, now that we've put them on the dead man?'

'Well, they remind me of something in *Macbeth*.' The Chief Constable smiled faintly. 'Something about a giant's robe on a dwarfish thief.'

'I'd call that poetic exaggeration. But the general picture is clear. It will be interesting to discover whether we have to go as far as Canada to come up with—'

Appleby broke off. The Chief Constable's chauffeur had appeared on the roof. He glanced askance at the body, and then spoke hastily. 'Excuse me, sir, but a gentleman has just driven up, asking for Mr Elwin. He says he's Mr Elwin's brother.'

'Thank you, Pengelly,' the Chief Constable said unemotionally. 'We'll come down.' But when the chauffeur had gone he turned to Appleby with a low whistle. 'Talk of the devil!' he said.

'Or, at least, of the villain in the hoary old melodrama?' Appleby glanced briefly at the body. 'Well, let's go and see.'

As they entered the small study downstairs, a lanky figure rose from a chair by the window. There could be no doubt that the visitor looked remarkably like the dead man.

'My name is Arnold Elwin,' he said. 'I have called to see my brother. May I ask—'

'Mr Elwin,' the Chief Constable said formally, 'I deeply regret to inform you that your brother is dead. He was found on the roof this morning, shot through the head.'

'Dead?' The lanky man sank into his chair again. 'I can't believe it! Who are you?'

'I am the Chief Constable of the County, and this is my guest Sir John Appleby, the Commissioner of Metropolitan Police. He is very kindly assisting me in my inquiries – as you, sir, may do. Did you see your brother yesterday?'

'Certainly. I had just arrived in England, and I came straight here, as soon as I learned that George was going in for one of his periodical turns as a recluse.'

'There was nobody else about the place when you made this call?'

'Nobody. George managed for himself, except for a woman who came in from the village early in the morning. His manner of life was extremely eccentric. And solitude was the very last thing that a man of his morbid temperament should have allowed himself.'

'It was a suicidal temperament?'

'Of course it was. And what point is there in dodging the thing? George had made one attempt on his own life already.'

'That is true. May I ask whether you had – well, a satisfactory interview with him?'

'Nothing of the kind. George and I disagreed. So I said good day to him, and cleared out.'

'Your disagreement would be about family affairs? Money – that kind of thing?'

'I'm damned if I see what business it is of yours.'

There was a moment's silence, during which the Chief Constable appeared to brood darkly. Then he tried to catch Appleby's eye, but failed to do so. Finally he advanced firmly on the lanky man.

'George Elwin—' he began.

'What the deuce do you mean? My name, sir, as you very well know, is Arnold Elwin, not—'

'George Elwin, by virtue of my commission and office I arrest you in the Queen's name. You will be brought before the magistrate, and charged with the wilful murder of your brother, Arnold Elwin.'

Appleby had been prowling round the room, peering at the books, opening and shutting drawers. Now he came to a halt, and spoke with distinguishable caution.

'It may be irregular,' he said to the Chief Constable. 'But I think we might explain to Mr Elwin, as we can safely call him, just what is in our minds.'

'As you please, Appleby.' The Chief Constable was a shade stiff. 'But be good enough to do it yourself.'

Appleby nodded, and then spent a moment in thought.

'Mr Elwin,' he said gravely, 'it is within our knowledge

that Mr George Elwin, the owner of this house, was, or is, subject to phases of acute melancholia. Last year, one of these attacks led him to an actual attempt at suicide – to which, indeed, you have just referred. That is our first fact.

'The second is this: the wrist watch found on the dead man's hand was not fastened as it would normally have been fastened on the wrist of its owner. The dead man's is a slimmer wrist.

'A third fact connects with the second. The clothes in this house are too big for the dead man.' Appleby paused. 'But the Chief Constable and I are obliged to reflect that they would fit you very well.'

'You're mad!' the lanky man got to his feet again. 'There's not a word of truth—'

'I can only give you what has been in our minds – emphasise the tentative nature of what I am advancing. Having said so much, I come to a fourth fact. George and Arnold Elwin were not readily distinguishable. You agree?'

'Of course I agree. George and I were twins.'

'Or Arnold and you were twins – for we must continue to bear an open mind. And now, what I shall call our hypothesis is as follows: you, George Elwin, living in solitude in this house, were visited by your brother Arnold, just back from Canada. He demanded money or the like, perhaps under some threat of damaging disclosure. There was a violent quarrel between you, and you shot him dead – at hideously close quarters.

'Now, sir, what could you do? The wound was compatible with suicide. But who would believe that Arnold had arrived here, gained possession of your gun, and shot himself?

'Fortunately there was somebody who *would* readily be

believed to have committed suicide, since he was known to have made an attempt at it only a year ago. That somebody was yourself, George Elwin.'

Appleby paused for a moment – not, it might have been perceived, for the sake of effect, but in the interest of achieving concentrated statement.

'So you, George Elwin, arranged the body of your brother Arnold, and arranged the weapon you had used, in such a way as to suggest something fairly close to a repetition of that known attempt at suicide. You strapped your own watch to the dead man's wrist. The clothes in the house would hang loosely on him – but he would be found naked, sunbathing in a fashion you were known to go in for – and who would ever be likely to notice the discrepancy with clothes tidily laid away in their wardrobes and drawers?

'The dead body, maimed in the face as it was, would pass unquestioned as *yours:* as George Elwin's, the owner of this house, that is to say. And that's all! You had abruptly lost your true identity. And, ceasing to be George, you had lost what is probably a substantial fortune. But at least you had an identity to fall back on – that of your brother Arnold, whom you had killed – and you weren't going to be charged and convicted of murder.'

'But it's not *true!*' The lanky man seemed to be in blind panic. 'You've framed me. It's a plot. I can prove—'

'Ah,' Appleby said, 'there's the point! If you are, in fact, George pretending to be an Arnold who is really dead, you'll have a very stiff fight to sustain the impersonation. But if, as you claim, you are really Arnold, that's a different matter. Have you a dentist?'

'Of course I have a dentist – in Montreal. I wander about the world a good deal, but I always go back to the same dentist. At one time or another he's done something to nearly every tooth in my head.'

'I'm uncommonly glad to hear it.' Appleby glanced at the Chief Constable. 'I don't think,' he murmured, 'that we ought to detain Mr Arnold Elwin further. I hope he will forget a little of what has been – well, shall we say, conjectured?' He turned back to Elwin himself. 'I'm sure,' he said blandly, 'you will forgive our exploring the matter in the interests of truth. You arrived, you know, when we had not quite sorted out all the clues. Will you please accept our sympathy on the tragic suicide of your brother George?'

'You mean to say,' the Chief Constable asked half an hour later, 'that I was right in the first place? That there was no mystery?'

'There was none whatever. George Elwin's gloom was deepened by the visit of his useless brother, and he killed himself. That's the whole story.'

'But dash it all—'

'Mind you, up to the moment of your charging that fellow with murder, I was entirely with you. And then I suddenly remembered something that didn't fit – that £5,000 you found here in an unlocked drawer. If George had killed Arnold and was planning to *become* Arnold – or anybody else – he'd certainly have taken that money. So why didn't he take it?'

'I can see the force of that. But surely—'

'And then there was something else – something I ought to have seen the significance of at once. The dexamphetamine in the medicine cupboard. It's a highly efficient appetite depressant, used for dieting and losing weight. George Elwin was slimming. On this occasion, I imagine, he'd come down here principally to do so. It was the latest expression of his hypochondria.

'He could lose fourteen pounds in a fortnight, you know – which would be quite enough to require his taking up one hole in the strap of his watch. And in a month he could lose thirty pounds – which would very decidedly produce your effect of the giant's robe on the dwarfish thief. George Elwin's first call, had he ever left here, would have been on his tailor – to get his suits taken in.'

The Chief Constable was silent for a moment.

'I say!' he said. 'We did give that unfortunate chap rather a bad fifteen minutes.'

Appleby nodded soberly.

'Perfectly true,' he said. 'But let us be thankful that one of Her Majesty's judges isn't burdened with the job of giving somebody a bad fifteen years.'

Credits

'The Entertaining Episode of the Article in Question' by Dorothy L. Sayers, from *Lord Peter Views the Body*, Victor Gollancz, 1928, reprinted by permission of David Higham Ltd

'The Mystery of Horne's Copse' by Anthony Berkeley, reprinted by permission of The Society of Authors as the Literary Representative of the Estate of Anthony Berkeley

'Invisible Hands' by John Dickson Carr, from *The Men Who Explained Miracles*, Hamish Hamilton, 1964, reprinted by permission of David Higham Ltd

'Chapter and Verse' by Ngaio Marsh, reprinted by permission of HarperCollins Publishers Ltd © 1989, Ngaio Marsh

'A Case in Camera' by Edmund Crispin reprinted by permission of Peters Fraser & Dunlop (www. petersfraserdunlop.com) on behalf of Rights Limited